"PREPARE TO SURFACE."

The sea was calm, placid. The sky was gray with no clouds, although a film of dust seemed to hover in the upper atmosphere. Land on both sides of the Bering Strait could be seen, and on both shores smoke rose listlessly from countless fires.

The world was burning. And no one remained to put out the flames.

Donovan watched in silence. One by one, the crew members came up on deck, walking to and fro, letting the magnitude of the tragedy sink in. At last Chief Engineer Smith spoke, calling up to the tower. "How could this happen, Captain?"

"We may never know," Donovan said.

J.D. CAMERON

AVON BOOKS ◆ NEW YORK

OMEGA SUB is an original publication of Avon Books. This work has never before appeared in book form. This work is a novel. Any similarity to actual persons or events is purely coincidental.

AVON BOOKS
A division of
The Hearst Corporation
105 Madison Avenue
New York, New York 10016

Copyright © 1991 by Michael Jahn
Command Decision excerpt copyright © 1991 by David Robbins
Published by arrangement with the author
Library of Congress Catalog Card Number: 90-93419
ISBN: 0-380-76049-5

First Avon Books Printing: April 1991

AVON TRADEMARK REG. U.S. PAT. OFF. AND IN OTHER COUNTRIES, MARCA REGISTRADA, HECHO EN U.S.A.

Printed in the U.S.A.

RA 10 9 8 7 6 5 4 3 2 1

The twin 1,350-shp General Electric T58-GE-SF turboshaft engines roared steadily as the old HH-2G LAMPS helicopter raced over the icy waters of the Bering Strait. The American chopper frayed nerves on the Russian side of the border as it chased down the bizarre sonar contact.

The strange submarine had been picked up an hour earlier. It was crossing the Northern Bering SOSUS barrier at an impossibly high rate of speed, especially considering the shallowness of the strait's waters and the certainty that unannounced passage through seas dense with Russian and American submarine detectors would send both sides into a frenzy of sub-hunting.

But something had roared southward through the strait faster than had ever been recorded before, and it was a phantom. Both Russian and American naval commanders in the area denied ownership and blamed the other in what was only the latest in an increasingly bitter series of "incidents" between the superpowers.

The overthrow of the liberal Russian premier and the return to power of Kremlin hard-liners had given the whole world's military structure a bad case of nerves. Every Soviet regional commander was hot to prove himself most loyal to the old ways of military paranoia and America-hating. That eagerness to grip the trigger was most evident in the Pacific, especially the North Pacific up into the Bering Strait, where American military bases in the Aleutians and Alaska rubbed up against Russian installations in Kamchatka. The American military, correspondingly, was defensive and wary, peering hard at radar screens, launch detection monitors and SOSUS screens in search of an expected Soviet aggression.

The HH-2G had been dispatched from the deck of the frigate F.F.G. *John Quevedo* to locate and identify the phantom sub contact that was disrupting the very fragile peace between Soviet and American forces in the North Pacific. Hovering close enough to the water for the rotor blades to roil the surface to foam, the chopper lowered a sonobuoy and listened as the phantom approached.

Technician First Class Charles Donovan was the LAMPS operator. The Light Airborne Multi-Purpose System had for years been the Navy's principal mobile ASW (Anti-Submarine Warfare) detector carried on helicopters. The two LAMPS choppers aboard the *Quevedo* had been scrambled fifteen minutes earlier when SOSUS/Alaska announced a sub detection heading fast through the Bering Strait. One headed north to intercept and the other south to cut off the contact. Charlie Donovan, on the northern LAMPS, was the first to colorfully express his amazement over the capabilities of the phantom.

"Jesus Fucking Christ, she can move," he said, staring wide-eyed at his instruments.

"How fast?" asked the copilot.

"Sixty knots. That's impossible in this water."

"That's impossible under any water. Are you sure?"

"Sixty knots, maybe more. Heading this way on

course zero-eight-seven. Right on course for the restricted area."

The restricted area was a thousand miles to the southwest, but was so sensitive that all ships in the North Pacific had been warned to keep away. The defense ministers of Japan, the United States, the newly reunited Germany, and the People's Republic of China were meeting on a carrier in the Sea of Japan to work out strategies for dealing with the new hard-liners in Moscow, and the last thing anyone in the West wanted was a disruption. So the *Quevedo* and her choppers were joining hundreds of other ships in making sure that nothing untoward happened in the Sea of Japan.

"How far from us?"

"Ten miles and closing. She's showing up on MAD," Charlie Donovan said, thumping the Magnetic Anomaly Detector.

The pilot cranked up the radio and called the ship, reporting the unidentified contact. After a moment he turned and said, "Captain wants us to ping her, find out who she is."

Charlie nodded and pressed the button that sent a request-identification signal racing from the hydrophone toward the phantom.

Nothing came back. Less than nothing. He might as well have been talking to a dolphin. At least dolphins occasionally talked back, though no one was really sure what they had on their minds. Instead of a signal, the submarine raced through the water beneath the chopper, moving so fast it created a perceptible ripple in the water, rather like a great white shark does while making a near-surface run on prey.

"Jesus Fucking Christ," Charlie said again, this time reeling in the sonobuoy before the gigantic shark could nip it off. "She's a big mother, four

3

hundred feet I guess, moving at sixty-two knots. Impossible. Not one of ours, anyway."

"Not Russian," the copilot said. "At least not in the book."

"Something new," Charlie said.

The pilot radioed: *"Quevedo,* the target just blew by us at six-two knots bearing zero-eight-seven. Refused acknowledge signal."

The ship's answer unnerved everyone. "You are instructed to arm a Mark 48 ASW torpedo and await instructions."

On the other side of the world, another submarine, a majestic submarine, cruised lazily north in no hurry to get anywhere. The *Liberator* was a new boat, the prototype of the new Omega class of nuclear-powered tactical submarines that the president and Congress ordered built to usher in the millennium.

Captain Thomas P. Donovan ordered a dive to seven hundred feet and levelled off the ship, heading on a course that would take the *Liberator* across the Greenland Sea beneath the Arctic ice pack. The ice was a mass in constant motion, and not a uniform chunk of frozen water. In places it was only chunks of brash—broken ice, some bits too small to cool a scotch and soda. Most of the pack ice consisted of odd-shaped floes from a foot or two to a dozen feet wide. Occasionally there were small "ponds" of open water surrounded by ice. These ponds were called *polynyas,* a Siberian word.

"Leave it to the Russians to have a word for 'water surrounded by ice,' " Donovan told the crew.

Few *polynyas* were large enough for a sub to surface in, at least in the Arctic. A *polyna* in the Weddell Sea in the Antarctic grows to more than 100,000 square miles, but ice at the South Pole has the advantage of being partly on land and therefore able to grow bigger. Antarctica was a continent with land (that a few dozen million years ago was tropical) but the Arctic was only ice and water.

A lot of ice and water. In places the ice cap is thirty feet deep and covers waters five thousand feet deep. Extending from Wrangel Island in the Chukchi Sea north of Point Barrow in Alaska and Mys-Shelagskiy in Siberia to Cape Stallworthy in the Queen Elizabeth Islands, Canada; to Shannon Island in Greenland across the Greenland Sea to Aleksandra Ostrova in Franz Josef Land and Severnaya Zemla back in the U.S.S.R., the ice pack is far from being a forbidden wasteland. The Arctic has long attracted adventurers. The European quest for a Northwest Passage around the Americas began in the sixteenth century and culminated in the great explorations of the late nineteenth century and early twentieth centuries. The Greeley Expedition nearly perished in 1884, and the Nansen exploration in the ship *Fran* first penetrated the pack ice in 1896, reaching 86 degrees 14 minutes north. Peary reached the North Pole—90 degrees north—in 1909 by dog sled, and the pole was attained by airplane in 1926. In 1958 the American nuclear submarine *Nautilus* traversed the ice pack, sailing from the Bering Strait to Iceland in four days.

Liberator took a more leisurely pace, for her orders were to remain submerged for two weeks under the polar ice cap, testing her ability to hide from enemy detection while observing complete radio silence. After departing Iceland and sailing north up the Greenland Sea, Donovan took her under the ice pack at 80 degrees north, 0 degrees west. She sailed past Nordauslandet and across the Wandels Sea, crossing 85 degrees north, and over the Angara Basin, the broad, deep basin that lay beneath the ice to the Eurasian side of the pole. *Liberator* passed over the North Pole on her seventh day under the

5

ice, and Donovan was chagrined at being unable to send a message home—"*Liberator* 90 north," or something similarly historic. Instead he contented himself with overseeing the continuing peaceful mission of the *Liberator:* making the best-yet underwater maps of the subsea terrain while studying the proliferation of microscopic life beneath the ice.

The ship crossed the Lomonosov Ridge, a mountain chain that rose to within one thousand feet of the surface and ran from the Lincoln Sea off Ellesmere Island, between Greenland and the Queen Elizabeth Islands, and reached nearly to the New Siberian Islands. She crossed the Mendeleyev Ridge and cruised over the flat Laurentian Basin, heading for the north Alaskan shore while completing her main mission.

Donovan was sure he was being successful in remaining hidden from the eyes of satellites and the ears of the Canadian and American Arctic SOSUS barriers. None of the several ships that had been sent to the Arctic as part of the game had any luck in finding the new submarine. The only things that remained to be evaded were three ice stations—in the ice pack in the Beaufort Sea and north of the Chukchi Sea—that had drilled through the ice and dropped detectors in *Liberator*'s expected path. Donovan knew that one of them would find him. In fact, he was ordered to contact Beaufort West Station and check in even if the detectors failed to pick him up, just so Washington would know its newest ship was okay.

The captain of the *Liberator* looked forward to contacting Beaufort West to tease them for failing to detect his ship.

With Charlie Donovan holding on for dear life and monitoring the MAD display, the HH-2G raced south on course one-eight-seven, and even at 152 knots maximum level speed took half an hour to overtake and get far enough ahead of the phantom to hover and wait. The crew was hyper, more than on edge. They had been ordered to fire on and destroy a submarine whose only crime was going faster than subs were supposed to and refusing to say who she was. The phantom could be American or Russian. She could be Martian. One thing was for sure—if she didn't start behaving there would be fireworks.

Charlie lowered the sonobuoy back into the water and listened. At nine miles the phantom was picked up, still maintaining course and speed. On instructions from the *Quevedo* he sent another message, this time with a warning—stop or be fired on. But once again there was no reply, only a 1,420-hertz drone that made no sense whatsoever. The drone came from the phantom, maybe from the engines or maybe from some bizarre type of sonar, but it definitely came from the ship, changing as it got nearer.

"This ship is fast, it makes no sense, and it's not stopping," Charlie reported, tossing up his hands.

He wondered for an instant if the phantom was *Liberator*. The mysterious new boat commanded by his big brother was supposed to be in the Arctic but also on the Atlantic side of the polar ice cap, and few knew what she could do. Maybe big brother did, but he was purposefully mysterious about her. Maybe *Liberator* can do what this boat is doing, Charlie thought. Maybe she *is* *Liberator*, having some fun with the Pacific ASW fleet.

Wouldn't that be strange, Charlie thought, and held his breath as the Mark 48 ASW torpedo was readied to fire.

Then things happened: the 1,420-hertz emission from the phantom changed to 1,500 hertz and then

1,750. The ship slowed while holding course, then turned ten degrees to west.

"Target is slowing," Charlie reported excitedly. "She is dead slow in the water and turning to starboard."

"Hold the torpedo," the pilot snapped.

All three men in the chopper looked out the windows and down. Bristling with detection antennas, weapons and armor, the HH-2G resembled a giant black bug hovering menacingly over the icy water, its human occupants uneasy witnesses to the drama unfolding below the sea.

"She's surfacing," Charlie announced, more excitedly than before.

"Surfacing?" the copilot asked.

"No, coming to launch depth and holding." He added, with a gasp, "Launch detection!"

The cruise missile broke the frothy surface of the Bering Strait in a geyser of white spray, then rocketed into the atmosphere as her main engines kicked in.

"Oh shit!" the pilot said, and that was the last thing he said, as the HH-2G was grabbed by the jet wash and slammed into the sea.

On the last day of the silent part of the mission, Donovan had only to contact Beaufort West and claim the satisfaction of having evaded the best efforts of Canadian and American submarine-catchers. He felt certain that he had succeeded. The silence from the rest of the world was deafening. They hadn't heard a peep of any kind in days, and they were listening with the finest equipment in the world.

Liberator started her design life as the prototype of the Omega-class submarines, an advance on the San Diego class, with an added forty feet in length for a total of 400 LOA. The extra beam of thirty-seven feet allowed the ship to carry forty Mark 70 long-range, laser-guided, acoustic-homing torpedoes with a range of 25,000 yards; twenty-four antiship missiles with a 250-mile range; and the experimental weapon that was conceivably the biggest advance in submarine warfare in decades, the blue-green laser.

The laser was an outgrowth of blue-green laser technology originally meant for surface-to-sub communications. Never before tested in battle, the weapon (two of them, actually) was fired from turrets mounted fore and aft on the tower. They could fire up to strike the hulls of surface targets or down (to the plane of the deck) to hit submerged targets. The range of effectiveness as a weapon was only 1,000 yards and the damage it could cause was mainly the disruption of electrical circuits, but that was damaging enough to a submarine. And at longer ranges, up to 10,000 yards, the laser was highly effective as an information probe. When tied into the *Liberator*'s Cyclops information-display system, the laser provided pinpoint accuracy on the location of items ranging from other ships to floating debris—and even the location of thermoclines.

Everything aboard ship was named by the men and with logic in mind. The engines not only were called simply "the engines," they were located in the engine room, which was reached by walking down the engine room corridor. The same went for the reactors, and there was no other place to find the torpedoes but in the torpedo room. The front of the boat was the bow and the back was the stern. There was no conning tower to speak of, only a hydrodynamic blister that was planned as a topsides extension of the bridge. It was called, simply, the bridge, and it was assumed that the men were smart enough to realize that, when the ship was submerged, the captain meant that part of it inside the main hull. Throughout *Liberator,* practice was to call things by the names that the men were most likely to use. Few confusing post–World War II Navy acronyms survived into the age of *Liberator.*

The exception was Cyclops, the tactical eyes and ears of *Liberator.* A marvel of advanced electronic and holographic technology, it took information from the sub's sensors—primarily sonar when under water but including radar, UHF and satellite information when surfaced—and used it to construct a three-dimensional image of the ship and its environment. The name was derived from Cycle Optics, the idea being that Cyclops presented a visual reconstruction of entire cycles of data available on course, the condition of the sea, subsea terrain and surface threats—ranging from icebergs to flotsam. Cyclops used mainly sonar images, but enhanced them with whatever information was available, and then some. The operator could even plug in the captain's intuition; if Donovan thought that an enemy submarine was hiding behind a nearby seamount, that intuition could be displayed on Cyclops. The operator—and the rest of the bridge crew—would see a three-dimensional visualization of seamount and enemy submarine and the *Liberator*'s position in relation to them, all displayed in shimmery blue and green light that hovered in front of and partly surrounded the helmsman and captain. In battle, Donovan could remain at his station, watch the Cyclops visuals, and guide the *Liberator* through the hazards. In peace and in an interesting subsea terrain, he could take the helm just to enjoy the view. In that way *Liberator* could fulfill both missions—as warship and as research vessel, studying and recording the life of the sea while preparing for the defense of the nation.

Liberator's main advance over the San Diego-class submarines that preceded her lay in the extent to which she was automated. Shipboard systems and procedures that once took three shifts of three or four men each were computerized, roboticized and manageable by one man per shift. Instead of 120 or more men, *Liberator* was manned by 45 men working in three shifts of 15 each. There was a large computer and systems repair crew to ensure that the automated systems kept running well, and crew accommodations were correspondingly large. Because *Liberator* was designed to stay submerged nearly all the time, a lot of effort went into designing comfortable living spaces. Most American nuclear submarines were comfortable in comparison with their conventionally powered ancestors, because the nuclear power plant took up so much less space than a diesel propulsion system with its bulky fuel tanks and battery space. *Liberator* was almost luxurious, designed to be a home away from home, a seaborne colony as well as a warship. Space was also important, because, with a few exceptions, her crew was older than the norm, better paid and better trained. Such men (and women, or so it was planned for future staffing) would not likely be attracted by Spartan accommodations. Everyone had his own cabin and the officers their own heads and showers. There was no old-Navy hot-bunking aboard *Liberator,* and since the ship was so highly computerized, everyone had his own monitor (for use in recreational viewing as well as in monitoring ship's systems).

In all, *Liberator* was the first submarine constructed to be a home and research laboratory as well as a boat. She was almost entirely self-sufficient and could prowl the world at will, exploring as well as defending herself and the nation. Her existence presumed a new era of submarine life, one where military significance time-shared with global research and undersea living.

Thomas P. Donovan was a wise choice as her captain. The thirty-seven-year-old son of a highly decorated New York City police detective, he mixed nautical savvy with a mild temperament that instilled confidence in the crew. Donovan cut his teeth on Los Angeles–class submarines, where he rose to the rank of captain and enjoyed his first command. He was given the helm of *Liberator* because of his combination of experience, temperament and adaptability. He had little problem adjusting to new conditions, and that was a quality judged of vast importance to the commander of a radically new design of submarine.

As he sat in the captain's chair behind the helm, Donovan watched the Cyclops display: white-blue pinnacles of light from the ice pack above, blue-black open water to port, starboard and ahead, and black below the ship, with the flat bottom of the Beaufort Sea being displayed as a hint of lime green that showed few features. In the two weeks that *Liberator* had been below the ice, Donovan couldn't get over the view. It reminded him of video games he'd played on the Upper West Side of Manhattan as a kid, the games where you drove a spaceship through a tunnel of light and sound. Only this time the game was real, and the white-blue light above him was filtered through fifteen feet of ice floating on top of the world.

John Percy, the executive officer, also admired Cyclops, and said so often. "I can't wait to test this in maneuvers," he said, pointing out a thirty-five-foot stalactite of ice that whizzed by the hull, tiny numbers alongside it showing its dimensions.

"It's a new concept in battle," Donovan agreed. "Cyclops is supposed to give us a clear picture of every ship within firing range. I'll believe that when I see it. However, its performance under the ice is impressive."

"There's no way we could make forty knots under the ice without it."

Donovan liked all his men, even Percy and the question mark that hung silently over his head, placed there by COMSUBPAC. The young man, barely thirty, was hotheaded, so went the legend, and thus had been passed over for command several times. It was said he longed too much for the old days of armed combat at sea, days nearly forgotten in the active-duty Navy. No current sub commander had ever fired a shot in anger, at least not at another ship.

Percy dreamed of the glory of war and excelled at war games but lacked the depth of temperament to be a submarine commander, or so believed the admirals who made such decisions. It was thought that a year or two under Donovan would mellow him for command. Donovan found him an able officer with a lot of eagerness for the job. Sometimes it was hard to get him off the bridge, and he certainly didn't subscribe to the one-shift-on, two-shifts-off design for *Liberator* officers. But then, all the members of the crew seemed, at times, to be zealots with a highly personal interest in the ship, almost as if they owned her.

The real "principal owner" in the crew was Dave Hooper, the nineteen-year-old helmsman who in a brief time had become Donovan's protégé. If all officers felt they had a personal stake in the ship, Hooper claimed actual ownership and spent enough time learning all her systems to know more about her than anyone, with the possible exception of Carl "Flazy" Smith, the chief engineer. Hooper and Smith, whose nickname meant "fat and lazy," spent most of their time arguing over who knew more about *Liberator* and was more dedicated. Smith probably knew more, since he'd participated in cru-

13

cial design decisions, but Hooper had a louder voice. Anyway, he was younger.

Donovan consulted his watch. "How long has it been since we last tried raising Beaufort West?" he asked.

"Fifteen minutes, Captain," Percy replied.

"Try again. They should have responded by now. They know we're here."

"After we told them, only after we told them," Hooper said.

Percy agreed. "We evaded all attempts to find us. The acquisition exercise was a failure from their point of view, a success from ours."

It was true. *Liberator* had evaded detection by the best of the West. Satellite detection, MAD sensors implanted in the ice pack, SOSUS barriers along the Canadian and Alaskan coasts, and listening devices dropped through holes in the ice at the ice stations, all had failed to pick up the presence of the sub. By all standards available, the first mission of *Liberator* was a howling success.

Then why was Donovan uneasy? He stood at the helm of arguably the greatest warship ever created, one that could take the defense of the nation into the next century with ease. He and his forty-five men could go anywhere, do anything, and live indefinitely. They were a ship for the present and future, capable of projecting both power and civilization and doing it without help.

What worried him? All he knew was that the small hairs on the back of his arms were tingling, a sure sign that something indefinable was wrong.

"Try Beaufort West again," he snapped.

"They most likely burned a fuse trying to find us," Hooper said, and emitted a gasp of admiration as an uncharted seamount passed beneath them and was displayed, measured, and recorded on 3-D charts for the reference of future generations. *Lib-*

erator's Cray-9 computer stored the information in files destined for the nation's civilian and military oceanographers and mapmakers, all those with an abiding interest in subsea places where submarines could hide.

Dave Jennings, chief communications officer and Cyclops operator, reported back: "Nothing, Skipper. No response. No noise at all from Beaufort West."

"No nothing?"

"Not even normal background emissions. They use a lot of electricity keeping systems up in the cold. No way they can mask the generators."

"Distance to Beaufort West?" Donovan asked.

"Ten miles dead ahead," Hooper replied.

"Reduce speed and take us there. We'll stop."

"Stop, Captain?" Percy asked.

"There's something wrong. I can feel it."

"What's wrong, Captain?"

"A whole lot of silence from the ice station we're supposed to contact," Donovan said. "We're going in to investigate."

2

"Mr. Hooper, distance to Beaufort West?"

"Seven miles. Slowing to one-quarter. There is still no indication from Beaufort West."

"Call them again, Mr. Jennings. Tell them we're here and we're hungry for barbecue."

Jennings smiled. "I'll ask them to light the hibachi, sir."

But a minute and a mile closer there still was no response.

"This is damned peculiar," Donovan said. "Do we have sonobuoy detection?"

"Affirmative, marked on the screen."

Donovan looked and saw a representation of the sonobuoy, marked in blue-green light on the forward viewscreen.

"Well, it's there at least. Is it alive?"

Jennings shook his head. "Dead as a doornail. No emissions, no feedback."

He studied his console, made some adjustments, then looked at the rest of the bridge personnel with furrowed brow.

"This has got to be wrong. The instruments must be off."

"Explain," Donovan said.

"The atmospheric temperature is all off. I've been reading eighteen to eighteen-five above for the past

16

two weeks. On the quarter-day reading this morning the temperature showed fifty-two."

He looked around the bridge at the assortment of puzzled faces.

"Fifty-two, in the Arctic!" Percy said. "The temperature sensor has got to be out of whack."

"Check it," Donovan said.

Jennings fed commands into the computer and waited a few seconds for it to come back.

"The error factor is point-seven-five. It's in the fifties up there."

"Impossible," Percy said.

Hooper said, "The Cray computer takes ambient readings of sunlight filtered through the ice for a six-hour period, factors in the mean density and opacity of the ice over the same time frame and compares it with the bounceback from a laser burst fired through the ice. It's the latest in remote detection."

"But how can that be?" Percy asked.

"I don't know but mean to find out," Donovan said. "How far is it to the edge of the ice?"

Percy said, "We should be able to break through at seventy-five degrees north a hundred and sixty-eight degrees west. That's the last known position of the Chukchi Sea ice pack."

"How fast can we get there?"

"Maintaining forty knots we can be there in two hours."

Jennings made yet another check of his sensors, then tossed up his hands. "There's nothing up there, Captain," he said. "Nothing but melting ice. The base is deserted."

"Best possible speed to the edge of the ice pack," Donovan said tersely.

The following two hours dragged on a year, or so it seemed. There was only one explanation for the unusually high temperature reading above the Arc-

17

tic ice, but nobody wanted to say it out loud. Barring the impossible coincidence that the Earth had suddenly tilted to point the North Pole toward the sun, the only conclusion to be drawn from the high temperature coupled with the desertion of Beaufort West was that, as feared, something had gone terribly wrong with the summit meeting in the Sea of Japan.

Donovan had feared that. Everyone had. Knowing that his kid brother, Charlie, was flying ASW in the North Pacific and hence in the danger zone made matters worse.

As the edge of the ice beckoned, the white-blue color from above as displayed on Cyclops changed to bright white and then some gray. As visualized on the viewscreen, the more-or-less solid ice broke up into growlers and cold water, and three hours after making the decision to head for open water, *Liberator* found it.

Donovan ordered the ship to periscope depth and raised the radar-receiving mast as well as the periscope. A visual sweep of the horizon revealed nothing for ten miles in all directions, and the radar showed nothing.

"There's nothing, Skipper," Jennings said. "No radar transmissions at all."

"And this is one of the busiest radar zones in the world," Hooper added, referring to the only common border between the United States and the Soviet Union.

"Even the Russian transmitter on Bering Island is silent," Donovan said.

"It's quiet as a grave up there," Jennings said. Almost immediately, he regretted his choice of words and sought to lose himself in work. "Shall we try radio?"

"And the satellite, please. Let's see if we got any messages."

Liberator was due to get a congratulatory tele-gram of sorts off the PSCS (Pacific Submarine Com-munications Satellite) upon completion of her mission. In return for successfully hiding from the world's prying eyes and bad news for two weeks, upon surfacing in the Bering the crew would hear the greetings and congratulations of their country.

But when Jennings tried to log on the satellite, all he got was more silence.

"The carrier frequency is alive. At least the sat-ellite is still there."

Donovan ordered, "Send to Washington: 'U.S.S. *Liberator* in Bering after successful completion of North Polar Ice Pack silence episode. Please ex-plain radio silence of Beaufort West and atypical atmospheric temperatures.' Give our current posi-tion and heading."

"Aye, Captain."

The message was encoded and burst-transmitted to PSCS, which was in a parking orbit 23,500 miles above the equator. From there the message would be relayed to ground stations in the States. But once again, *Liberator* was met only by silence.

After a short time, Jennings tossed up his hands in despair.

"I've never heard of them not responding," he said.

"Listen on radio. All frequencies."

As the ship's radio receivers scanned all frequen-cies and got only static, the enormity of their soli-tude began to sink in. All off-duty personnel who could fit crowded onto the bridge, and the rest gath-ered in corridors, exchanging looks of disbelief.

Jennings said, "Nothing, Captain. We're all alone."

Donovan nodded, then asked, quietly, "How hot is it up there?"

"Sixty-two degrees."

Whistles of disbelief and cries of anguish ran throughout the ship, followed by concern for country, family, and world. Donovan said, "Let's see how bad it is. Prepare to surface."

Sullenly, almost mechanically, the crew watched as the automated control systems brought *Liberator* flawlessly to the surface. When the upper bridge broke surface and a crewman opened the hatch, Donovan led the way.

The sea was calm, placid. There was no ice despite being a short distance south of the limit of the permanent ice pack, and the air was warm and dry as a bone. The sky was gray with no clouds, although a film of dust seemed to hover in the upper atmosphere. Land on both sides of the Bering Strait could be seen, and on both shores smoke rose listlessly from countless fires.

The communications lines that once tied *Liberator* to civilization were dead. Radio and radar revealed nothing. The satellite was alive but no one remained on land to talk to it. Both America and the Soviet Union were burning, and no one remained to put out the fires. They were quite alone.

Donovan watched the untended fires in silence while each and every member of the crew took turns coming up on deck and walking to and fro, letting the magnitude of the tragedy sink in. At last Chief Engineer Smith, speaking for the crew, called up to the tower: "How could it happen, Captain?"

Donovan said, "We may never know. We were under the ice, sleeping."

A small group of men milled about on the foredeck, not talking as *Liberator* moved slowly south, her automation system holding course out of the Arctic and through the Bering Strait. A flight of shearwater, seagull-like birds with hooked beaks, skimmed the surface of the strait en route to Little Diomede Island.

"Send a message on all frequencies," Donovan ordered. " 'U.S.S. *Liberator* requesting communications.' Do not give our location. Not all survivors may be friendly."

Jennings gave the captain a sharp look, but said only, "Is that all?"

"Yes. Program the transmitters to send it every fifteen minutes. Still nothing coming in?"

"Only background noise on the radio and radar. The sonar is reporting a steady hum on the 1,420 hertz frequency. We can't pinpoint the origin except that it's outside the ship. It may be a harmonic off the automation system."

"Filter it out," Donovan ordered. "And try to raise the U.S.S. *Quevedo*, reported operating in these waters."

"Your kid brother?"

Donovan nodded. "He may have a better idea what happened . . . if he's still alive."

For five hours, through most of the afternoon until sundown approached, Donovan stood on the foredeck of *Liberator* and spoke with his men.

They came to him individually and in groups, and all came more than once. Their questions were different and the same: How could World War III have started, been fought, and ended in less than two weeks? What happened to their families, their nations, the world? Is this the end? Are we the only ones left alive, and why us?

"I should have gone into the priesthood after all," Donovan thought, and sat alone on the bow, staring across the endless stretch of sea while the ship moved south through waters deprived of human life.

That nearly happened, his entering the priesthood. When he was thirteen and flirting with manhood, Donovan was called into the Mother

Superior's study and told that she had a vision from God. She said that God had visited her the night before and told her that Donovan had a vocation to become a priest, and that if he denied his vocation he would condemn himself, and her, to hell.

Even at age thirteen he knew he didn't want to go into the priesthood, he wanted to go to sea. At that time he thought of the surface navy, perhaps a good big battleship. But by the time he reached real manhood the battleships were gone and submarines were the real power at sea. After graduating from the Academy he went to sub school and soon was prowling the corridors of a nuclear attack submarine.

Donovan never looked back, at least not until the day after the world ended. Sitting on the bow of *Liberator,* listening to the hum of her engines and thinking of all the angers and fears of his men, he wondered if the priesthood wasn't really for him, after all. He was good at it, being father confessor and big brother. Donovan had the ability to put people at ease and instill them with confidence, to make them see the best in themselves and their situation.

But there were limits. He could find no "up side" to the end of the world, or if not to the end of the world, to the days after World War III. When they were sailing down through the Bering Strait from a suddenly warm Arctic, moving along through an apparently empty world, it was hard to find good things to talk about. Hope? For what? Loyalty? To whom? Duty? Well, maybe they had a duty to themselves.

And that was to pick up the pieces. Find out what happened and rescue survivors. Make the best of what mankind had done to itself. If need be, find a safe haven and start civilization over. Their duty was to make sure that their lives weren't in vain, that they did some good in the world. And no one was better equipped to do it. They had the world's most advanced submarine—really, a home and laboratory as well as warship, able to go anywhere and do anything.

But where to start? Donovan sat on the bow, surveying the dismal gray sky, knowing that forty-five pairs of eyes were on him, looking to him for leadership and counsel.

He stood, straightened his jacket, and turned to face a dozen men who lingered in the middle of the foredeck. He reached into his shirt pocket and pulled out a pack of Lucky Strikes and was about to light up when Jennings came running forward from the tower, pushing his way through the men.

"A signal, Captain," he said excitedly. "I'm reading an automatic distress locator beacon from a life raft—it's one of the *Quevedo*'s."

"Charlie," Donovan said, and ran aft to the upper bridge.

The signal was from an ELB, an Emergency Locator Beacon carried as standard equipment aboard life rafts on Navy ships and naval aircraft. The odds that it was Charlie were 164 to 1, that being the number of men on a guided missile frigate that carried two choppers. But Donovans had a survival instinct. Their father had survived several shooting incidents to become the most highly decorated detective in New York Police Department history. And Tom Donovan had survived the political infighting that raged for years over who would be chosen to skipper *Liberator*. And Charlie had shown his own stubborn determination, preferring the life of an airborne ASW technician to more stable but less gratifying ways of earning a living.

"A man like that deserves to be saved," Donovan said, climbing to the upper bridge.

"Captain?" Jennings asked.

"Nothing. What about the distress call?"

"Coming in from a hundred ninety-four degrees and about seven miles out. That way," he said, pointing out to sea.

Donovan scanned the area through high-powered binoculars.

"I don't see anything."

"The raft may be low in the water. The message is faint."

"Move toward it," the captain said. "Rescue party on deck."

Donovan watched as a four-man party inflated a life raft and prepared it for launching while other crew members stood by. The rescue and the chance that there was a survivor raised everyone's hopes. The glimpse of another human, alive and well and possibly offering explanations, meant that there was hope for their own loved ones.

The teal-colored hull of *Liberator* moved swiftly, almost silently, across the calm surface of the Bering Strait. Her lines were gently rounded, like the back of a porpoise, and unmarred by ballistic missile tubes. Even the four torpedo tubes and the planes blended into the ship's overall gracefulness, which was made even more pronounced by the silence of her motion through the sea. *Liberator* exuded power and control, and instilled all aboard her with confidence, as much of it as could be expected given the circumstances.

A bridge lookout cried, "Raft in the water, bearing one-nine-zero."

All eyes shifted in that direction, and Donovan found himself filling with excitement.

Through the binoculars he made out a speck that hung low in the water, orange with neon blue stripes, barely moving.

"Come to course one-nine-zero," he ordered.

Liberator moved swiftly to a position a hundred

24

yards from the raft and stopped. Donovan watched through the binoculars but could see nothing inside the raft. The sides were high to shelter survivors and a body lying prone would not be seen.

The rescue boat was put into the water and the party of four cranked up the outboard and hurried over to the life raft. Unable to wait, Donovan went back down to the foredeck and hopped down onto the starboard diving plane. He was the first to grab the line when the boat returned.

Two sailors lifted an ill-shaven head into the gray sunlight.

"Charlie!" Donovan exclaimed.

3

Liberator's sick bay was large enough for the crew of a ballistic missile submarine, and the main operating room dwarfed the men in it. Donovan and Executive Officer Percy stood by a bed looking down at the captain's brother.

Charlie Donovan had a three-day growth of beard over skin that was curiously grayed. The skin was ashen, as if it had been lightly burned by a searing heat, and the tips of his eyelashes and eyebrows were curled. His hair too had been singed in patches, mainly on the front and top of his head, which were exposed to the open air while he lay in a thin layer of water in the raft.

He wasn't seriously hurt, mainly exposed to the elements, hungry, and frightened. He was dazed enough to have acquiesced to being carried onto *Liberator* and down to sick bay without uttering a word, and was having trouble focusing on his rescuers.

"Are you guys American?" he asked, rubbing his eyes.

"That we are, Pirate," Donovan said, using the nickname his younger brother had adopted after seeing the legend "Air Pirates" on the back of a seaplane pilot's shirt way back when in the movie

Raiders of the Lost Ark and deciding to enter a life of flight.

Charlie focused on Donovan's face. "Tom?"

"Hi, kid."

"I'll be damned . . . what kept you?"

Donovan smiled. The family perseverance always showed through.

"How are you feeling?"

He tried to sit up, but was restrained by the hand of the ship's surgeon.

"I'm weak in the knees and hungry as hell. I got chills now and then, mainly during the night. But since the sky calmed down things haven't been so bad. Is there anything to eat?"

"Tell me about the sky," Donovan said. "What do you mean 'after it calmed down'?"

Once again Charlie rubbed his eyes. "Things got weird fast. I was lying in the raft and feeling pretty sorry for myself because I was the only one to make it when the chopper got splashed. Then a couple of minutes later things started popping. There were flashes on the horizon and low rumbles, kinda like a herd of elephants in the sky."

"Flashes all over the sky?"

"East and west, mainly. To the south is ocean and to the north, ice. Nothing to burn. But the people areas of the planet were lit up pretty good. That went on for half an hour maybe. Then the wind . . ."

"Wind?"

"I don't know . . . a hot wind, like you walked out of an icebox and into the desert. It blew like hell for three or four hours, then stopped and the fires on shore began. That's it."

"That's it?" Percy asked, an anger rising as if he were disappointed.

"What do you say about the end of the world?" Donovan said.

"It's not the end of the world," Charlie said. "We're still here. Are you sure there's nothing to eat?"

He sat up, and this time the surgeon didn't restrain him.

"He'll live, Captain. I gave him a vitamin shot and some antibiotics. His radiation count isn't too bad and will drop more. I suggest you feed him."

"See? What did I say? Steak and eggs."

"In modest portions to start."

"What about the military action?" Percy demanded.

Charlie shrugged. "We may have been all there was, at least in the conventional sense. We were tracking a phantom sub that came down outta the Chukchi like a bat out of hell and fired a missile. The jet wash splashed the chopper and only I got out. I don't know what happened to the sub, but we had been ordered to fire on her after she ignored warnings to stay out of the threat zone."

Donovan said, *"Quevedo* was sailing a picket line to keep unidentified ships from coming out of the Arctic through the Bering and getting into a position to threaten the Sea of Japan, where the military summit was taking place."

"Which the Russians wanted to sabotage," Percy said, his temper rising.

"We don't know that," Donovan said.

"Come on, Captain. The summit was on how to deal with the Russian threat."

"At any rate," Charlie went on, "the sub was a big mother, over four hundred feet and moving at better than sixty-two knots, which don't make sense in any man's navy. She didn't respond to hails and just when we were going to fire on her, she fired a missile. That's pretty much the end of my story."

"That's the end of a lot of stories," Donovan said.

Charlie was easing himself out of the hospital bed

when the quiet of the operating theater was broken by the sound of the ship's alarm. Then a voice came over the speakers. It was Jennings, the communications officer.

"Captain to the bridge! Aircraft approaching bearing two-two-nine."

"From Russia," Percy said, and followed the captain out of the sick bay and down the corridor to the bridge. They ran up the stairs that led to the upper bridge, and then went up into the late afternoon air. A lookout pointed at the plane, a growing speck flying low over the water and coming from the Russian mainland.

Donovan grabbed a pair of binoculars. After glancing at the plane, his brow furrowed.

"What the hell is *that?*" he said out loud.

Charlie had followed him to the bridge, and took the binoculars. Right away he said, "It's him, Old Ivan. He's back."

"Who?"

"Old Ivan, flying a vintage Mikoyan-Gurevich 15 with no bullets."

"What?"

"A MIG-15, first flown in 1947 and used extensively in the Korean War."

"The Korean War was over fifty-five years ago," Donovan exclaimed.

"Yeah, it beats the hell outta me too how the damned thing is still flying. Maybe it's from the Siberian Air Show. Anyway, Old Ivan buzzed me yesterday and again this morning. Tried to strafe me, too. But he isn't armed. I'll bet the guns don't work, but he insists on trying. He's crazy as they come. Blames me for the war, I guess. Now he's got *Liberator* to imagine he's shooting at."

"Shall we dive, Captain?" Percy asked.

"No. What harm can he do?"

"He can report our position."

"To whom?" Donovan asked. His comment fell over the bridge like a shroud, and as it was repeated throughout the ship in the hours, weeks and years that followed, the captain's "To whom?" came to symbolize their situation: alone or nearly alone in the world after the apocalypse, roaming the seas, picking up the pieces.

The old jet roared overhead, its bulbous wing tanks and donut-hole nose intake making it look nearly as ancient as the Wright brothers' apparatus. The pilot could be seen briefly, with pure-white hair and no helmet, waving a fist at the submarine, which continued south as land faded from view.

He "attacked" *Liberator* for half an hour, coming in low above the water and trying to fire empty and nonworking guns while the submarine's officers watched helplessly from the tower. The MIG circled between passes, climbing to five thousand feet and then coming in for another run. Eventually, though, the engine spat, faltered, and ran dry of gas. At the top of his climb the pilot bailed out and a white parachute blossomed in the gray air.

"All stop! Rescue party to the deck!"

The vintage aircraft spun down to a watery grave, splashing in a geyser of seawater. The parachute fluttered to the sea, where it was met by four *Liberator* sailors in the same raft used to rescue Charlie. Forty-five minutes after the jet began its attack, the pilot was lying in the same hospital bed.

Besieged by the unheard-of occurrence of two legitimate patients on the same day, and confronted with his first terminal case since signing on board the ship, Chief Medical Officer Paul Martin plugged the symptoms into the medical computer and frowned.

"Radiation poisoning complicated by exposure and general systemic shock," he said. "In lay language, the man's whole world was blown away; he's dead but hasn't dropped yet."

"Can he talk?" Donovan asked.

"No. But what's there to say?"

"Why did he try to attack us?" Percy asked.

"We're the last visible symbol of the old order," Martin said. "He was lashing out."

"But attacking us makes no sense."

"He knew he was dying," Donovan said. "The guy is forty years old going on four hundred and fifty years old. Look at him—white hair and half his teeth gone, half-starved and pissed off."

"Undoubtedly experiencing paranoid delusions," Martin added.

"You're really not paranoid when the world is demonstrably out to get you," Donovan said. "I think that we can expect to be targets of this kind of anger wherever we go."

"Where are we going?" the doctor asked.

Donovan checked his watch, then said, "I'm calling a meeting of all off-duty hands—in the mess in half an hour. In the meantime, I'm diving and taking us south, away from land. Let's have no more surprises today."

The medical monitor flashed and emitted the straight-line tone of death. Martin tossed up his hands as an orderly pulled a sheet up over the body.

"We'd better bury him," the doctor said. "He's hot."

Donovan had confirmed for him that day why he declined to enter the priesthood at age thirteen. As a kid he told the Mother Superior—as an explanation of why he was condemning himself, and her, to hell—that he wanted to have a life filled with adventure, excitement, and helping people, and that he didn't see himself accomplishing it while sitting in a cloister.

She argued. The church was the best place, for souls came in to be saved. Donovan knew even then that souls who were truly lost never came in, that he would have to go and find them. He would have to venture into the wilderness, preferably one covered with oceans, seeking out people to help, and that this could be accomplished while having adventures.

"The first step is to find out how badly we've been hurt," he told the assembled crew. "The step after that is to see what we can do to help. We'll steer east of Saint Lawrence Island, bypassing the shipping lanes and other routes where we might be expected. Our first port of call will be Navy Harbor in the Aleutians."

"What's there?" an anonymous voice asked.

"An outpost of civilization, or what's left of it. To put it bluntly, we have to find out what's left of the world."

"And find out what happened to our families," said Flazy Smith. A romantic at heart and very much a family man, his anguish in the hours after *Liberator* recognized the enormity of the tragedy was most visible among the crew. If Donovan symbolized courage and hope, and Percy their anger and wish for revenge, Smith expressed their loss. His wounds were visible; with him around, no one else needed to mourn out loud.

"We'll try to do that," Donovan said, though he had doubts. How do you find out what happened to a wife and kids in San Diego, when San Diego itself has been wiped off the face of the planet? "We'll gather as much information as we can and go from there. Navy Harbor is the logical first place to look.

"There's no point in speculating about what happened to our loved ones. The best thing is to keep hoping and keep looking. Right now we have only a tiny piece of the picture. Let's start learning more, then we can figure out the best way to help."

"Come on, Captain," said another anonymous voice. "We went to war with the Russians and lost."

"Somebody fought somebody. We all lost. We were kept out of the battle because we were under the ice. If you believe in God, you might think that he had a purpose in putting us there. And furthermore, he has a purpose for us now—to pick up the pieces."

Percy had done a good job of keeping in check his reputed hotheadedness, having uttered only a few comments that hinted at a desire for revenge. Now it came fully to bloom.

"Begging the captain's pardon, but we're still at war," he said. "The Russians are still the enemy."

"We don't know that they ever were."

"Come on, a Russian pilot just attacked us."

"A solitary lunatic in an antique plane with no bullets," Donovan said, thinking almost fondly of the lost soul they had just buried at sea. "The only way we'll find out what happened in the war is to ask, and we can't do that submerged in the Arctic with no communications. Let's go to America."

"I vote for revenge," Percy said, more forcefully that time, and several voices responded in agreement.

Donovan bristled, and said, "I'll take that under consideration, Mr. Percy—when this becomes a democracy."

The executive officer was piqued but kept his thoughts to himself, and Donovan didn't pursue the matter of command prerogatives any further. If the crazy Russian pilot had no one to report home to, neither did he. There was no command structure, no garrulous admirals, no brass at all. There was no ground support, and probably no functioning naval bases. Fortunately, *Liberator* was largely self-supporting, with essentially unlimited power and life support. Sure, Donovan would have to conserve torpedos and missiles and scrounge for food after the current three months' supply was exhausted. Scrounging for food would at least give them something to do to keep their minds off their woes.

His main problem was keeping up the crew's hopes, and keeping their loyalty. With no command structure to back him up—for one thing, Donovan couldn't even guarantee his men their paychecks— the possibility of mutiny was always there. Not that *Liberator* crewmen were even vaguely inclined toward rebelliousness, but what do you tell them they should be loyal to? An armed forces that failed to win World War III, and maybe even started it? Their families, who are almost certainly dead?

Donovan knew he would have to convince them to carry on for the sake of humanity's future, and he would have to do it man-to-man. No speeches would work.

"Let's do what I said, go to America and find out how bad we were hurt. Once we know, we can decide what to do next. We're setting course for the Aleutians. After we visit Navy Harbor, we'll have a good idea. In the meantime and from here on in, I'm available to talk to you one-to-one. Any time you need to talk, you know where to find me."

"Probably stealing a smoke," Flazy said, and the others laughed. Donovan's long-running and losing battle to give up smoking had suddenly achieved new dimensions.

"Why should I stop now?" he asked, to the nervous laughter of the crew.

To accent the point, he pulled out a Lucky Strike and lit up.

Back on the bridge, Donovan sat in the captain's chair behind Dave Hooper's helm and looked ahead. The Cyclops displayed the white-blue sea surface above, blue-green vastness to port and starboard, and, increasingly far below, the subsea terrain. Far below the keel, the shallow Bering Sea gave way to the deep Aleutian Basin as *Liberator* steered south toward the island arc of the Aleutians. That westernmost extension of North America reached to 173 west longitude, closer to the Soviet Union than to the United States.

"Our first real indication of how bad it is will be there," Donovan said, and got no arguments.

"The ship is level at seven hundred feet and steering one-eight-zero," Hooper reported. "All systems are showing nominal. Automation is up and ready. Shall I engage?"

"Any contacts, Mr. Jennings?"

"No sir. The ship is clear of traffic and free to navigate."

"Very well, Mr. Hooper, engage automation—"

The communications officer interrupted with a staccato, "Contact, Captain."

"Belay that last order," Donovan snapped.

"The contact is on the seafloor, bearing twenty degrees off the bow ... It's a ship, Captain, and recently sunk."

"Put her on visual," Donovan said, leaning forward in his seat to watch her come up on the starboard Cyclops screen.

The ship appeared as a colored stick figure, little more than a one-inch outline on the starboard viewscreen. She lay on her port side, her bow partly buried in silt. Next to the figure, Cyclops displayed her name, as determined from the encoded laser reflector installed on all U.S. warships in the late 1990s. It read FFG97 U.S.S. *Quevedo.*

"Beam forty-five feet, LOA four forty-five feet, and no significant sedimentation topsides. She's a recent victim, Captain."

Donovan spoke into the intercom, "Charlie Donovan to the bridge."

WIthin a minute, his younger brother was there and staring sadly at the visualization of his old ship. "So that's where the *Quevedo* wound up? Damn. Any idea what happened?"

Jennings said, "She's two miles down, so Cyclops can't see many details, but there's no gross damage. She may have burned."

"Sunk with all hands, almost," Donovan said grimly, and detected an angry look on Executive Officer Percy's face.

Charlie touched his brother's shoulder and left the bridge without saying anything more.

Donovan cleared his throat and said, "Engage automation, Mr. Hooper. Ahead full. Steady as she goes for Navy Harbor."

Donovan felt the gentle rolling of the old wooden sailboat as she lay in her berth at the Seventy-ninth Street Boat Basin in New York City. Even at thirty-seven years of age he could pop himself back into his childhood, which even in the concrete vastness of Manhattan included a boat.

Donovan's father, the police detective, lived alternately in a big old apartment on Riverside Drive overlooking the Hudson and on a wooden boat at the marina. This was when he wasn't being shot at or having another medal pinned on him by the mayor. Such was Donovan's childhood that his father was ever off in some act of selfless derring-do or lounging on the bow of the yacht, the *West Wind,* listening to rock and roll disks on a portable player that in those days was called a "ghetto blaster."

The effect of this upbringing was to give Donovan his father's talent for successful adventures coupled with a love of the sea. The old man's boat never left the dock, though many were the daydreams in which it did. Donovan fulfilled his dad's dream by going to sea, and right up to the *Liberator*'s last mission enjoyed sending his father postcards and nautical memorabilia from afar.

Donovan flipped through the images on his monitor. The laser disk gave him a block-by-block picture of the Manhattan neighborhood in which he grew up: the ivy-covered walls of Columbia University, the rolling green of Central Park and Riverside Park, and the tall spires of the Cathedral of St. John the Divine, where his father capped his career by tracking down a mad killer.

"What's it like now?" he thought. "Rubble? Melted down? Under water or still standing but devoid of human life? And my parents, dead?"

There was a voice in the doorway. It was Charlie. "Postcards from home?" he asked.

"Something like that," Donovan said. "Can I get you a Coke?"

"You have Coke?"

"For the time being. We'll run out in a month and have to go to recycled water, so enjoy."

He reached into the deskside minifridge and pulled out two cans of Coke Classic.

"Dad's brand," Charlie said, popping the can.

"Yeah, just one of his habits I've got. Sit down and relax. We haven't had time to talk."

"Are you free?" Charlie asked, helping himself to a seat on the bunk.

"Yeah. The ship pretty much runs herself. A standard bridge watch while running in open water makes for a good poker game: exec, helm, communications, and systems."

"No navigator?"

"Helm does that when the ship's on automation, and the exec backs up. On automation the only really essential guy is the systems officer, and he mainly watches the indicators to make sure everything's nominal."

"Sounds easy."

"As long as nothing breaks. So, are you recovered?"

"Doc says my radiation count is down," Charlie said, holding up his hand and inspecting it. "I think

I've stopped glowing in the dark. Thanks for rescuing me, by the way."

"My pleasure, Pirate. Tell me the story on that sub you were chasing."

"She was four hundred feet easy, and coming down out of the Chukchi making sixty-two knots. That's unheard of."

Donovan sipped his Coke, a look of benign satisfaction on him.

Charlie read it. "That's not unheard of?" he asked.

"We've done sixty, flank speed. It's not recommended as an everyday thing, though. And I'm positive we're the only ones who can do it. Are you sure your readings were right?"

"I calibrated those instruments myself. She was doing *better* than sixty knots."

"And four hundred feet long?"

"Maybe more."

"There's only one ship I ever heard of that fits that description," Donovan said. "That's us. To move something this big through the water that fast takes a fuck of a lot of power. We can do it, but the designers had to shrink the tower to a blister to get the last five knots. What kind of missile did she fire?"

"Hard to tell. Cruise, maybe. She came to firing depth and let one fly. I was swimming within seconds. I can tell you this, though: she burned hot. Damn near vaporized the chopper."

"How did you get out?"

"I was lucky. Blown out of the chopper while we were still hovering. The bird sank as soon as it hit. The other guys never had a chance. Like I said, that was some hot missile."

Donovan flipped through the images on his screen until he came to a video that showed two New York City storefronts, including a Chinese restaurant and an Irish bar. He pressed his finger against the screen.

"I guess Riley's is gone, too."

"The bar Dad used to hang out at? I suppose so. Look, Thomas, I had three days lying in that raft with nothing better to do than think about it, and I've come to terms with it. Mom and Dad are dead, and so is everyone else but you and me and what you see in this boat."

"There may be others," Donovan said.

"Yeah, the crew of that other submarine, unless they too were blown away. It seems that everything that wasn't under the ice is dead."

"There are others. You. That Russian pilot. There may be more. We have to find them."

Charlie thought for a few seconds, then agreed. "I may have been in a pocket that was relatively untouched by the war. There could be others. Will that be your mission now, to look for survivors?"

"What else can I do? We'll find out when we get to America if we have a home to go to. I suspect there's no one for us to fight, though my executive officer would have it otherwise. *Liberator* began her life as a warship and research vessel. Now she'll be a rescue ship."

Donovan sat on the bunk next to his brother and stared across the room at the monitor until the images his father had sent him burned into his brain. Then, abruptly, he crossed the room and the screen went black. Charlie looked up at his big brother and, for perhaps the first time, saw tears in his eyes.

"I had lots of time to come to terms with it," he said again.

"I'm trying, Pirate," Donovan said. "I'm really trying."

Navy Harbor was built up during World War II on the site of a gold rush mining debarkation port on Unalaska Island near the midpoint of the Aleutian arc.

The original channel, which derived from the runoff of a river that had its origins in the volcanic mountains twenty miles inland, was widened by the Corps of Engineers so that it could accommodate frigate-sized vessels dockside and larger ships moored in the harbor. The harbor was a natural one, and had a sand spit that curved out from one mouth of the river. Engineers built piers on the lee of the spit and a medium-sized dry dock as far up the river as it was possible to navigate.

A good road system connected the harbor with the town, which began at the north end of the harbor and went upstream for three miles. It was a Navy town, by and large, with a sizeable resident population of fishermen manning a fleet of shrimp, salmon, and herring boats. There was no land access to the Alaskan mainland, but a good airport with an asphalt runway and a cargo-and-passenger line that flew the Aleutians to Seward and Anchorage. All in all, Navy Harbor was the picture of a thriving Alaskan city that lived in cooperation with the sea.

It was to this idyllic setting that *Liberator* made her appearance.

With his brother by his side and Executive Officer Percy watching like a hawk, Donovan guided the submarine into the shipping channel ten miles south of the entrance to Navy Harbor and ordered her to periscope depth. When the 'scope and antenna mast were above the surface, Donovan waited for the reports from communications to come in.

"Nothing again, Captain," Jennings said. "No radar emissions of any kind."

This time the report surprised no one. The trip down from the Bering had been made in almost complete silence. No one wanted to talk about possibilities, knowing that what they might find when they reached America could be ghastly.

Donovan made a visual sweep of the horizon, two of them, then three. Then he turned the 'scope over to Percy, shaking his head.

"Nothing living apparent on the horizon in all directions. Nothing human. Birds."

Jennings said, "Further on that, Captain. I'm getting hydrophone sounds—humpback whales, a school of them off the port quarter."

"So we're not entirely alone," Donovan said. "Bring the ship to the surface. Small arms party on deck."

This time, Donovan was the first out of the hatch and onto the topside bridge, which rose not quite two stories above the foredeck. The topside bridge was teardrop shaped, with the broad end facing forward, tapering back to a fine point aft. Like the rest of *Liberator,* it was completely hydrodynamic—even the splash rails and the ladders leading to the deck retracted when the ship dived. The low profile of the blister gave *Liberator* an added five knots in submerged speed, but it took its toll when running on the surface: everyone atop it got soaked in all but the calmest seas, and even the splash rail served only to keep men from falling overboard. Fortunately, the boat was designed to stay submerged most of the time.

Two men ran forward and two aft, armed with assault rifles. Donovan wanted no repetition of the incident where the Russian pilot "strafed" the ship, at least not without the ability to fire back. With rifles pointed to port and starboard on the bow and stern, *Liberator* headed up the shipping channel.

Donovan scanned the mountainous terrain. Makushin Volcano, 6,680 feet high, which dominated the island, was but one of dozens of volcanos that by their outpourings of lava helped build the Aleu-

42

tians. As the floor of the Pacific pushed north, it pushed up a curved string of volcanos that became the Aleutian Islands, a bulwark between the Bering Sea and the Pacific Ocean.

The sky had changed more in the time since *Liberator* headed south. The gray of the postwar had cleared, apart from a trace of high atmospheric haze. The days were again sunny, and a few cumulus clouds formed over the mountainous arc of the Aleutians. The school of humpback whales drew nearer to the ship and, for a brief time, swam languorously alongside, before satisfying their curiosity and heading once again for deep water. Seabirds wheeled overhead and, as the shore drew nearer, songbirds ventured out over the water, hunting insects. Closer in to land, a butterfly fluttered past the bridge.

"There's everything but people," Donovan said.

"Weird, isn't it?" Charlie agreed, trying his own binoculars on the landscape, with no more luck than his brother.

Percy was on the bridge, as was Systems Chief Smith. Both were agitated for different reasons—Percy in his impatience to find Russians to exact vengeance on, and Smith in his desire to return to San Diego to look for loved ones. Both used binoculars on the landscape, which the closer they got to shore looked even more bereft of human life.

"Still nothing on the radio or satellite, Captain," Jennings said. "I get a little static on the UHF, but it reads like far-off lightning. The satellite is still emitting a carrier, but no one's talking to it."

"Any reply to the message we sent from the Bering?"

"Not a word."

"Send a UHF: 'U.S.S. *Liberator* requesting communications.' Try all known frequencies for Navy Harbor."

43

"Aye, Captain," Jennings said, and tried everything he could think of or could pull out of the Cray computerized list of radio frequencies for the Aleutians: Coast Guard, local police, state police, harbor master, dry dock master, even the control tower for the airport. Nothing came back. There was no one to send a reply.

Percy said, "Coming up on a channel entrance buoy, Captain. Flashing red at two-second intervals."

"Slow to one-quarter. Take us up the channel slowly."

As the bridge party and small arms party watched, *Liberator* crept into the channel, leaving the red entrance buoy to starboard.

"Green number five passing to port," Percy reported. "Forty feet under the keel—we have plenty of water, Captain."

"Steady as she goes," Donovan said, not taking his eyes away from his binoculars.

Jennings said, "I make out two tanks, bearing two-niner-seven, and one radio tower, bearing three-one-two. Still nothing on the UHF and no radar, Captain."

"This is like a fucking Hitchcock movie," Donovan said, and no one argued.

"A red number four to starboard," Percy said. "Small waves breaking over shoals a quarter mile off the starboard bow."

"Thirty feet under the keel. The chart shows a clear channel right up to the dry dock."

The channel narrowed and passed through a bulkheaded opening in the sand spit. Moving deliberately slow, *Liberator* came close enough to the eastern bulkhead to smell the creosote used to preserve the timbers. Atop the bulkhead a one-lane asphalt road dead-ended in a yellow-painted barricade. A several-years-old Buick sat up there, all four doors open to the gentle morning breeze.

The small hairs on the back of Donovan's neck stood up.

Off to starboard, the harbor curved sharply around and culminated in the first of a succession of piers, with boats tied up at all of them. There were dozens of shrimpers and eight medium-sized trawlers, their nets neatly packed and ready to catch herring. At the large dock was an old and rusting cargo ship of the Eltanin class, 256 feet on the waterline and 4,000 loaded tons. Designed for Arctic operation and with her hull strengthened against ice, she lay quietly rusting in her berth, with no one on deck.

Alongside her was a seagoing tug, the *Cherokee*, 240 feet and 2,400 tons, commissioned in 1979 and in Arctic service for two decades, hauling disabled ships from one part of the coastline to another. She rested easy at her dock, bobbing up and down gently in *Liberator*'s wake. Up and down Navy Harbor, boats large and small reacted to the wake as if it were the only thing to move them in weeks.

On a long commercial dock, a long block's worth of quayside buildings stood as deserted as an old movie set. The ship's chandler, two freight forwarders, a long and ancient fish and shellfish market, a dingy restaurant and a dingier bar stared past a row of parked cars, their doors open. And the doors to all the stores were open, as were the windows.

"Do you see that?" Donovan said. "There's nobody home but all the windows are open."

"The doors are open on the boats too," Smith noticed.

"Weirder and weirder. And no answers to our radio messages?"

"Not a peep," Jennings reported.

"Where the hell *is* everyone? Dammit, I mean to get to the bottom of this. All stop!"

"All stop," Percy replied.

"We'll anchor here and send a party ashore," Donovan said. "I'll lead it myself. We'll take the large boat with the Merc on it. I'll need two men armed with automatic weapons, Dr. Martin, Chief Smith, and my brother."

Percy bristled. "Begging the captain's pardon, but I should go instead of your brother."

"Negative. You're needed on board. In case anything happens to us, get the ship to safety out of the harbor. For your information, I'm bringing Charlie because he's very intuitive. He's also the best shot in the Navy, and that's not a small consideration."

That was true. The Donovan brothers picked up their father's traits, with Tom taking the lion's share of the intuitiveness and all of the curiosity, and Charlie picking up some of the intuition and all of the marksmanship. A two-time Navy pistol champion, he excelled at guessing where and when targets would pop up and then plugging them. Tom could think of no one more qualified than his kid brother to ride shotgun on a shore party that was venturing into the unknown.

With *Liberator* resting at anchor and small arms parties positioned fore and aft, the crew broke out the six-man raft and slipped it into the water from the starboard plane. Donovan sat in the bow holding his 9-mm Colt, while Charlie crouched beside him, cradling a 9-mm Kurzweill-Benz automatic, as the Mercury outboard motor was fired up and propelled the boat to shore.

As the teal hull of *Liberator* slipped behind them, Donovan again noted the normality—everything was as it should be, except that all the windows and doors were open and no one was home. Even the smooth surface of the harbor had the requisite fine coating of oil, which broke up the sunlight into a spectrum. Three needlefish swam swiftly by, and a large school of bait fish broke the surface of the water a stone's throw from the raft.

On shore, a mangy old brown dog crept nervously down the quayside, alternately looking in doorways and out at the approaching boat. Seagulls perched on mooring posts, some of them eyeballing a black-and-white cat that sunned itself atop an empty oil barrel.

"Everything looks right, but . . ." he said, and Charlie nodded.

"This could be any town in the United States," Smith said.

"Any town in the world," the doctor replied.

Donovan found himself unconsciously tightening his grip on the handle of his Colt.

He didn't like guns, at least not in the way Charlie did. To him they were tools, to his brother they were wonderful toys. Carrying a gun embarrassed Donovan a little, as if it meant he couldn't talk his way out of a bad situation.

The boat made a slow arc and pulled alongside a floating dock at which a 120-foot fishing trawler was tied up. The boat was secured and all hopped out, with one man standing guard by their means of escape back to the submarine. *Liberator* lay at anchor a few hundred yards away, not far as ships go but a world away as concerned the tiny boat they came ashore in.

Donovan hadn't been on a dock in a month, given two weeks for maneuvers and another two weeks under the polar ice cap. Something felt creepy. He couldn't pin down what it was or come up with a better way of describing it. He only knew that he had a creepy feeling, and that it pervaded the atmosphere around him, from the floating dock up across the quay and into the town of Navy Harbor.

The trawler was named the *Ellie B,* printed in block letters where the black paint was fading from years of casual maintenance. Rust stains ran down from the gunwale railing nearly to the waterline, and the bow and spring lines, both four-inch cotton, were fraying. As it was with everywhere else, the bridge and cabin windows and doors were open, and the only motion was a bright orange plastic milk carton that had been suspended from a signal halyard, for no apparent reason.

Pushing his Colt ahead of him, Donovan moved up the gangway and peeked over the rail. Left unguarded almost within arm's reach was a portable 110-volt generator and, nearby, a newly purchased hawser.

"Nobody's afraid of thieves," Donovan said.

"The generator is worth five hundred dollars," Smith noted. "And two guys could carry it right off."

Charlie came around from behind his brother, the automatic at the ready, his head cocked like a spaniel does when he hears something. Donovan recognized the symptoms of intuition in his brother. Charlie, too, sensed that something was wrong in the air.

"What is it?" Donovan asked.

"All I know is I got a bad feeling about this. Let's check out the wheelhouse."

"The rest of you stay here," Donovan ordered, then followed his brother, who crept catlike across the deck of the trawler to the wheelhouse, then stuck his head in the open door. They nearly jumped out of their skins when the radio sprang to life.

First there was the crackling of static, then a familiar voice. It belonged to Dave Jennings, and it said: "This is the U.S.S. *Liberator* requesting communications. Anyone listening please respond."

Donovan scooped up the mike.

"Liberator, this is Donovan, calling from the trawler *Ellie B.* How do you copy?"

"Five by, Captain. Are you okay?"

"Yeah. The skipper of the trawler had his radio on but no one was listening to it. There's nobody on board, so we're going into the town."

"Mr. Percy recommends caution."

"I'm fond of it myself," Donovan said. "Have there been any readings or communications?"

"Negative, Captain. It's still quiet as a grave."

In the time since he first made that remark, the communications chief had lost his fear of stating the obvious.

"Keep her in idle with your hand on the gearshift. We may be coming home in a hurry."

Donovan hung up the mike, and Smith, who had joined them, said, "Why in a hurry?"

"This place gives me the creeps."

"It's a general condition. I looked at the engine room and everything is in order. They even have a cassette deck in there with a country and western tape on 'play.' The batteries had run down with it on."

"So they were playing music when they died? Interesting that nobody remained to shut it off."

"This place is *very* creepy," Charlie said. "Let's try the dock."

Once again they crept up the dock with Charlie and his automatic in the lead, but this time Donovan had his finger on the trigger of the Colt. Guns, he decided, had become more of a necessity than he thought during the many boring hours on the practice range. And, come to think of it, he wasn't that bad a shot either.

Halfway up the dock they found a fishing setup.

Apparently a man and his son had set up a bamboo pole alongside a spinning rig and cast their lines into the harbor. There were all the makings of a pleasant afternoon fishing: a bucket with bait, now largely consumed by bugs; a pair of sandwiches and a Twinkie, also eaten by insects; two pairs of sunglasses; a Walkman that contained a tape of *Bat Out of Hell,* a vintage rock and roll album (the batteries of this player also ran down while it was running); and a Styrofoam cooler containing five cans of Olympia Beer. A fifth can, opened and half drunk, sat atop a mooring post. Flies buzzed around it.

Donovan took in the scene, then picked up the spinning rod and reeled in a bobber and an empty hook. "His bait's gone."

"What was he using?"

"Squid. There's some in the bucket."

He put down the rod and looked up onto the quay. Still nothing stirred, apart from a few seagulls, and the mangy dog had gone on his way. All the doors and windows on the block were open, and through the door of the freight forwarders a light was burning.

"The power is on. At least something's working."

Smith said, "Basic systems could be relatively untouched. The Aleutians are on the Alaskan Nuclear Power Grid, which could supply power automatically for a short period of time."

"Which leaves only one excuse for not being on the radio, TV, or radar," Donovan said. "They're all dead."

Smith shot Donovan a dirty look, and the captain replied, "I don't like it, but I have to admit the truth."

Charlie went ahead of the rest, not relaxing his caution a bit, and the group followed him across the dock and street and along the row of parked cars. All had their doors left open and windows rolled down, and all the keys were in the locks.

Donovan poked his head in the front seat of a '97 Toyota and tried the ignition. The engine cranked for ten seconds, then started. Immediately the cassette player came on, full blast, Beethoven's *Eroica.*

Donovan shut it off. The noise was like a jet taking off, coming as it did after the deadly silence. "This was fascinating back on the trawler," he said. "Now it's getting scary. What did they do, party their way through World War III?"

"With the doors and windows open," Dr. Martin said. "But where *are* they?"

"Here!" Charlie shouted from the door of the ship's chandler.

They ran to him and then recoiled at the sight. In a shop that specialized in selling ship's supplies, including rope, nine corpses dangled from crude nooses strung from the rafters.

The bodies hung straight down, limp as wet rags, and were frozen in the still air. The shoes were neatly tied. On the counter, between the cash register and a book entitled *Arts of the Sailor,* an old record player cranked on, the needle wearing a groove in an ancient 45 rpm record, "Two Out of Three Ain't Bad." The stench of decaying flesh reached the ceiling and fanned out through the store.

"God," Donovan gasped, and stumbled outside into the clear Aleutian air.

Martin joined him, wiping his suddenly sweaty brow with a handkerchief. "Those people didn't kill themselves," he said.

"There was nothing for them to jump off of," Donovan said.

"Someone hung them."

51

Shaking, Donovan made his way down the sidewalk, past the fish market, to the saloon, the General Quarters. A static-y sound crept from the doorway, as did an eery blue glow. The creepy feeling that had been building in Donovan and was confirmed in the chandler's shop turned to a flush of shock and rage: inside the bar the bodies were stacked like cordwood, clothes neatly arranged, illuminated by the glow from a large-screen TV that had been left on.

Donovan felt his stomach coming up, and once again staggered out onto the sidewalk. Dr. Martin held his arm, tentatively. Then there came a shriek and, from behind the building, came a man pallid white in a white T-shirt holding a shotgun at the ready.

Donovan gasped and raised his pistol and there came a roar from Charlie's Kurzweill-Benz. The man was cut in half and thrown back into the saloon's big front window, smashing it. He came to rest in a pile of glass and neon beer signs.

"One o'clock!" Charlie yelled, and fired again.

Before Donovan could turn in that direction, another white-shirted corpse was sprawled on the sidewalk. Another shotgun rolled from another set of fingers.

"Three!" Charlie yelled, and this time Donovan was fast enough. He caught the third attacker with a solo shot from the Colt that hit him squarely in the chest and spun him around to the pavement. A Bowie knife clattered to the ground.

"Get back!" Charlie yelled, and shoved his brother in the direction of the line of cars.

Two more men, both dressed in white, came from behind the saloon. One held a small revolver. A shot crackled and smashed the windshield of the Toyota. Charlie yelled "Freeze right there," but the words made no difference. The man with the gun swung

52

it toward Chief Smith and, in turn, was cut down by automatic weapons fire.

The fourth attacker stood, facing Donovan, a scythe in his hand. His skin was ghostly white and mottled with black sores. His nails were black and most of his hair had fallen out. His T-shirt was bleached almost white but the original design could still be seen. It read "Superbowl XXXI." Donovan held up an empty palm in the universal gesture of peace.

"We mean you no harm," he said.

The man hesitated, then let out a bellow and raised the scythe and charged Donovan.

Charlie shot him and he fell across the hood of the Toyota, then rolled off onto the ground. Dr. Martin bent over him. "Severe radiation poisoning and God knows what else," he said.

Then the harbor air was shattered by the voice of Executive Officer Percy, his electronically amplified voice warning from the ship, his crisp military style suddenly very welcome: "Shore party return to the ship! You! On the rooftops! Stay where you are and don't move!"

Donovan looked up at the row of white, sore-encrusted faces looking down at him, an assortment of weapons held in gnarled hands.

"Holy shit!" he said.

"Let's g-get outta here!" Chief Smith stammered.

As they ran across the road and back out onto the dock, they heard Percy again, this time in a sharp order the tone of which was unmistakable. Then the *Liberator* opened fire, the small arms parties on deck raking the Navy Harbor rooftops with bullets. Several shotgun bursts also filled the air, and there were no cries of pain as bodies dropped.

The crew member who had stayed with the boat had the engine revved up and ready to go when the landing party ran down the dock and hopped aboard. As they raced back to the welcome deck of *Liberator*, they could see a handful of white-clad figures standing atop the row of storefronts, waving rifles and knives.

5

When Percy extended a hand to help the captain back onto the deck, Donovan said, "It wasn't quick. It wasn't painless."

"What wasn't?"

"World War III."

"Did you think it would be?"

"All the propaganda held that a nuclear war would be quick and painless. It wasn't either. Those people are dying as slowly as it's possible to die. They're in incredible pain."

"Captain . . . they nearly killed you."

"They think they have a right. Thanks for saving us, by the way."

Percy said, "You were right about your brother. He's some shot. I watched it all from the bridge."

"How many were there?"

"Seven or eight on the roof of the saloon. Another bunch on top of the chandlery. All wearing white shirts. Did they say anything?"

"Not in so many words," Donovan said. "The doctor says it's radiation poisoning."

"That and a generalized madness," Martin cut in, straightening his jacket. "Probably driven by shock and fear."

"They know they're dying."

"How can you say that?" Percy asked.

"I felt it," the captain said. "I felt the desperation. They have nothing to lose."

Chief Smith said, "What I don't understand is why the buildings are still standing."

"Yeah, and the radiation count is just slightly above normal background," Donovan added. "Does anyone have a speculation?"

"There has been some speculation about nuclear war creating a devastating climate effect," Jennings cut in. "Maybe the nuclear effects are elsewhere . . . no, that wouldn't explain the radiation poisoning."

"I said that it *looked like* radiation poisoning," Dr. Martin said. "The bottom line is that I need to autopsy one of those bodies."

"A shame we didn't have time to bring one back to the ship," Donovan added. "Maybe if they weren't shooting at us . . ."

Chief Smith was silent for a moment, lost amidst a speculation about buildings that shouldn't be standing, power grids that remained on, and war-maddened corpses that not only didn't have the sense to fall down, but became homicidal. "My God," he said. "If it happened here, in the Aleutians . . ."

"It could be happening back home," Jennings added.

"In America. Where our families are. Captain, we've got to go home."

"There's nothing we can do for them."

"But our families . . ."

"There's nothing we can do," Donovan repeated, more emphatically. "Let's gather information . . . as much as we can . . . and go back to the States once we know what we're dealing with. In the meantime, let's get the hell out of here."

He ran up the ladder to the topside bridge and reclaimed his binoculars. Through them, he watched as the white shirts faded back into the streets and alleys of Navy Harbor. Fifteen minutes after their attack, they were as invisible as they had been when the ship sailed into the harbor.

Donovan watched them with grim fascination. Were they the last dying remnants of the old world, or the infants of the new? Surely they'd killed all those in Navy Harbor who weren't killed in the war, but who *were* they? The survivors from among ordinary men, turned keepers of the corpses and vengeance-seekers against all newcomers, especially those in warships?

If so could they be an isolated example of the worst effects of the war, or were they only the first such creatures the *Liberator* would encounter? If there were others throughout the world, there could be no hope for finding civilized survivors—the white shirts or others like them would kill any civilized survivors.

Whatever the ultimate answer, word of the white shirts spread quickly throughout the ship and the crew's concern came back to the captain, who remained on the bridge with the executive officer, the systems chief, the communications officer, and two lookouts.

"The men want to know, Captain," Chief Smith said. "They heard what happened from the lookouts and the small arms party. They want to see for themselves."

"The tape?" Donovan asked. "Yes, I guess I owe them that."

Liberator was equipped with a complete system for recording all action from research to cartography to military action. Most of it was computerized and contained within the ship's Cray computer banks. It recorded digitally all information from external sensors—sonar, radio, radar, and lasers—and saved it along with data from scientific detectors and such odd but useful sensors as thermal probes to detect and record the pattern of thermoclines. But the data banks also included an old-fashioned videotape recorder that took feeds from scientific labs as well as blister-mounted cameras designed to record visual information from the ship's immediate surroundings.

After settling back on the bridge, Donovan reviewed the tape of the fighting in the harbor. It was shot from a distance and a little grainy, but the image of ghastly white-shirted men trying to kill the landing party was real enough. It was just as well, he decided, that no pictures existed of the bodies hung in the chandlery or stacked in the General Quarters.

"Show it on all monitors," he said.

"Aye, Captain," Smith said, and passed an order down to his subordinate inside the hull.

"*Liberator*'s first military action would have to be shooting deranged civilians," Donovan muttered.

"This is not what the Navy had in mind," Percy agreed.

"Raise anchor. Get us out of here."

"Aye, Captain. Raising anchor and leaving Navy Harbor at eighteen fifteen hours."

"Take us out the channel on course one-seven-zero and inform me when we are in enough water to dive," Donovan said.

"Aye, Captain. And our course after that?"

"I don't know where we're going," Donovan said. "I'll be on the bow, thinking about it."

This time Donovan sat on the bow looking back at the ship as it sailed out the channel and toward the deep ocean. Navy Harbor faded fast and soon was the picture-postcard fishing village it seemed when *Liberator* sailed up to it a short while before. Then Unalaska Island itself faded lower and lower

58

on the horizon until it was little more than a ghost of mountains cast against a setting sun.

Soon the ship was again alone in the ocean, but this time in the Pacific and making her way south. Donovan pondered the hull of *Liberator* for half an hour, chain-smoking Lucky Strikes and flicking the butts into the ocean. From the day of the keel-laying ceremony at the Newport News Shipping and Dry Dock Company in Virginia to her first sea trials, *Liberator* had the mark of destiny on her. Even her advanced design, which built upon the best elements of Soviet and American submarine design, was forward-looking. Donovan sometimes called the design a "stretch version of the Victor III," the fast Russian attack submarine, because the conning tower had been streamlined to a blister and the tail fin sported a bulb that contained sensors.

But the American ship was longer and faster and, because she was designed almost exclusively for submerged speed, was quieter (the full-flood vents were reduced to a shielded few, so that when she was on the surface her lines were almost unbroken by vents). *Liberator*'s design was a compromise. The Navy wanted an ultrafast hunter-killer, the National Academy of Sciences wanted a do-anything research vessel, and the White House wanted a ship built for war but capable of carrying science into the new century.

It was ironic, Donovan thought. The one ship in the American merchant or military fleet best capable of thriving in the postnuclear age was the one that survived. While he was sitting on the bow, smoking and looking back on the sleek teal lines of his ship, Donovan thought that surely *someone* meant for *Liberator* to live on.

Charlie wandered out, wearing a uniform shirt that was one of a half dozen procured for him by the systems chief. He took his time, hands in pockets, shuffling his feet on the deck plates and poking his toe at bits of spray that came over the bow. When he got near, Donovan offered him a cigarette.

"Smoke?"

"Filthy habit. I never did get used to it. Maybe if you ask me again next year."

"You think we'll be here next year?"

"Who's gonna kill us?" Charlie asked, with a slightly gleeful tone of voice, proud of his grim realization.

"You have a point," Donovan admitted.

Charlie extended a hand down to his brother, and Donovan got up and straightened his pants.

"She's a good ship . . . made it through the war . . . didn't even fire a shot . . . now she has to pick up the pieces."

"Where do we start?"

"Let's work our way south along the coast," Donovan said. "Puget Sound will be a good beginning."

"Do they have beer in Puget Sound?" Charlie asked.

"They always did. I don't know what shape it'll be in, though."

"Beer in any condition is okay. So, when are we gonna shove off?"

"Right now," Donovan said.

They walked astern to the topside bridge and climbed the ladder. The sun was setting over a sea that was still placid—Pacific, in fact, just as it looked when given its name by Ferdinand Magellan in 1520. The ship was in deep water, having just crossed over the boundary between the Aleutian coastal shelf and the trench beyond, where the water dropped sharply to a depth of several miles.

There, the northward moving Pacific tectonic plate dived and thrust under the North American plate, creating the Aleutians as well as the deep trench. Geologically the area was of great interest, and as such had been fed into the ship's computer bank as something to check out when in that part of the world.

It came as a welcome relief, then, when the system worked and Communications Officer Jennings announced, "A Cyclops reading, Captain. Sonar is picking up the sensors placed in the Aleutian trench five years ago by the Scripps Institute. Indications are that the one below us has migrated two-point-seven centimeters since placement. The seafloor is still descending into the trench."

Donovan smiled and called down from the topside bridge, "Save that video. I want to look at it later."

"Very good, Captain. We're now in 7,250 meters and cleared to dive."

"Say good-bye to the sun for a while, gentlemen."

Charlie looked at the others on the topside bridge and replied, "I'm looking forward to taking some time to learn the ship."

"There will be lots for you to do. Mr. Percy, clear the topside bridge and take us to seven hundred feet."

Donovan and his brother went down the ladder as the diving alarm was sounded. The others followed, and soon *Liberator* was levelled off and cruising easily seven hundred feet below the sea.

"Heading, Captain?" Percy asked.

"Puget Sound on the direct route. We'll check out the general status as well as the shipyards at Seattle and Bremerton and the Naval Air Station on Whidbey Island."

"Course is set for the Swiftsure Bank Lightship," Percy announced.

"Ahead full," Donovan said, then leaned back in his chair to feel the gentle surge as *Liberator*'s engines thrust the ship ahead toward the continental United States.

* * *

Donovan awoke at 0500 feeling hung over; an odd feeling, since he hadn't had a drink since the Christmas party at Flazy's house on the Calle Morelos in San Diego.

He took two Advil and made a cup of Sanka and sipped it while shaving mechanically. Donovan had given up regular coffee since he found that his thirty-seven-year-old nerves were better off with fewer chemicals in his veins. Not that his nerves were ever so bad, just that nothing worked quite as well as it did when he was twenty-seven and pumped iron daily. Serving on submarines had its down side—he got neither the exercise he once did nor the sunshine he needed, and once he reached thirty-seven found that he had to try harder to stay in shape.

Still, he hadn't done badly for himself. He smoked too much, but that was his only vice. He lived alone—Flazy told him that was another vice, the one that would kill him. Flazy was always promoting marriage and the family as the cure for all a man's ills. Certainly it worked for him: Susan was a real turn-on and the kids a treat. But Donovan didn't see it working for him. He was at sea too much and for too long, and when he wasn't at sea was flying around the country consulting on submarine design and programs.

He finished shaving and buttoned his shirt, then left his quarters and walked aft down the corridor toward the engine room, running his fingers over the ubiquitous pipes and conduits. If there was one thing universal among Navy ships, it was corridors. They all looked alike, be they on nuclear submarine or coastal cutter. Pipes and conduits lined walls and ceilings, and lighting fixtures were seldom more than barely covered bulbs.

Light bulbs, he thought; one thing we can't make and will run out of someday is light bulbs. *Libera-*

tor recycled water and air and could find food anywhere, but light bulbs had to be bought in stores. Were there any more stores, he wondered, and who was operating them? Torpedos, too, had to be bought. But he didn't expect to use torpedos. After all, there seemed to be no one left to fight. But light bulbs, they could be a problem.

Liberator's aft engine room was large and spartan, packed to the rafters to accommodate the three T7W steam turbines manufactured especially for the ship by General Dynamics. Only two of the engines were in use at a given time, but all three fed the single shaft. One T7W was kept in reserve for emergency replacement and/or normal rotation out of service for inspection and overhaul. Since an engine was not rotated out of service until after an operational year and *Liberator* was only at sea for a total of a month, the entire power plant was working at peak design efficiency.

The Westinghouse NCS Superfluid Metal Coolant Reactor occupied the room forward of the engine rooms (fore and aft engine rooms), and took up the portion of the ship just aft of amidships. Like so much of *Liberator,* the reactor design was dictated by considerations of quiet operation, simplicity, and longevity. The basic design had been in flawless operation for a decade at the Fermi National Laboratory in Batavia, Illinois. By using superfluid dibarium as a coolant in a natural convection design, engineers eliminated the primary coolant pump, which after the steam turbines was the main source of noise in nuclear submarines.

The reactor core had a life span of thirty years and could probably go indefinitely on the fuel with which it entered service. It ran quietly and reliably, nowhere near redlining. The efficiency of the heat-transfer mechanism on the nuclear-steam link was such that the NCS reactor and T7W turbines could work effortlessly at two-thirds peak while driving the hydrodynamic hull at sixty knots. She could certainly do better than that at flank speed and full power on reactor and engines, but had never been tested. It was deemed that there was no need, *Liberator* already being the fastest submersible in the world by a long shot.

Donovan went through the reactor room to the aft engine room, where he found Systems Chief Smith taking readings from the Master Control Board, which controlled both reactor and engines. Master Control was a fifteen-foot curved control panel mounted in the fore end of the engine room just to one side of the door. The turbines took up the rest of the compartment, secure in their two-tier array where one turbine was suspended on a web of girders above the other two. Two engineers poured over the reserve turbine, checking computer attachment points.

One thing that the designers of *Liberator* had not been able to conquer was the noise of the engines as heard within the engine room. Donovan said, "Hi, Flaze," and pulled the systems chief out into the corridor.

"Catch you at a bad time?"

"Nothing's good or bad anymore," Smith said, sticking his clipboard under his arm. "Look, Tom, I'm sorry about the way I acted up on deck before."

"Forget it."

"No, I shouldn't go shooting my mouth off in front of the crew. It's bad enough that I use our friendship to do it."

"You're entitled, and I want the crew to hear everything," Donovan said. "Technically, there's no command structure anymore. There's no higher authority to back up my orders and, hell, I can't even pay these guys. The only hope I have for keeping

64

their loyalty is trust. That and the fact they have nowhere to go but where the ship does."

"Maybe they want to find that out for themselves."

"Maybe, and I plan to offer them that. We're on course for Seattle, which would have been a triple-A target what with all the military bases around Puget Sound."

"What do you expect to find there?" Smith asked.

"Not much, frankly. I hope I'll be surprised. But we owe it to ourselves to see how badly the country was hurt, and the fastest way to do that it is to check out what happened to a primary target."

Smith took a deep breath, and said "San Diego is a primary target too."

"I know that, and I'm sorry about Susan and the kids. New York is a primary target too, and I've admitted to myself that Mom and Dad are dead."

"Don't you want to find out for sure?"

"How?" Donovan asked. "In a city of ten million, halfway around the world."

"We have the means to get there."

"Yeah, and I'll go there someday, and I hope I find them. But *Liberator* will be better used helping the survivors we find right here, in the Pacific. I hope we find some in Seattle, and when we get to San Diego I hope your family is among them. But . . ."

"You don't have much hope."

"No, I don't. I have to say it."

Smith nodded his head and leaned against the wall. "Okay, Tom, what do you want from me?"

"Your support with the men. Help convince them to go along with me. We've got to turn our attention to rescue."

"Percy is already rabble-rousing. Politely, of course. He wants to sail to Russia and blow the damned place up."

65

"We already did that once," Donovan said. "I see no need to do it again. Unless, of course, there are still Russians around who come after us."

"Percy thinks there may be Russian warships still afloat," Smith said.

"Not unless there was a Russian sub hiding under the polar ice with us. I ran the problem through the Cray, all the probabilities of various types of craft surviving the war under various conditions, and came up with one thesis: we're alone. Furthermore—"

Donovan was interrupted by the ship's intercom, which blared out the voice of Executive Officer Percy. The voice said: "Captain to the bridge! Surface contacts bearing two-six-nine, fifteen miles."

"Come with me," Donovan said, and ran forward.

6

Hooper was at the helm with Percy standing beside him, looking over his shoulder at the Cyclops display, when Donovan and Smith barrelled onto the bridge.

"What do you have?" Donovan asked, moving Percy aside and taking his chair.

"Single contact, Captain. A ship, a small one, fourteen miles and closing."

"Come to course two-six-nine. Periscope depth."

"Two-six-nine, coming to periscope depth."

"Mr. Jennings, is she making any noise?"

"Not a sound, Captain. And I'm getting no sonar registry plate—she's not one of ours."

"Put her on the screen," Donovan ordered, and bent forward to look at the top Cyclops screen. A blip appeared on the horizon, just a splash of color at first, then as *Liberator* drew nearer and came closer to the surface, the splash was resolved into a shiplike icon framed on the surface, apparently dead in the water.

"More readings, Captain. I get nothing—no engines, no sonar or depth sounding, and the only heat generation is the temperature differential with the surface water. She's a dead one, no doubt."

"Not baiting a trap?"

"I get no more thermal readings than would be generated by a floating log."

Charlie said, "She's dead all right."

"More intuition?"

"Common sense. It's a small boat in the middle of nowhere. Too small from coastal ASW to have ventured this far at sea."

"Just where are we?"

"About nine hundred miles west-northwest of Vancouver Island, on course for Puget Sound," Percy reported.

"Charlie's right. That's too far out for a solitary ASW ship."

Jennings said, "Target is now seven miles and closing."

"We're at periscope depth," Percy said.

"Slow to one-quarter. Any more readings?"

"Yes sir. She's still as quiet as before and now reading about two hundred feet over all. Practically a rowboat."

Donovan consulted his watch. "The sun is almost up. Raise periscope and antenna mast."

He waited while his order was carried out and Jennings used the radar receiver to check for signals coming from above the surface.

The communications officer shook his head. "No signals, Captain."

Donovan made a sweep of the horizon with the periscope, then focused on the ship, making his own observations as well as pressing the button that videotaped what he saw.

The ship was a shade over two hundred feet and broad of beam, a fishing boat, and in none too good shape. "A trawler," Donovan reported. "A Japanese boat, burned to the waterline. There's nothing on deck but scorch marks. Mr. Jennings, show the tape to all quarters."

Donovan didn't exaggerate. The trawler looked

as if a giant blowtorch had descended from the sky and blasted her from all directions. The wheelhouse was still standing, but all glass was melted. Two masts read as if they were no more than willow twigs that had been used to roast marshmallows. The haul-in drum for nets showed some residue from scorched cable.

"Take readings, Mr. Jennings. I want to see what our science labs can do. Figure out from wind and drift how far that boat has come since she was dead in the water. Let's begin to get a picture of what occurred where and when."

"Aye, Captain. But we could do more if we had a full science crew aboard."

"A bit late to think of that," Donovan said. "Maybe I'll hit the books myself."

"Do you want to surface and look at her?" Percy asked.

"No. Down scope and resume course for Puget Sound."

Jennings said, abruptly, "More contacts, Captain."

"Belay the course change," Donovan snapped.

"Multiple contacts off the port bow."

"What?"

"A task force, Captain, approximately ten miles wide and fifteen miles long. I'm reading fourteen ships, formation indefinite."

Donovan felt the small hairs on the back of his neck stand up. "Call alert stations, Mr. Percy," he said.

Percy pressed the button that sent the alarm—previously heard only in drills by all the men aboard and everyone else they knew—sounding throughout the ship. As men tumbled out of their bunks and to their stations, monitors placed at strategic locations in corridors, work spaces, and living quarters flashed the message dictated by the captain and programmed by the communications officer: "Multiple contacts off the port bow, a task force of fourteen ships."

"What do you want me to do?" Charlie asked.

"Stick around. I'll think of something."

Jennings said, "Make that twelve ships. One carrier, bearing two-seven-four, distance ten miles, is the central contact. The escort ships are arrayed around her, in no obvious pattern."

"What the hell is a carrier task force doing nine hundred miles west-nor'west of Vancouver?" Donovan asked.

"Good question," Charlie agreed.

"Mr. Percy?"

"Unknown, Captain. The best Russian carrier-borne planes are the Yaks operating off the *Kuril,* and they don't have the range to reach a target in the States from here. Besides, the *Kuril*—"

"I'm getting sonar registry," Jennings said excitedly. "They're ours."

"Ours? An American task force south of the Aleutians doesn't make any more sense than the Russians being here."

"Protecting the oil shipping lanes from North Slope as well as our northwestern flank."

"There's no time for that in nuclear war," Donovan said.

"Reading the carrier . . . she's the *Roosevelt!*"

Donovan pounded his fist on his armrest and said, "Dammit, the *Roosevelt* is in the Sea of Japan, protecting the summit conference."

"Or was a week ago," Charlie added.

"What the fuck is going on? She couldn't get here that fast . . . well, maybe she could, but *why?*"

"I have no idea," Percy said, truly astonished for the first time in his life.

"Course and speed for the task force," Donovan said.

70

"None, Captain."

"What did you say?"

"They're dead in the water, too," Jennings replied.

"Dead? Like the trawler?"

"Exactly like the trawler. No energy readings at all. No temperature. Floating logs."

"Show it to me," Donovan ordered, and within seconds the Cyclops displayed twelve icons representing as many ships. He got to his feet and leaned over Hooper's shoulder to look at them. The largest reading, the one for the carrier, stood out.

The *Roosevelt* was the second of the new CVV class of medium aircraft carriers, 780 feet long and carrying V/STOL aircraft, mainly Advanced Harriers, and the Sea King and LAMPS helicopters. She had distinguished herself in action in the Persian Gulf, the Indian Ocean, and for her support role in the Central American War. She was sent to the Sea of Japan because her ASW abilities were unmatched. At that time, no one imagined a threat from a sub-launched cruise missile.

"Up scope."

Donovan increased the power and swept across the field of view that included the group of ships. They were laid out just as Cyclops displayed them, not prettily and in a rough circle surrounding the *Roosevelt*. There was no visual indication of life, nothing at all. No planes or choppers, no smoke from the stacks of the escorts, nothing.

"I don't get it. Let's surface and take a look."

"This could be dangerous," Dr. Martin said, recalling the scene they had just survived in Navy Harbor.

"That's what we're here for, Doctor. Gentlemen, we'll need another small arms party to go on deck. I need a volunteer to lead it."

"I'm here, Captain," Charlie said, his eyes bulging with excitement at finally having been given an assignment.

"I had you in mind, Mr. Donovan," the captain said, with a smile.

Percy looked alarmed. "Captain . . . the whole task force up there . . . dead?"

"But still afloat. See for yourself."

He offered the executive officer the periscope, then sat back and watched with arms folded. As Percy went over the dozen ships, looking at each with low, medium and high magnifications, Donovan watched the bridge monitor and saw what Percy saw. So did the rest of the crew. The decision to build real-time video monitoring into all quarters was one of the important ones in the design of *Liberator*. It took some of the power away from the role of captain—the ability to hand down decisions that didn't have to be backed up with evidence. But it also increased the stake that each crew member had in the day-to-day operations of the ship; made him, in effect, a partner.

Watching the task force appearing like, in Jennings's words, "floating logs," and sharing their feelings simultaneously, brought home once again the horror of their situation. At Navy Harbor a medium-sized Alaskan town had been decimated. Now it was a carrier task force, with all its might, that was reduced to burning hulks.

"There's not so much as a deckhand," Percy gasped, and relinquished the periscope.

"Down scope," Donovan ordered. "Surface."

The second that the topside bridge broke water, Charlie Donovan—newly named First Gunnery Officer—broke out of the hatch and onto the foredeck, brandishing the new Navy version of the Luigi Franchi 9-mm automatic.

As issued to submariners, the compact submachine gun had a thirty-two-round box magazine, an eight-inch barrel, and a 250-rounds-per-minute rate of fire when on automatic. The Franchi was constructed from rectangular welded tubing for easy handling by machine shops that do not have advanced manufacturing capabilities, and for years was favored by guerilla groups in Latin America, Africa, and Southeast Asia. It was issued to sub crews because it was repairable in their machine shops.

Superstitious after the experience in Navy Harbor, Donovan issued himself a Franchi and carried it with him onto the topside bridge.

Liberator surfaced five miles west-northwest of the task force and crept right down its throat, moving slowly. The area of sea was more than calm; it was flat as a mirror and covered by a misty gray air. The sun was determined not to come out that day, and just as well. The task force lay half on and half under the sea, one or two of the hulks still smoking, the rest simply blasted by an unearthly fire and left to drift.

Donovan took the ship down the middle, too struck by the devastation on all sides of him to talk, and the crew felt the same. There was no conversation, other than an occasional choked sob. For good reason—the might of the United States Navy lay before them, smoldering, dead but not yet buried.

An Oliver Hazard Perry—class guided missile frigate, the *Edders,* had lost her main antenna mast and three radar antennas. The Mark 14 Harpoon missile launcher was partly melted, as was the 20-mm Mark 16 Phalanx CIWS automatic gun. All of the superstructure was burned as if in a blast furnace, and in places the steel sheeting was oxidized.

An Aegis guided missile destroyer, the *Tompkiss,* was in worse shape. The extensive mast system that supported the Mark 2 Aegis Weapons Control System looked like broken twigs, and the Spruance-type sharply defined bow was encrusted with carbon scarring from the fire. Less than a mile away an ASW destroyer floated low in the water, injured in a collision with a still-burning tender.

The *Roosevelt* stood amidst it all, her flight deck buckled by heat and resembling an asphalt road that had been blistered by an August Texas sun. The superstructure was almost entirely gone, simply blasted away and then melted down. A solitary aircraft sat on the flight deck, a LAMPS helicopter similar to Charlie's. It was merely a roasted metal shell with no rotor.

The sea around the ships was littered with flotsam, ship junk. Parts of ships and launches bobbed quietly in the still sea, along with flotation devices and food wrappers. Everything, even the oil-slicked water, bore a coat of gray ash.

"My God," Donovan said as *Liberator* swept quietly by the carrier.

"There is no God," Smith snarled.

"Can we board one of these ships. I mean, is there a *point?*"

Percy said, "To look for survivors?"

Jennings shook his head. "There aren't any," he said. "The computer estimates that the heat outside the hulls of those ships was high enough to vaporize anyone inside. There are no bodies."

To which Dr. Martin added, "Those ships are hot, Captain. There's too much radiation for us to go there, except in protective suits. And there's far too much for any of those crews to have survived."

"What about this area of sea?" Donovan asked.

"Also hot, especially in the middle of the task force. We shouldn't stick around more than a few more minutes."

Liberator passed close enough to the bow of *Roo-*

sevelt to see that the heat scarring included even the underside of where the flight deck overhung the prow. The links of the anchor chains were scorched even where they overlapped.

Donovan looked down at his brother, who stood on the rise of the foredeck, where the topside curve reached its height before plummeting toward the bow, cradling his Franchi and looking out in bewilderment at the floating mausoleum. There could be no doubt now that their loved ones were dead, that everything had been turned upside down, that it was a new world in which *Liberator* was their only home. If no one could survive in a carrier task force, men and women in mere buildings had no chance whatsoever. The planned visits to the States would be formalities, courtesies to the feelings of the crew.

The captain spoke through the bridge speakers: "Mr. Donovan, take your men back into the ship."

And to the bridge personnel he said, "Mr. Jennings, do a drift analysis on this task force. See how long and far they drifted. Compute their original position."

"Aye, Captain."

"Mr. Percy, get us the hell out of here. Shortest possible route."

"Gladly, Captain. On the surface?"

"Yes. I need the air. Let's go where it's fresh."

"Course?"

"Back on our original heading—Puget Sound."

Percy made some computations, then announced, "Come to course two-three-six. Ahead one-half."

As *Liberator* swung temporarily to the south to clear the remaining hulks and picked up speed, water began to crash over the bow, which was scarcely designed for surface running. By the time the ship was free and clear once again in the open sea, only the blister bridge and a stretch of deck fore and aft of it stayed relatively dry.

Donovan stayed topsides with Percy and the lookouts and took off his cap, letting the salt spray of the Pacific soak his hair, clothes and skin, and he stayed there until the desolation they had found was far behind.

Liberator had only one mess, the distinction between officers and men having become so blurred that it was nearly meaningless, at least as far as day-to-day living was concerned.

Titles remained, to an extent. Donovan was "Captain" and the doctor was "Doctor," but from them down titles evolved with the man. Percy liked titles more than anyone and was called "Mr. Percy" by one and all. Smith was "Flazy" to Donovan, Martin and, lately, Charlie, and "Chief" to everyone else.

Hooper was occasionally called "Helmsman," but that title went with the chair the man sat in. Other titles ebbed and flowed depending on who was on the bridge. When Smith was there orders were given to "Chief," but when one of the other systems officers was on duty orders went to "Systems." Jennings was a workaholic and seldom off the bridge, but when he was off orders went to "Sonar" even though that was only a part of the job (the word "Communications" was too long). Donovan's practice was to call everyone on the bridge "Mr.," and that caught on. Charlie's new title, Chief Gunnery Officer, started as a joke on him and the fact that *Liberator* was poorly equipped as far as small arms went, but it too caught on.

The mess was located forward of the bridge and the officers' quarters and was big, with several tables and plenty of stretch-out room. It was in a complex with the galley, workout room, library, and sick bay, so designed in a conscious attempt to put all the living areas together (the crew quarters were just forward, followed by the torpedo room and bow sonar pocket). The mess was part reading room and part dining room, and a logical gathering spot for off-duty personnel.

Donovan, over his third cup of coffee, was staring evilly at the Styrofoam cup in his hand. "We're gonna have to give this up," he said.

"What, coffee?" Jennings asked.

"No, Styrofoam cups."

"We can go back to the old metal ones. I have the report you asked for."

Jennings laid a batch of papers on the table, and said, "We'll have to give up paper, too."

"Yeah. Another thing we can't recycle. What's the bottom line on this?"

"The bottom line is that the trawler was attacked a distance off the Queen Charlotte Islands and drifted northwest on the Alaska Current. The task force was attacked in the Pacific north of the Hawaiian Islands and drifted east-nor'east on the North Pacific Current."

"And wound up ten miles apart," Donovan said, putting out a cigarette in his coffee. "That's one fuck of a drift."

Jennings agreed. "Very fast but not impossible. However, the only computer projection that adds up makes no sense."

"How long ago was the attack?"

"Ten days to two weeks. A day or two after we submerged beneath the ice."

"You're telling me that there were two horrendous firestorms—"

"That we know about so far. One in the Pacific north of Hawaii and the other in the Northwest/ Seattle area, that's what I'm saying."

"And the remains of the trawler and the task force were pushed toward the Alaskan coast? That's weird."

"The computer makes allowance for the current effects of nuclear firestorms. One model holds that simultaneous or near-simultaneous nuclear firestorms in neighboring parts of the ocean could result in temporary current shifts and other extraordinary phenomena."

Donovan smiled at his communications officer's newly displayed scientific acumen. "Very impressive," he said.

"I'm only repeating what the computer said," Jennings replied, a bit stiffly. "Really, Captain . . . you're going to have to find a science expert."

"I'll shop around at our next port of call."

"My point . . . the computer's point . . . is that the firestorm model could account for blazing infernos in two sections of sea . . ."

"Where the ships were."

"Yes, and relative lack of destruction elsewhere. No destruction, not of property anyway, in Navy Harbor."

"But most of the population dead," Donovan mused. "I wonder what we'll find in Seattle."

"The Puget Sound area has long had one of the largest concentrations of civilian and military nuclear targets in the world," Jennings said, reading from another paper. "The trawler was on the edge of that region when it was attacked. We may not find much in Seattle itself."

"We may find nothing," Dr. Martin said, pulling up with a cup of coffee and taking a chair. He too dropped a sheaf of papers on the table in front of his captain, then scowled at the just-lit cigarette.

"That's going to kill you," he said.

"We'll run out eventually," Donovan replied. "I only have one carton left. The ship can't recycle tobacco, either."

"Well, I still need one of those bodies to autopsy before I can tell you what happened to people in Navy Harbor, but . . ."

"But?" Donovan said, interested.

"I just spent two hours going through the medical records in the computer, plugging symptoms and probable symptoms into the epidemiology modelling software. Radiation insanity."

"What?"

"Radiation insanity. It was first reported in the immediate aftermath of the nuclear shelling ten years ago in the Andean coca fields. Symptoms developed incredibly fast: fever, sores, dementia, paranoid delusions and hyperaggressive behavior. Surprisingly, death was not the ultimate result. Some lived on, but always under conditions that would be hard to consider as ideal. They were hopelessly psychotic."

"It was an especially bad nuclear shelling," Donovan said.

"Now, I don't know that the same thing is operative here. I will need a body or two. But it *could be*."

"I didn't hear about anyone surviving that shelling," Jennings said.

"It was a carefully kept secret. Out of one hundred who survived the immediate fire and blast effects, ten developed radiation insanity. Two of them survived *that*, but not the insanity. They became hopelessly homicidal and had to be put away."

"How fast did symptoms develop?"

"The fastest reported was two weeks. Of course, they could have developed sooner, but relief workers didn't want to go into the fields to find them.

Actually, no one expected to find survivors. And those were only field-grade weapons."

"Good killing power, though," Donovan said.

"Neutron bombs, they used to be called," Dr. Martin said. "The enhanced weapons kill people but leave relatively little structural damage. That was the justification for their development—people died but man's works remained."

"Why would the Russians want to save American buildings?" Jennings asked.

"Enhanced radiation has a very short half-life. The buildings and cities become habitable after a few months," Donovan said. "New coca workers were back in the fields planting by the end of the year. I suppose the Russians could want to live in Seattle, if it was the Russians who started World War III. Mr. Percy is sure that's the case. I'm awaiting more evidence."

Dr. Martin reached over and plucked the captain's cigarettes from his pocket, then took one and lit it. He puffed long and with satisfaction.

"The bottom line is two percent of the surviving population is affected with radiation insanity," he said. "Of a hundred thousand survivors in a large city, two thousand will be hopelessly psychotic. Not an enviable prospect."

"Hardly," Donovan agreed.

"That's *if* the medical evidence gathered after the fighting in South America ten years ago holds true for now. Why don't you consider switching to a filtered cigarette?"

"We're out."

"Anyway," Dr. Martin said, "when we get to Seattle, I'd appreciate it if you could dig up a body."

"Doctor, your ghoulish tendencies are not serving us well in this situation," Donovan said, hoping to change the subject as two crewmen drifted into the room, got coffee and cake, then left.

The mood of the crew had shifted noticeably since *Liberator* sailed through the remains of the carrier task force. Men who previously cried out to return home to search for loved ones no longer were so sure. The certainty of death hung over them. Why go back if there's no hope? Making matters worse was the peculiar nature of the killing. The sea targets encountered thus far, the task force and the trawler, were totally devastated, with 100 percent mortality but bizarre structural damage (the hulls were completely burned out but remained afloat, indicating a searing but brief firestorm). But Navy Harbor had all its buildings intact—even the fisherman's beer cooler was undamaged—but mortality was high and radiation insanity affected the few who survived.

Donovan had drifted in his thoughts a bit, musing about the future and how to manage the crew, and the doctor and Jennings, both of whom could be considered his friends, picked up on it.

"Captain?" Dr. Martin asked. "Tom?"

"The truth is, I make jokes about the war but at heart I'm like anyone else—a bit lost for what to do."

"What you have to do . . . carry on," the doctor said.

"I know what we'll find in Seattle—complete devastation. I don't know why I feel compelled to see it myself."

"Because there's no other way to believe it," Jennings offered. "There are no newspapers to tell us what happened, and supposition and probability aren't good enough. You have to know. I have to know. *We all* have to know what's left of the world."

"And if there's nothing there?"

"Then we go looking for survivors elsewhere," Dr. Martin said. "We have to do that. We have food and shelter. We have medicine. We can help."

"We have weapons," Donovan added.

"Yes, and they may be needed," Jennings said. "Mr. Percy has a point—we don't *know* who started this, but one thing's for sure—we'll have to shoot at *someone* before the job is done."

"You're both right, of course. We're only a day's sail from Swiftsure Bank Lightship and the entrance to Puget Sound. Running into the remains of the task force threw me, that's all."

Donovan stubbed out his cigarette, stood, and was about to excuse himself when the room shook with the voice of Executive Officer Percy over the intercom: "Captain to the bridge! Surface contact dead ahead, ten miles!"

"A guy goes to have a smoke," Donovan grumbled, then took off aft toward the bridge.

Jennings had barely retaken control of sensors from the communications duty officer when he was asked to make his report.

"What is it, Mr. Jennings?"

"A ship, captain, another one dead in the water. Readings coming in: length approximately four hundred feet overall, narrow beam, configuration uncertain. I am getting no sonar registry. She's not ours."

"Is she making any noise?"

"Nothing."

"Let's see her," Donovan said, and looked at the top Cyclops screen.

As seen on the gently curving viewscreen, the contact was a splash of light roughly shaped like a long, thin ship with no distinguishing characteristics.

"It's the same as with the trawler, Captain. No engines, no sonar or depth sounding, and no heat generation noted yet. Hold on . . ."

One of the captain's eyebrows arched toward the ceiling.

"Negative heat generation," Jennings said, a bit hesitantly. "She's colder than the surrounding water."

"Colder? Impossible!"

"Nevertheless, those are the readings."

"Captain, thermal profiling of targets is only three years old, a relatively new military science," Percy said. "We don't even have a catalogue of the heat signatures of all major American naval vessels, and almost nothing on the Russians, except that their subs run hotter than ours . . . as a general rule."

"Meaning?"

"Meaning that the Russians are concerned enough about heat profiling to develop countermeasures. That's what Naval Intelligence thinks, anyway."

Donovan said, "Mr. Jennings, are you comfortable with your readings?"

"Aye, Captain. But I can't explain a negative temperature reading. Every other reading we've taken has been right on the mark, including the atmospheric readings through the ice. I'm willing to bet on my instruments. If it's reading negative that means it's below water temperature, which at the surface at this place and time is . . ."

He consulted a small monitor.

". . . Fifty-one-point-three degrees."

Hooper, the helmsman, reminded them, "Target is seven miles and closing."

"Still no motion, Captain," Jennings said.

"Slow to one-quarter," Donovan ordered. "Come to periscope depth."

"The ship is rising at ten degrees," the duty officer manning the diving station announced. "Holding on ten degrees . . . levelling off."

84

"Up scope. Communications officer check for radar emissions."

As the periscope and antenna mast broke surface, Jennings watched his monitors and soon announced, "No radar emissions. Reading other monitors, that ship looks dead. Her hull temperature is still holding at fifty degrees. Very unusual, Captain. I'll have to ask the computer for an analysis."

"Do so."

"What's unusual about another floating wreck?" said Charlie Donovan, newly arrived on the bridge and straining to see the Cyclops display.

"She's cold, about one-point-three degrees below the water temperature," Donovan said.

"Carrying a load of ice?"

"Maybe. Let's have a look."

He went to the periscope, adjusted the light level for the mid-afternoon sun, and homed in on the target.

The ship was still miles away and not entirely clear. But what Donovan made out of her shook him. He stared at the image for half a minute, then said, "She's a sub ... on the surface. Not one of ours."

Percy took the periscope and scrutinized the target. "She's got a blister bridge like ours, and a tail bulb. Captain, she's the mirror image of *Liberator*."

"Is she Russian?" Donovan asked.

"I can't say. She looks a bit like a Victor III."

"So do we," Donovan said. "That ship does look like *Liberator*. I do not like this one bit."

"Me neither," Percy agreed.

"I also got a bad feeling," Charlie said. "How big did you say that thing is?"

"Sonar reads four hundred feet," Jennings said.

"This feels weird," Charlie went on, rubbing his chin. "When I was laying for three days in the raft thinking about the sub that launched that missile I had this creepy feeling that I was being watched."

"So?"

"I got the same feeling now."

Donovan took back the periscope and pressed his face against the light shield. "All stop," he ordered, and watched while the ship slowed to a halt.

He switched to high magnification and trained the laser rangefinder on the tower of the strange submarine, which lay perfectly still on the glassy surface of the Pacific.

"Five thousand, two hundred and forty-seven yards," Percy said, reading off a small monitor on the periscope housing.

"I make out five masts, none with any markings. No markings on the hull, which is gunmetal gray. The forward edge of the tower has a slit that may be a window. The deck is porpoise-back, like ours . . . maybe even a bit more so. And . . . hold on . . ."

"What is it?" Percy asked.

"The deck is wet!" Donovan said, clenching the handles.

"Wet?"

"She's been submerged within the hour! Damn, I think she's starting to move! Sonar, are you getting anything?"

"Nothing," Jennings replied.

Charlie stammered, "Listen on fourteen-twenty hertz."

"I know that frequency," Jennings said, groping for a memory.

"Me too. Listen on it."

"Do it," Donovan ordered.

Jennings gave an order to the sonar duty officer and soon one of the Cyclops monitors flashed new information.

"Damned if she isn't emitting *something* on fourteen-twenty hertz."

86

"Down scope and antenna!" Donovan snapped. "Ahead full! Dive to one thousand! Alert stations!"

As *Liberator* leaped ahead and down, Donovan sank back into his seat and grabbed the armrests and wished that his ship was faster, better armed. In the final seconds that he watched the strange submarine, he saw her surge forward, cutting a distinct wake in the calm sea. She had been waiting for him, baiting a trap. There he was, in command of what everyone had told him was the world's most advanced submarine. But who was this stranger and what did she want?

"Charlie, what do you remember?"

"Three frequencies as she ran down the Bering toward the Pacific—fourteen-twenty at first contact, then fifteen hundred and seventeen-fifty. I have no idea what they represent. Maybe a propulsion system."

"I'm not getting any screw signature," Jennings reported.

"Just the fourteen-twenty?"

"Yeah, and it's coming from the ship. The locus is identical with the sonar contact. And you were right, she is moving. Moving forward and diving."

"What's her position?"

"Four thousand, eight hundred and ninety yards. Crossing our bow from starboard to port and still diving."

"Levelling off at one thousand," Hooper said from the helmsman's spot.

"Slot to one-half. Hooper, keep turning with her. Come up astern of her, distance thirty-five hundred yards. Mr. Percy, is the torpedo room ready?"

"Torpedo room shows ready, Captain," Percy replied, glad to have a fight on his hands.

"Switch off active sonar when you get a laser lock."

"Aye, Captain, we have a laser lock. Tying in Cyclops with Weapons Control."

Percy said, "Weapons Control indicates receipt of laser lock. Feeding in to torpedo guidance."

"Make ready two torpedoes," Donovan ordered.

"Torpedoes ready," was the reply.

"Dim the lights more."

The red lights on the bridge came down a few steps more, until all that could easily be seen were monitors—more monitors than the ten men in the room could seem to handle in a day—and the multi-colored arch formed by the three viewscreens that made up the Cyclops display. Leaning into the display and looking over Hooper's shoulder, he saw the target growing in size and continuing toward the bottom . . . five hundred, five hundred fifty, six hundred feet . . .

The display was magical, almost. Logically, Donovan knew that it was only a fancy TV image. He realized that the curvature of the three screens was designed to give the illusion of real-time target and terrain plotting. That the quarter-inch depth of the liquid crystal medium only gave the impression of three dimensions. That the image of the foreign submarine, now at eight hundred fifty feet, was only a computer-generated icon. But it looked so damned real.

"Target is levelling off," Jennings said. "She's at one thousand feet."

"The same as us," Donovan noted.

"Turning to starboard, Captain."

"Stay with her, Mr. Hooper."

What was she doing? First she sat on the surface while he got a good look at her. Then she dived to the same depth as *Liberator*, levelled off and now was turning and presenting her flank, which considering her radical stern taper could hardly contain weapons. Was she running away or being defiant?

Could *Liberator* beat her in a fair fight? The attack systems were working perfectly, a designer's dream. As planned, everything was integrated and tied in to the ship's automation system. Sensors that gathered information routinely on the condition of the ship and the sea around it and all it contained now were channeling data into Weapons Control, which was manned by an eager young adventurer reporting to Percy. Weapons, designed to be unobtrusive until called upon, were showing nominal. Would the ship's Mark 70 long-range, laser-guided, acoustic-homing torpedoes be up to the task of punching a hole in the foreign sub? On paper it was no problem. But something felt wrong, a feeling Donovan also noted on the face of his always-intuitive brother.

"Any other readings, Mr. Jennings?" Donovan asked.

"Negative, Captain. She's at one thousand feet bearing two-eight-two. Dead ahead of us and making thirty knots. She's running away."

"Maybe. Distance to target?"

"Three thousand, five hundred and holding, sir." Hooper said proudly. In his first action, he was doing just fine.

"Enemy making thirty-two knots," Jennings reported.

"Stay with her," Donovan ordered. "Mr. Hooper, you have the helm. Put the pedal to the metal and stay with her."

"Aye, Captain," he said, prouder still.

"A new reading, fifteen hundred hertz," Jennings said.

"That's the second one I heard," Charlie said. "It happened when she speeded up coming through the Bering."

"Damn me. I ordered her noises filtered out of Cyclops. Thought it was a reflection off our own propulsion. What the fuck is powering that boat?"

"Unknown, Captain. I'm still getting no screw noises. No engine noises either."

"Both could be reduced substantially," Percy said. "Both the Russians and us were working on it."

"Noises can't be eliminated," Donovan said. "If there are working parts, there is noise. And our sonar is state-of-the-art. We're supposed to be experts on silent running, remember? We just spent two weeks under the Arctic ice proving how good we are."

"Reading the stern, Captain," Jennings said. "Sensors report a tall vertical fin topped with a bulb, and two smaller stern planes. We're getting indeterminate readings regarding propulsion—sonar might be reflecting off some sort of screw shield. I call tell you this, though: that ship is sailing the straightest course I've ever seen, heading for the deep ocean."

"Try lasers, Mr. Jennings."

The command structure of *Liberator* used a section structure with duty officers in each reporting to the bridge officers. The torpedo room reported to Weapons Control, which reported to the exec. Reactor Control reported to the systems chief. Communications was a broad command that included Sensors (sonar, lasers, and radio/radar), Computers, and Research. Overlapping areas were shared, as a result of which lasers were a joint responsibility of Sensors and Weapons Control.

Liberator's blue-green laser, fired from turrets mounted fore and aft on the tower, was designed for use against either surface or submerged targets, which it could hit down to the plane of the deck. The effective range as a weapon was only one thousand yards (more, up to fifteen hundred yards, as depth increased) within which it caused the disruption of electrical circuits. At ranges up to ten thousand yards the laser functioned as an information probe. Like sonar it ran almost continuously, feeding information about thermoclines into the computer. By accurately reading those layers within the sea that were best for silent running and speed, *Liberator* was able to push its top end speed up close to sixty knots.

Scanning a target only thirty-five hundred yards away in clear water was a snap. But almost the second he was instructed to read the stern of the foreign submarine and report findings, the laser operator offered only consternation.

"I'm getting reflection signals," he said. "but no picture. I'm reading a blur where I know there's a ship."

"Explanation?" Jennings asked.

"None, sir. When we did trials against the *Danson* we could read every rivet in her hull, and she was making twenty-four knots at the time."

Jennings turned to Donovan and tossed up his hands. "The computer needs time to analyze," he said.

Hooper announced, "Target is making forty knots."

"Stay on her tail. Mr. Jennings, how strong was that first burst?"

"Scanning strength, Captain. Zero-point-ten."

"Increase strength to weapons status. Poke a hole in that blur."

A second later, a second-long pulse of blue-green light flashed from the forward laser turret and struck the stern of the retreating submarine. The reaction was immediate.

"Target is increasing to forty-five knots," Hooper said. "She sure didn't like that last one."

"Flank speed, Mr. Hooper. Keep us in firing range."

"Aye, Captain."

"Laser, keep firing," Donovan ordered. "Mr. Percy, ready tube one for firing."

"Yes *sir!*" the executive officer said, and gave orders to Weapons Control. After a moment, he reported back, "Torpedo is set for fifteen hundred cycles. That's the only sound we're getting from her."

Donovan grasped the armrests tightly and said, "Mr. Jennings, hold the laser. Mr. Percy, fire one."

"Fire one." Percy echoed the command.

The Mark 70 torpedo burst out of the tube and kicked into life precious feet from the bow of *Liberator*.

"One launched," Percy said. "She is running true with all systems nominal." He watched his monitors, then said, "Her sonar targeting has captured the enemy."

"Is there any jamming?"

"None, Captain."

Jennings said, "Target now emitting on seventeen-fifty."

"She did that to me in the Bering," Charlie said.

Excited, a little scared, Hooper said, "She's increasing speed to fifty and diving! Heading down at ten degrees . . . speed now fifty-three!"

"Lost the l-lock, sir," Weapons Control stammered.

"Damn!" Donovan swore, and banged a hand into a fist.

"What's the matter?" Charlie asked, noting the proliferation of sudden downcast eyes on the bridge.

"The targeting computer can't focus on only one sound source, which is what we're getting from the target," Percy explained.

"I'm reading fifty-seven on the enemy," Hooper

92

said. "She's crossing twelve hundred feet and diving. We're starting to fall behind."

After a particularly long consultation with Weapons Control, Percy confirmed. "We missed her. Fish one was high. Fish two is reset and ready."

"Hold on."

Hooper said, "Target is at sixty knots, Captain. We're at fifty-five but now three thousand yards behind and falling back. We don't accelerate anywhere near like her, and we're knocking our heads into the absolute top end. And she's deeper—presently two thousand feet and diving."

"Reduce speed," Donovan said reluctantly. "We'll continue following her until contact is lost."

Percy was aghast. "We have another fish ready to fire! That Russian sub—"

"Is making sixty knots and our torpedos only make seventy. Not only that but we have a limited number of torpedos and no way to replace them. And how do you know she's Russian? She didn't identify herself."

"What else could she be?"

"Unknown. There's a lot more we need to know."

"Target is at sixty-two knots and five thousand yards," Hooper announced. "Still heading for the deep sea. Presently twenty-five hundred feet."

"Where we'll never find her," Percy said.

"She seems to have the ability to find us," Donovan noted. "And not only to find us, but to play dead on the surface, waiting. She's already had a good look at our weapons and gotten away free and clear, going faster and diving deeper than we can. We've been snookered, and that's enough for one day. Mr. Hooper, reduce speed to one-half."

"Captain, I protest in the strongest possible terms," Percy said. "We owe it to our loved ones to destroy that submarine."

"We owe it to the survivors of the war to avoid

being destroyed," Donovan said. "Gentlemen, continue to track the target. Communications and executive officers please feed all data into the Cray. Who is she and where did she come from? Where can she be going? What the hell kind of engines is she using?"

"We'll never get that much out of the computer," Jennings protested.

"I'll buy speculation," Donovan said.

"Target is holding at sixty-two knots and has pulled away to ten thousand yards," Hooper reported, rather mechanically. "We have slowed to twenty-seven knots."

"We're losing her," Percy said, earning himself a scowl from the captain.

"Switching the laser from weapons status back to probe," Jennings dutifully reported. "Feeding data into the computer. We'll find out all we can about the target."

"Thank you, Mr. Jennings," Donovan said.

Charlie, who had been silent through most of the chase and abortive battle, rested a hand on his big brother's shoulder.

"There will be other days," he said.

"We know one thing now," Donovan said.

"What's that?"

"We're not alone."

8

On orders from the captain, Hooper steered *Liberator* deeper into the Pacific, following the strange submarine. She had levelled off at three thousand feet and was holding at sixty-two knots on a course that led into the central Pacific and the general direction of the Hawaiian archipelago. Jennings and his sensing crew began to lose contact at fifteen thousand yards and by twenty thousand the target was gone. The sea was once again free and clear of odd emissions in the thousand-plus range of the hertz scale, and the humpback whales resumed their domination of the medium frequencies.

Donovan ordered *Liberator* back on course for Swiftsure Bank Lightship at the entrance to Puget Sound and repaired to the library, where he found Smith and Hooper, both having gone off duty, pouring over a CD ROM and engaging in the latest of their many arguments.

The library was large, by submariner standards, but there were no books in it, perhaps the one oversight in *Liberator*'s design that Donovan had not been able to overrule. The library was stocked with computers and storage devices, mainly CD ROMs (Compact Disk—Read-Only Memory) and monitors that were designed for easy reading. Archived materials included basic library reading—science, history, art, literature, and of course, sports. That last-mentioned category had become so popular—the library contained records of playoffs in all major sports from World Cup soccer to the America's Cup yacht racing and the Superbowl (CDs of the last thirty-five Superbowl games were especially popular with the younger crew members).

And there were the scientific and technical journals, including the specs on all American warships of the late twentieth century and what was known about foreign navies. Donovan found Smith and Hooper toggling between two monitors. On one was displayed the bare-hull specifications for *Liberator*. On the other was the latest edition of *Jane's Fighting Ships*. An argument was joined, an old one that had been updated by the knowledge that another submarine, and one that looked like their own, had survived the war.

The existence of a ship known variously as the second prototype, *Liberator II*, "Battleship *Liberator*," or, after the rumors wouldn't die, *Nemesis*, had long been the stuff of off-duty gossip. The ship that many superstitious crewmen believed was created at the same time as *Liberator* was meant to be the second in the class. But after the devastation caused by the South American War and the consequent public reaction against defense budgets in general and nuclear power in particular, plans to build her were scrapped.

The keel and partial hull of the second prototype were nearly scrapped, too. Then the Navy, eager to save money following the debacle off Cartagena, sold them to the Greater Germany Defense Force (GDF). Germany, eager to flex its newly reborn muscles on the world stage, moved the second prototype to its leased shipyard at Gdansk with the idea of building the first of a fleet of fast nuclear attack submarines bristling with weapons so it could take advantage of the waning power of the Soviet Union.

But the Crash of '99 hit Europe especially hard. More specifically, the people of Poland voted overwhelmingly to return to the sphere of influence of the Soviet Union, as a result of which Gdansk was named a sovereign city, neither East nor West, but existing as an anything-goes trade zone. Rumors swirled that the shipyard would build anything for anybody and at times was working for both local navies—the Soviet and the GDF. Hard evidence of the disposition of the second prototype disappeared, replaced with rumor and innuendo.

The GDF's advanced satellite jamming capability prevented surveillance of the shipyard, and some said that the second prototype was launched as a fast nuclear attack submarine. American naval intelligence discounted that rumor and the ship was never observed, let alone photographed. Shipyard officials claimed, to the belief of no one, that the prototype was destroyed in a fire. But three years worth of silence convinced nearly everyone that *Nemesis*—that was what she was called by that time—was no longer a threat, whatever her status.

"No one even knows who she sails for," Hooper argued, waving a coffee mug.

"The Germans, of course," Smith retorted. "Why am I not surprised that, once reunited, the fuckers took less than a decade to start World War III."

"Don't drink coffee in the library," Donovan snarled. "We have no way of replacing those keyboards if you spill coffee on them."

"Sorry, Captain," Hooper said. "But the Chief is being stubborn, as usual."

"It's one of his more endearing qualities. Now, do we have to replay the scuttlebutt over *Nemesis*? My considered opinion is that the keel and hull were turned into paving material for the Warsaw Freeway."

"The GDF has the fastest frigates in the world and their destroyers are near the top," Smith maintained. "And there's her fleet of conventionally powered pocket subs."

"You're describing a coastal defense fleet, and mainly a surface fleet at that," Hooper retorted.

"The GDF has no need for a nuclear attack sub," Donovan agreed. "Their sphere of influence is still central and northern Europe. That part of it that isn't too shallow for nuclear submarines is socked in by ice most of the year. Besides, all computer models for World War III show total devastation of Europe."

"*Nemesis* could have been at sea," Smith maintained, stubbornly.

"She's beneath the freeway," Donovan insisted.

"Then what *was* it we were chasing?" Hooper asked.

"I was hoping you could speculate about propulsion. What was powering that ship?"

"All we have to go on is her noise," Smith said. "And I ain't seen nothing that produces a fourteen-twenty hertz whine."

"Did you look it up on the computer?"

"I did that, and I looked it up in my gut reactions. The computer says it's some sort of motor. BFD—Big Fuckin' Deal, I need a computer to tell me *that?*"

"An electric motor?" Donovan asked.

"Probably, maybe a big Erector set or something. Sure it's a motor. But what *kind* and what does it do? That I can't tell you."

"It could be a pump sound. Our tertiary coolant pumps make a whine," Hooper chipped in.

"My balls whine," Smith thundered. "The noise

we heard was coming to us through a couple miles of water."

"And probably through a hull that is otherwise shielded," Donovan said.

"You got it."

"The implications are weird. If the ship was noise-shielded well enough to silence the main engines, why let us hear a pump?"

"It don't make sense."

"In fact, why let us hear anything?"

"Nothing about it makes sense," Smith said, his voice carrying a finality that suggested he was tired of arguing the matter logically and would prefer a verbal fistfight. Or another hour spent reminiscing over the specs of World War II battlewagons, always a favorite pastime of crews everywhere.

"It doesn't make sense to the Cray, either," Jennings said, taking a seat and switching on a third monitor. Within a few seconds he was reading data off the display.

"I did as complete an analysis as I know how," he continued. "Remember that sensors reported a tall vertical fin topped with a bulb, and two smaller stern planes?"

"I remember," Donovan said. "That was the sonic sensor—the laser didn't read squat."

"It's the best we have, but you aren't going to like the results."

"I already don't," Donovan said, a bit forlornly.

"There is no computer match to any known submarine. Based on the tail structure and what we know of existing ships in other navies, this one is, well . . . weird."

"Not a scientific category, Mr. Jennings."

"I'm not a scientist. I think I said that."

"Well, until I find one you'll have to do. Carry on."

"The tail is similar to *Liberator*'s but between three and five meters higher."

"There are taller tails than ours," Smith cut in.

"Maybe, but the lateral fins aren't bigger in proportion. They're *a lot* bigger than they should be. The Cray theorizes a design for optimum diving ability and speed."

"What the hell is that all about?" Hooper asked.

"Beats me," Smith said. "The damn thing seems overdesigned."

"When you can make sixty-plus knots, who needs to dive fast and deep?"

"On that score, the computer analysis of her diving ability shows extraordinary talent. Figure a dive angle of fifteen to twenty degrees plus the fact she dropped two thousand feet in the same time it takes us to drop five hundred."

"Four times our diving ability!" Hooper exclaimed.

"That's what the big fins are about," Donovan said.

"This don't make sense," Smith insisted.

"No it doesn't," Donovan agreed. *"Liberator* is designed pretty well—the best minds in the country spent ten years on the project—and still they built us to optimize speed and silence. Our diving ability is only so-so. The old Skipjacks could dive better than us. We sacrificed that for speed. This target we just chased is faster than us by at least a few knots, can dive four times faster and carries cruise missiles—if she's the same boat that Charlie chased up in the Bering."

"She's got to be the same one," Hooper said. "There can't be *three* boats capable of sixty knots."

"I hope not. Two is enough of a challenge. And I was just getting used to the idea of being alone in the world when these guys came along. What does the Cray say about her propulsion?"

"No data," Jennings said.

"I'll buy speculation," Donovan said again.

"I'd sell if I had any. The whines at fourteen-twenty going up to fifteen hundred hertz are unique."

"What about turbine-electric propulsion, like they used in the old *Lipscomb?*" Hooper asked.

"Too big and too underpowered," Smith said, shaking his head. "What this ship has is something else. Damned if I know what it is."

"The computer has no idea either," Jennings said, flicking off the monitor as if he were closing a book. "And one other thing—there's no explanation of how we could read all of the tail structure except that part where the propulsion presumably is located."

"The area that read fuzzy."

"Yeah, that. No record exists of a technology that can shield from laser probe under these circumstances."

Donovan agreed. "In maneuvers in the Atlantic we had no trouble detailing the underwater structure of war games target vessels. Remember the pseudo–3-D printout of the keel of *Danson?*"

"That was something," Smith agreed.

"It gave them a big justification for our last-year's appropriation when it was shown to the Joint House-Senate Committee. I wonder where we'll get our money now."

Nobody said anything in reply, and Donovan was about to break up the meeting when Hooper tossed up his hands and said, "She's got to be *Nemesis.*"

"Not again," Jennings said. "I don't want to hear that rumor surfacing again."

"It already has," the captain reported. "Mr. Hooper is convinced that we're chasing *Nemesis.*"

"C'mon guys, why not? *Nemesis* is the best explanation of what we're talking about. The reason that the computer couldn't come up with answers is that *Nemesis* was never logged into American defense computers."

"She doesn't exist and that's final," Donovan said. "Next you'll have us chasing *The Flying Dutchman.*"

As if on cue, the intercom sprang to life, again with the voice of the executive officer.

"Captain to the bridge," Percy said. "More surface contacts."

Donovan, Percy, Jennings, Smith, and Martin were the officers on the topside bridge when *Liberator* surfaced fifty miles west of Swiftsure Bank Lightship.

It was 0500 and dawn's early light was turning the sky from dark to pale blue. The sky was brilliant. There were stars, more stars than Donovan had seen in years. The gray cast that had hung over the earth since the final days of the war had finally given way to the richness of the blue that nature intended.

As if in response, the sea began to offer up waves for the first time since. Little waves they were that lapped against the teal hull and occasionally broke over the arched foredeck. A gentle early morning offshore breeze was kicking up, and Donovan swore he could smell land. A pair of seagulls cruised above the bow, wheeling and squawking when they saw the men on the bridge.

Smith looked up at them and smiled. "Gulls," he said. "American gulls. There's still things alive."

"Yeah," Donovan said, and couldn't avoid a smile as a Monarch butterfly floated by on the breeze.

Liberator sailed slowly but relentlessly toward shore and before long the surface contacts came into view. There were many and they were all over the place. Bits and pieces of boats. Pleasure boats,

Chris-Crafts and Sea Rays. Boston Whalers. Chunks of fiberglass hull scorched and floating in the water, their jagged torn edges melted and curled over, the flat parts the color of gray toast.

As Hooper, steering from the topside bridge, picked his way through the debris that was all that remained of the Seattle-area seafront, the officers watched their emotions migrate from horror and anger to quiet desperation and, at last, resolve. Debris in large chunks including bits of houses and docks turned to smaller patches of garbage. That came in all sorts—kitchen refuse, paper, bottles, Styrofoam, cotton and diapers—everything that didn't burn in the firestorm that swept over the city and could still float.

The remains of the Swiftsure Bank Lightship passed by, melted steel burned nearly to the waterline and clinging to life on the surface by a thread. As *Liberator* moved within five miles of shore, having passed through intermittent bands of garbage and debris for fifteen miles, the waters cleared again. The sun rose over the ashes of North America after the fires had gone out. Seagulls again swirled in the skies and so did shore birds, making cheerful mating cries above the ruins.

On the horizon there was nothing higher than a tree, and most of those were stripped of branches and leaves. Donovan swept it with his binoculars. There were no buildings to be seen from the sea, only the girders and brickwork of a few small ones along the waterfront. Apart from the birds and the sound of the waves as *Liberator* moved up the channel, once again the crew was greeted with silence.

There was nothing at all in all of the electromagnetic spectrum: no radio, no TV, no radar, nothing. No cars roamed the land; there were no streets to keep clear. All of the multimillion-dollar systems built into *Liberator* to detect threats found nothing, and even the small arms party that once again patrolled the deck found nothing to do but stare at the nothingness.

On the bridge Smith stared at this vision of a burned and wasted land and said, softly, "My family."

"I'm sorry, Flaze," Donovan replied, gently laying a hand on the big man's arm.

9

The entrance to Puget Sound lay inland up the Strait of Juan de Fuca, a narrow channel from Cape Flattery in Washington to Port Renfrew on Vancouver Island. *Liberator* proceeded cautiously with all sensors functioning nominally, even though the chance was decreasing that the ship's eyes and ears would detect a threat.

Staying close to the Washington side and with the small arms party on deck, Hooper steered south of east, passing the chokepoint between Port Angeles and the Race Rocks Light House, which, like all other navigational aids in the harbor, was merely a memory. *Liberator* slipped through Admiralty Inlet off Port Townsend and turned farther to the south into Puget Sound proper.

Donovan took the ship around the sound in a counterclockwise direction, passing the approach to Bremerton and then turning sharply to port and heading back in a northerly direction.

The Seattle waterfront was, simply, levelled. Bricks and mortar from blown-down buildings spilled over into the harbor, totally obscuring the roads and railway systems of the harbor infrastructure. Of the skyline, only Mt. Rainier remained. All the works of man were blown down and already nature was reclaiming the city. Fast-growing weeds and vines were poking their heads above the dust and ash. These were about the only living things—even the hardy Norway rats that locals had sworn they would never be rid of were exterminated. Vines grew and birds poked around in the ruins but that was it.

Donovan and Percy alone remained on the topside bridge, and both wore radiation-protective suits. Jennings's computer analysis showed far too much ambient radiation within the confines of Puget Sound for an unprotected man to breathe the air for more than a few minutes. Hooper steered *Liberator* along the computer track (laid out in the preceding decade, it allowed magnetometer readings of the local magnetic field to feed into the Cray and be turned into an accurate "track" into and out of most American harbors).

As the ship passed Fort Lawton. Donovan and Percy stared wordless from behind their protective shields. Once *Liberator* was back in the Strait of Juan de Fuca and aimed once again at the welcoming arms of the deep sea, the radiation suits came off and men again came up on deck, to wash off the radioactive dust and stand once again with small arms waiting for life, even hostile life, to show itself.

It came late in the ship's daylong tour of Seattle. Sonar picked it up first, a relatively high-speed drone coming out of the south. Then the port lookout, watching from the topside bridge, saw the Boston Whaler racing at them, powered by a ninety-horsepower Mercury outboard. Donovan warned, "Small craft approaching off the portside beam. Videocameras on. Dr. Martin to the bridge."

The boat had come out of Port Angeles and was roaring at *Liberator* at thirty-plus knots, the man at the helm wearing a tattered white formal shirt with ash-stained ruffles. Around his face was wrapped white gauze, it too stained with ash, dirt and pus. He carried a twelve-gauge shotgun.

"Charlie, he's got a twelve-gauge," Donovan yelled.

"Weapons party hit the deck!" Charlie hollered, raising his 9-mm Franchi to the ready position.

The man in the boat lashed the wheel amidships so that the Whaler was on a straight course for *Liberator*. With no waves or appreciable current the small craft zoomed in on the massive nuclear submarine, whose officers (with the exception of Donovan and Percy) crouched behind the splash rail and watched in fascination. Unlike his men, who were laying on the deck as ordered, Charlie stood proudly on the bow, waving the intruder to come and get him.

"Is this a pattern?" Percy asked, his voice showing admiration.

"I'm afraid so. When we played stickball back in New York, he used to dare guys to throw the ball at him."

"Can he duck as well as he shoots?"

"He can duck even better. Hold on."

As the boat swept in at *Liberator*, Charlie stood stock-still as the white-garbed intruder aimed the shotgun and pulled the trigger. As the gun discharged Charlie dropped to the deck, then jumped back up and aimed the Franchi.

"I want him *alive!*" Donovan yelled as his brother squeezed off a shot.

The man went down, thrown to the bilge of the small boat, which then went into a sharp turn, circled once, and splattered against the port beam of *Liberator*. Donovan and Percy watched as crewmen grabbed the gunwales and pulled the survivor out.

"Get the outboard! Get the outboard and tank!" Chief Smith hollered, running out onto the deck to supervise.

Once again sick bay had a customer. Chief Medical Officer Martin was confronted with his second terminal case since signing on board the ship, and this time he knew the symptoms before he plugged them into the medical computer.

"Radiation poisoning complicated by exposure and general systemic shock," he said. "Same as with the Russian pilot. The shot in the shoulder is, at this point, a minor inconvenience."

"Why can't he talk to us?" Donovan asked.

"He's in deep shock, and I doubt he'll pull out of it. This may be part of the history of the illness—rapid degeneration and death following any trauma."

"In other words," Donovan said, "the bullet in the shoulder killed him."

"He's dead already, for all intents and purposes. Charlie's bullet was the exclamation point. Look, there's something else."

"What?"

"This much radiation should have killed him a week ago. He should be as dead as the bodies in Navy Harbor by now."

"We *know* the date of onset," Donovan said.

"Yes and no. It's true that global nuclear war lasts something like six minutes and everyone should have received their fatal doses of radiation at more or less the same time. It's also true that those who received equivalent amounts of radiation should die at about the same time. *But this one didn't die on schedule.*"

"Meaning?"

"I looked in his pockets," Martin said, flashing a Sherlockian look of satisfaction. "He's not from Seattle. He lived in Cranbrook, in the mountains of British Columbia—nowhere near a prime target. He bought gas there three days ago. There's a receipt in his wallet. The computer estimates that the war was fought ten days ago, while we were still under the ice. This chap was in the mountains then, and quite safe. He came to Seattle a week after the city was devastated—"

"A looter," Donovan said, smacking his fist in his palm.

"Exactly, a looter come down from the safety of the mountains to see what he could find."

"He got a speedboat and motor. The shotgun may have been his."

"He also picked up a deadly disease," Martin said.

"Radiation insanity," Donovan said.

"Fever, sores, dementia, paranoid delusions and hyperaggressive behavior, in his case, looting and the attack on us. I see now that the Russian pilot, the mob in Navy Harbor, and this man were all affected the same way—all hopelessly psychotic."

Donovan quickly picked up the line of thought. "This means a lot," he said, "and none of it good. It shows some social organization . . ."

"The guys in Navy Harbor had a crude, brutal, but working organization. They worked together in a fashion," Martin said.

"The Russian pilot managed to fly the plane. This guy stole and operated a boat. They may all have been crazy, but they managed to function. I have to suppose there will be more of them."

"Especially in the remains of cities. Looters will come there and pick up radiation insanity."

"We have more of this to look forward to," Donovan said grimly.

"If only there was a cure," Martin said. "The researchers found none after the South American War, but they didn't have many victims to play with. We could have thousands wherever we go."

"Find an antidote, Doctor. You have your work cut out for you."

Martin checked the vital signs on his patient, then shook his head. "I drew blood from him and will run tests, but I'm no pathologist. I may never find an antidote to what's killing this man. It's weird—part radiation and part viral psychology. What the hell does the white shirt mean, and how did white shirts migrate from the Aleutians to here in a week. Did this guy wear white accidentally?"

"Not likely. He went out of his way to wear a white formal shirt. I like the ruffles."

"There must be some meaning. White is supposed to be pure. I suppose that's it. Radiation insanity must provoke some basic impulse yearning for cleansing action."

"Such as violence against warships," Donovan said, thinking back on the way the victims had attacked *Liberator* and its crew.

The medical monitor went straight-line. Martin pulled a sheet up over the latest body.

"Want to keep him?" Donovan asked.

"For a while. Let me get tissue and organ samples, then you can bury him. If there's an antidote to radiation insanity I'll find it."

"Tell me, Doctor. Are we in danger?"

"It's not catching," Martin said. "However, the victims are vicious and organized. They also have a big grudge against us. That's danger enough, wouldn't you say?"

"Oh yeah. One more thing—if you find an antidote, we can use it to save lives, you know."

"That occurred to me. We might save some lives among those who weren't seriously irradiated. That's if I find an antidote and if we can manufacture enough of it."

"We'll find a way," Donovan said. "We have to. We have a stronger mission now—we can really save lives."

"If the white shirts don't kill all the survivors first," Martin said.

"I will present the dilemma to Mr. Percy and the crew," Donovan said.

And that's exactly what he did. As *Liberator* sailed out into the Pacific and away from the ruins of Seattle, Donovan conferred first with his executive officer and then with the entire crew.

Donovan's problem was not so much avoiding mutiny but inspiring confidence in the direction he had chosen. Mutiny was never a real possibility, and it certainly was never talked about openly. There was some grumbling about "doing it Mr. Percy's way," though nobody had a clear idea what that way was. Percy was a hothead and a military adventurer, but none of that made sense without a clear and present target to take action against. The only Russian they had encountered was a madman who stole a plane and tried to strafe them without bullets.

Unless *Liberator* sailed straight to the Soviet Defense Zone surrounding the Kamchatka Peninsula she was not likely to encounter many Russians. Even if she did there was no reason to believe that Kamchatka—certainly a priority target in a nuclear war—would have fared any better than Seattle. Probably the Russian peninsula, with many military and few civilian targets, would have fared worse, if that were possible.

And the prospect of finding a Russian convoy was unlikely, too. *Liberator* was continuously sweeping the sea and skies for signs of other ships, and the only ones found were dead or, in the case of *Nemesis,* too mysterious to figure a port of call. So who was there for *Liberator* to fight, were the crew to take up Mr. Percy on his call to arms? And the increasingly dim prospect of finding a Russian alive enough to kill begged the issue of whether or not the Russians started the war. On the face of it Greater Germany was a probable aggressor, given the fact that its star was rising as the Russian empire faded.

Who or what was *Nemesis* and what did she want with *Liberator?* Those questions would await another day, when maybe the odds would be a little better. Or, at the very least, *Liberator* would be ready.

For more than three hours, as the ship coursed out into the North Pacific and as far away from Puget Sound as possible, Donovan met with the crew—all three shifts. He presented to them a choice. Assume, as Mr. Percy did, that Russia was to blame and begin roaming the seas in a probably fruitless search for Russians to kill. Or do the right thing and do what they could to help survivors. There was no doubt that the survivors needed help, what with semiorganized gangs of white-shirted crazies prowling the cities with homicidal intent. *Liberator* could help some of them. Dr. Martin could find the antidote to the radiation sickness that was destroying the remnant of mankind. If that happened, *Liberator* would have to set up a means of production and distribution.

In either case, it had become indisputable that *Liberator* could make a difference, could help. Two hundred miles off the shore of Washington State, the crew put it to a vote and rallied behind the captain. They would dedicate their lives to helping. They would start right away. The only question was where.

That was solved during the dinner hour on the first day out of Seattle. As the blue shift enjoyed muffins and the usual gallons of coffee and listened to country music on the disk player and the red shift took advantage of some surface running to take in the fresh ocean air, Communications Officer

Jennings scanned the heavens for radio transmissions. Normally the scanning was automatic, with radio-frequency and sonar receivers programmed to sample all known frequencies. The computer listened to everything—even the ubiquitous dolphins—and alerted its human operators to those it deemed worth hearing. So far that had amounted to nothing. Of all the radio frequencies and sounds that were known to naval communications experts and programmed into the computers, only two—the outboard motor in Puget Sound and the 1,420 hertz droning of *Nemesis,* had made themselves known.

Nothing infuriated communications officers so much as silence. It was antithetical to their very existence. The idea that no one was talking rendered pointless the hours they spent listening. It rendered obsolete the multimillion-dollar systems designed to listen for them. So Jennings had taken what was, for a modern nuclear submarine, the extraordinary step of putting on earphones and twirling the dial of the UHF to see if his own ears could hear what the computer could not.

He found it, barely audible (below the design tolerance level for weak-signal computer pickup) at 462.725 in the high police band, and instructed the receiver to boost the signal. Once it was processed and audible Jennings routed it to the PA system, where it was piped to all quarters.

"Calling for help from San Francisco. . . . I am in a police car on what remains of the Golden Gate Bridge . . . myself and other survivors are under attack by the gangs . . . we need medical supplies and help. . . . We need evacuation . . . is anyone listening? Can anyone help?"

On hearing this, Donovan sat up in his seat and said, "Mr. Hooper, set course for San Francisco. Ahead flank."

The approach to San Francisco was like the approach to a bonfire—in a desperate hurry with sirens wailing and lights flashing, but at the last moment, hesitatingly, to avoid getting burned.

A plea for help from a police car atop the remains of the Golden Gate Bridge? Donovan keyed on those words. "Remains" was telling; the bridge was wrecked, but not so badly that you couldn't sit in a car atop it. You could also sit down and have the time to figure a way to summon help. But the absence of policemen from the police car told Donovan that civil order was a shambles, if it existed at all. And the gangs? White-shirts, he imagined. It had to be them. And they had spread all the way down the coast from the Aleutians to Seattle to San Francisco.

It was a fortnight after armageddon and already the crazies were on the march.

Still, the good guys were still alive and organized enough to find a way to summon help. He had to let them know it was coming.

"I have it worked out, Captain," Jennings announced proudly. "I can boost the signal and lay it right down in their laps. If they're listening on 462.725 they'll hear us."

"They have batteries or gas or both," Percy said.

"Gas to drive up on the bridge," Donovan conjectured. "It makes no sense to walk all the way up onto a wrecked bridge hoping to find something useful. Downed bridges are dead ends."

"They could be defending themselves," Percy said. "We know the white-shirts migrated down from the Aleutians to Seattle. They could have reached Marin County by now."

"And be assaulting the ramparts of San Francisco," Donovan said. "The good guys could have gone up on the bridge to make sure it stays out."

"Or to erect defenses if it isn't entirely out."

"We have to find out who they are. Percy, how far are we from the Golden Gate?"

"Two hours, Captain. That's at flank speed."

"I need suggestions. You're the military strategist . . . give me your appraisal of the situation."

"The probable situation is a besieged community under attack from at least one direction," Percy said, proud at being taken seriously both as a partner in the enterprise of running the ship and as a military man. "If it were just a matter of crazies from the north, they could flee south. Something is barring the escape routes from San Francisco, probably white-shirts coming up from the south."

Donovan agreed. "San Francisco is easily isolated. In the earthquake of '89 the Bay Bridge was knocked out for a month."

"Throw a picket line across the narrow part of the peninsula near Pacifica and you have a prison," Percy said. "I recommend we make contact by radio, announce our arrival for noon the next day, and then . . ."

"Go in the night before to have a precautionary look around," Donovan agreed. "That's what we'll do. Jennings, send this message: 'U.S.S. *Liberator* steaming into San Francisco Bay noon tomorrow with medical supplies and assistance or evacuation.

115

Please identify self for rendezvous. State your numbers and identify enemy. How is he armed and where is he?' "

"Shall we say more about who we are? They won't expect a submarine."

"All the better," Percy said. "Just in case it's a trap."

"Who would think to trap a nuclear submarine? Besides, we're essentially invincible."

"That point can be made as long as we're at sea," Donovan said. "But San Francisco Bay is a lake. For us, anyway."

Liberator came to periscope depth and ran that way long enough to let Jennings send the message, repeatedly over the space of an hour, before it was received. The reply was enthusiastic, even ecstatic, and came in a new voice: that of a young woman. It went:

"This is Embarcadero calling *Liberator*. Who are you and can you help? We are one hundred under attack by gangs from the countryside. They have guns. We hold the waterfront from the Municipal Pier to the Trans-Bay Tube, North Beach and Telegraph Hill, HQ at Fisherman's Wharf."

Donovan grabbed the microphone and said, "This is Tom Donovan commanding *Liberator*. Those places are still standing?"

"Just barely, Donovan," was the reply. "The gangs are weak now but getting stronger. Our fortifications won't hold much longer. Can you help?"

"That's what we're here for, Embarcadero. Be waiting for us. Wear something with an *L* on it so we can recognize you. What kind of guns do the gangs have?"

"I don't know. I'm a scientist, not a goddam soldier. Guns that kill people."

Donovan gave the officers on the bridge a pained

116

look and told them, "I don't believe this—a rescue job with an attitude problem."

The radio spoke again, saying, "I have to get back to the wharf. It's getting dark out. Please hurry."

"On our way . . . *Liberator* out."

"What do you make of that?" Charlie asked.

"I don't know," Donovan said. "Down antenna, ahead flank. Mr. Hooper, take us to the outer channel marker and slow to one-half and call me. I'll be in my cabin with the exec and the chief gunnery officer, planning strategy."

Through the periscope and using night vision image intensifiers, the Golden Gate Bridge looked unscathed by the war. The nearly full moon glistened off its steel webbing, which shone from the droplets left behind by a daylong fog. There was no apparent sagging, and no cables were out of place.

But using 12x magnification and silhouette-comparison with the silhouette stored in the computer's bank of Pacific Coast shore landmarks revealed the flaws. Roadbed plates were buckled, making the northern segment of the bridge impassable by car. And all of it was treacherous, a walk through a minefield of holes. On the highest magnification Donovan could make out cars: hundreds of them, frozen in time as they were caught during the firestorm.

That kind of damage was hard to assess. The firestorm had been a brief and capricious one, echoing a pattern that was to prove true around the globe. The fires of war touched different places differently, sparing some the worst direct damage. The Golden Gate Bridge looked a bit singed, but no more affected by the initial fire. Instead, the blast damage was most apparent: the blown-apart roadbed and numerous cars tossed over on their roofs and sides. But most of the window glass was intact or shattered, but not melted. On the bridge, the fire-storm had been minimal.

That held true for the horizon. As Donovan swept the periscope across the horizon from the Golden Gate south down the shore, the horizon silhouette pretty much matched the one in the computer. The main difference was the total absence of electric lights. It was an eery sight—a long stretch of urbanized coastline without so much as a traffic light.

Instead, bonfires and campfires dotted the shore. Donovan thought it was a scene from an old pirate movie, where the heroes approach a hostile coast seeing only the fires of enemy encampments. Through image intensification, trails of smoke could be seen snaking their way upward from the largest fires, which burned in Golden Gate Park. There was no motion other than the smoke.

Donovan ordered the ship to the surface and from the slightly elevated topside bridge still could see no activity. Radar and sonar sweeps revealed nothing, and a lot of listening on the high police band found more silence. Whatever use the survivors made of that band, it was only during the day. At midnight, *Liberator* moved into the inbound shipping channel and shallow-dived to where the topside was just under the surface.

The shipping channels had been dredged down another forty feet five years before, and the Corps of Engineers had subsequently kept the silting to a minimum, so there was plenty of water. Hooper followed the computer track eastbound through the narrows and under the Golden Gate Bridge.

Jennings reported, "Numerous cars on the bottom under the bridge, Captain. This was dredged out five years ago and they must be new."

"Blown off the bridge," Donovan mused.

"It seems likely. Will we have enough water?"

"Reading ahead five thousand yards up the channel to the southbound turn. No significant obstructions."

"I'm getting a flux in the computer track," Hooper reported, a trace of concern in his voice. "The track I'm reading is not the one in the computer."

"Will it give you problems?"

"Negative, I can compensate."

"That deviation is confirmed, Captain," Jennings said, reading his monitors. "Analysis is a magnetic dispersal of recent origin. This happened since we went under the ice. The last navigational update by satellite into the computer was twenty days ago."

"Explanation?"

"A sudden flux in the geomagnetic field is best explained by seismic activity," Jennings said proudly.

"I thought you didn't know science."

"I don't. That's what the computer readout said."

"So the Bay Area had an earthquake recently?"

"There is some evidence for nuclear triggering of seismicity. It could have happened here."

"The earth's crust is fragile in these parts," Donovan translated.

"Analysis of the flux indicates recent earth motion to the near south, possibly beneath the city itself," Jennings said.

"The NaviComputer is stabilizing the signal," Hooper said. "We're still on track."

"Take us to anchorage seventeen off Fisherman's Wharf," Donovan said. "We'll drop anchor in the channel, bow heading outbound. I sense a fast getaway."

"The ship will be ready," Percy replied.

Hooper steered *Liberator* around the horn of the San Francisco peninsula and south into the bay. All the way, Donovan watched through the periscope while the shipboard computer compared what he saw of the skyline with the computer record of the same skyline, fed into *Liberator*'s memory a few months before she took to sea.

The comparison was startling. Of the once-great city, only the northern tip remained somewhat as the computer remembered. All of the area south of Market Street and Golden Gate Park lay in ruins, with few buildings poking above the three-story level. The devastation was nowhere nearly as total as it was in Seattle—buildings remained and were arguably habitable, but all of the streets were impassable to all but foot traffic. Dust and wreckage were everywhere, right up to a ten-foot sheer wall where the bomb-induced earthquake split the city from west to east. On about the line of Park from Haight to Market the earth was rended in two, forming a wall that was impossible to climb without help.

But north of Market the story was dramatically different. While the tall buildings were gone—the TransAmerican Pyramid was little more than a skeleton denuded of glass—many of the smaller buildings remained. Many were knocked down, too, and the streets here were no more passable than in the south. There was no electricity anywhere, and the waterfront along the Embarcadero was a shambles of crumbled brick buildings and trash piles that once were wooden and plaster houses.

There was another difference between north and south. To the south, in the wrecked portion of the city, campfires abounded, their smoke trails combining to form a hazy cloud that hung over the blackened ruins. But to the north there were few fires, apart from a controlled one on Fisherman's Wharf and a line of them that ran up Market and as deep into the city as Donovan could see.

After reaching the anchorage and assuring himself that they were unnoticed, Donovan brought the ship to the surface and had her anchored. With running lights off and an order of silence on deck, *Liberator* sat a few hundred yards off Fisherman's Wharf, impossible to see from the shore unless one was looking hard.

The officers and lookouts spilled onto the deck and topside bridge and scanned the shoreline with binoculars. Close-up, Fisherman's Wharf and the surrounding Embarcadero were alive with activity—at least more alive than the crew had seen in weeks. The windows of the main building on the wharf were lit, and smoke from some kind of internal fires spilled through makeshift chimneys poked in the roof. A solitary figure sat on a wooden chair propped against a mooring post at the northeast corner of the roof. To all appearances he was a normal human being—a welcome sight after Seattle and Navy Harbor—and doing what sentries throughout history have done, sleeping.

A small group of figures stood around a pile of burning wood at the foot of the pier. Another was out on the very end of the curving municipal pier (two figures near that group were fishing). Going eastward to Pier 43, another fire raged in a broad trash can and was kept going by one of a party of four men who were doing something that Donovan found to be extraordinary. They were working on *Priscilla,* an 1888 oyster schooner that had been a tourist attraction on the pier for years and was suddenly being readied for a long-delayed return to life as a functioning sailing ship.

"They're getting her ready for sea," Donovan said to Charlie, who like him admired the days of men and wooden boats. It was something both had learned from their father, who was fascinated with the lore of life under sail.

"It's a classic escape ... if they can keep her afloat and the sails fill."

"Where in hell are they going?" Donovan asked.

"Out," Percy replied, and gestured for his captain to look down the shoreline to the ruined zone.

There, at the base of the ruined Oakland Bay Bridge, was a scene of brutality so foul that the crew understood immediately the cruelty of what the survivors referred to as "the gangs."

Around a huge bonfire made of the walls of tumble-down buildings, a group of forty or fifty men milled, some standing dumbly, others moving in mechanical cadence carrying bodies. A snaking line of men carried corpses out of the ruined city to the bay edge, where they were thrown onto the fire, whose flames flickered and consumed. A second line of men carried wood, stripping it off the flattened buildings of the World Trade Center. This was food for the flames, as was the occasional squirming body of a live victim.

Donovan swore he heard the screams across the waters of San Francisco Bay.

"My God," he swore.

"There is no God," Charlie said. "The Chief was right."

"No wonder those people want to get out. They want it badly enough to ask us for help."

"I guess we have to give it to them. What say you put me ashore with a couple of men and let me take care of those guys over by the bridge?"

"Maybe before we leave," Donovan said. "First let's make contact with Embarcadero."

"Where will we find her?"

"On the wharf, I guess. Let's go ashore now. I don't think we can wait until noon. I've seen the situation and we can help."

"You're not going without me."

"Of course not. It looks like a jungle in there. I'll need you and two of your best shots. We'll take Percy and the Chief. I'll need them to evaluate Embarcadero's tactical and materiel situations."

11

Dressed in black and using oars instead of an outboard, Donovan led the shore party in a wide arc that swept in on Fisherman's Wharf from the blind side.

They tied the small boat to a floating dock on the cargo side of the wharf and, with Charlie in the lead, crept up the stairs to the pavement. Fisherman's Wharf had fallen on hard times. The block-long array of shops and restaurants was boarded up and ringed by abandoned cars, most of them late-model luxury cars.

The main building still bore the marks of its most recent upgrade, one that turned it from a slightly seedy tourist attraction to a modern, clean mélange of shops and eateries appealing to the rich. Behind the nailed-up barricades was a contemporary facade packed with stores of food and drink. No wonder the survivors were attracted to using it as a base, Donovan thought.

One shop near the corner was a tobacconist; Donovan thought, "Got to pick up some Luckies before I go home," then felt silly and continued creeping along the wall behind Charlie.

The plaza between the wharf building and the bulkhead had no cars but was a pedestrian mall, with a large concrete planter every thirty feet. The

124

planters had been stripped of plants and turned into huge pots for fires used both for cooking and for light and protection. Two burned past midnight on the day that the *Liberator* crew landed; three if you counted the bonfire nearest the Embarcadero where a group of men warmed hands and discussed strategy.

It was a crisp May night, unusually clear of fog, one that made it tempting to recall San Francisco on a good night in the tourist season when the Giants were playing at Candlestick Park. The lookout that Embarcadero had posted stirred slightly on his chair, which was a standard kitchen chair tilted back against a mooring post. Charlie and Donovan crept up to him and Charlie put a gun to the man's temple and a hand over his mouth.

"Freeze and shut up," Charlie said, in a loud whisper.

The man's eyes went wild and he struggled for a moment, then when he saw that his assailants could talk and were apparently normal he calmed down.

"Who are you?"

"The help you asked for. Where's Embarcadero?"

"In the wharf. Are you guys real?"

"You gonna shout?" Donovan asked.

"No. I swear."

"What's your name?"

"Bill."

"We're real," Donovan said, standing and pulling off his black jumpsuit. He had his uniform on beneath it. Bill focused on the insignia, then smiled in relief.

"I'll take you to her," he said.

He led them along the front of the wharf building to the midpoint, where a onetime crab-and-shrimp palace had been turned into the survivors' headquarters. As they approached the entrance, the group of men standing down the block took notice and began pointing and shouting. Bill waved at them as if to say "It's okay," but they ran tentatively toward the shore party. When he went into the HQ behind Bill, Donovan left Charlie and one other of the guards to keep the other men out.

Inside was an unlikely bunch of resistance fighters. They were sitting at what had been a thriving bar, going over a street map using shot glasses to mark key bulwarks and intersections. There were six men of all ages, all centered around a young white woman with curly black hair that was barely contained by a rakish bandanna.

She looked up, startled, and her eyes fixed on Donovan's face. She was so young. He couldn't suppress a smile.

"Donovan?" she asked.

"You're the attitude problem we came here to save?" he said.

"Is that you? We weren't expecting you until tomorrow."

"We caught a favorable wind and blew into town early. Do we have to worry about you guys? We'd like to put down our guns."

It was only then that she noticed his Colt and the Franchi automatics carried by the others.

"Guns? Oh, please do put them down. I don't like guns."

"That's why you're holed up in a bar," Donovan said, holstering his Colt. "My name is Tom Donovan, commanding the U.S.S. *Liberator.* We were under the polar ice pack when it happened. We appear to be the only game in town. What's your story?"

As she told it, the woman known to them as Embarcadero was Alexandra Fisher, the daughter of an Episcopalian minister who was the real leader of the survivors in San Francisco. Padre—that's what he was called by one and all—had managed to organize a resistance out of the survival movement that sprang up in the immediate aftermath of the war. His twin children, Alexandra and Peter, were his lieutenants. Alexandra was a computer whiz with an encyclopedic knowledge of history and politics; Peter a skilled surgeon and medical researcher. In the absence of charismatic figures other than himself, Padre relied on Alexandra to supervise the Fisherman's Wharf HQ while he tended to the outpost at Coit Tower, which was closer to the front.

"It was my idea to call for help," she explained, sitting at a large round table with her aides and the men of *Liberator* gathered around. "I hot-wired a cop car that had been abandoned on Powell and managed to get all the way up onto the Golden Gate."

"What are the roads like?" Smith asked.

"Roads? What roads? We're dealing with cow paths between busted-down buildings. This part of town is a little better now that the corpses have been cleaned up."

"Who did that?" Donovan asked.

"The white-shirts. They came on the seventh day and within a week had picked up all the bodies that the buzzards didn't get. They've moved off now and are cleaning up south of Market."

"We saw them. They were cleaning up corpses that weren't dead yet. How did they get here? Across the bridge?"

"Yeah, they came over the Golden Gate from the north. How did you know?"

"We've met them before," he said. "Up north."

"Anyway, there's no roads but I did manage to get the car up onto the bridge before it conked out. And I sent a message to you. Here you are."

"You mentioned gangs," Donovan said.

"Barbarosa," she said flatly.

127

"Who?"

"He started out as a preacher, like my father. But he was a fundamentalist, a real Bible-thumper. Somewhere during the war he went off the deep end, saw himself as the new Messiah. He's tried to kill my father and establish himself as the leader of San Francisco. He wouldn't mind running us into the sea and taking over our territory."

"Can't you negotiate with this guy?"

"We tried, and it worked for a while. Barbarosa and his men are the ones who drove the white-shirts to the other side of Market, and they still patrol all of the wall with the exception of the very east end, by the BART tube. That's ours. But when Barbarosa looted most of the firearms stores and set up a medieval-style rule in his territory, my father opposed him. That's when the trouble started. He's mad, Donovan, entirely mad."

"There's a lot of it around."

"He's worse than most. Did you ever read about Charles Manson?"

"That bad, is he?"

"Worse. He's efficient. And he's got his men—and women—organized into Manson-style killer bands who live in Golden Gate Park."

"What keeps him from just moving in and killing all of you?"

"Simple. He's got the brawn. We've got the brains. Me. I make things run, and I control the food supply. We've got all the emergency supplies locked safely in the BART tube that runs between here and Oakland. The survivors of San Francisco stored it there for the use of all right after the war. We parcel it out to one and all according to need. Barbarosa wants to take it all, but we manage to fulfill our mission."

Systems Chief Smith, who came along to make a

determination of the survivors' materiel needs and infrastructure, asked, "What's with this wall?"

"All I can do is conjecture, but it looks like a nuclear-induced seismic event. Specifically a five-or-greater Richter earthquake on the secondary east-west fault, which bisects the peninsula. There wasn't much primary bomb damage here—forget about Oakland and points east—but the quake flattened sixty percent of the buildings in this area and all of the ones south of Market. It also made a nifty strike-shift fault line that dropped the land south down ten feet. It's pretty nearly impassable; a major pain in the ass getting from one side to the other."

"At least it keeps the white-shirts away," Smith said.

"No it doesn't. I mean, it keeps them from coming back in hordes. But incursions are frequent. Barbarosa loses a lot of men, but he's programmed his followers to believe in romantic suicide. They get their rewards in the afterlife if they sacrifice themselves for him now."

"That saves on overtime," Donovan mused.

Smith said, "So Barbarosa is manning the ramparts and you guys have the harbor facilities and the food. You're refitting a ship to make it seaworthy enough to take you somewhere safe. Why not just pay off Barbarosa with food and buy enough time to let you split?"

"It's not just us, Chief. There are only a hundred of us in the front lines of the survivors' movement. We could get aboard *Priscilla* tomorrow and sail away."

"What's the problem, then?" Donovan asked.

"We have to think of the other *ten thousand!* That's the total number of survivors in our section. How can we leave town and leave them to the mercy of Barbarosa? If he doesn't kill them, the white-

129

shirts will. You can't evacuate ten thousand people."

"Are all of these people healthy?" Donovan asked.

"No. Seven out of ten will die within the next year. That's what Peter says, anyway. But the thousands that live will be able to rebuild this city."

Donovan felt a surge of excitement and saw the same thing in his fellow officers. The speeches he had made to them about doing what they could to help the world recover suddenly made real and present sense.

If *Liberator* could help make San Francisco safe for the good people who survived the war, it could serve as a safe haven for other northern California survivors. In that case, World War III wouldn't be the end of the world that so many had predicted.

There was no decision to be made. *Liberator* had to help. "What can we do?" he asked.

"We need guns and someone to show us how to use them."

"Charlie?" Donovan said, offering his young brother's services.

"Glad to help, ma'am. Are there any gun shops left?"

"A big one, but it's south of Market, on Mission and Seventh by the Greyhound bus terminal."

She lifted an Alcatraz souvenir shot glass and pressed a fingertip against the map to show the spot.

"The bus depot is the white-shirts' HQ. That part of town crawls with 'em. All I can do is get you a dozen men and show you the way over the wall."

"That's a start," Charlie said.

"What else do you need?" Donovan asked.

"My father needs medical supplies up at Coit Tower. We have plenty of supplies in the BART tube but no way of moving them."

"Do any of these cars work?" Smith asked. "I got my eye on a Mercedes down at the end of the dock."

"They work, but there's mostly no gas. I mean, I know where it is but none of the pumps work. There's no electricity either."

"Is there a power plant we could patch up?"

"No. Nothing."

"We passed a seagoing tug that didn't look in too bad shape," Donovan said.

"What about it?"

Smith said, "Tugs have generators. The captain has a point. If we can tow that tug to the wharf and patch her up, we'll solve your electric problems. Part of them, anyway."

"All we need is enough to power the hospital," she said.

"Consider it done," Donovan said.

Embarcadero smiled and relaxed momentarily, long enough to brush a few strands of hair from her eyes. Donovan sensed that she was beginning to see the light at the end of the tunnel. Maybe she was also beginning to think of herself as a woman again, for the first time since the war.

He thought the whole thing was quite amazing. Here was a major American city struggling to emerge from the ashes of the war, and its fate was being guided by a twenty-five-year-old computer expert who happened to be a girl. And not a bad-looking one at that.

Computer expert, he thought. That's interesting. "What kind of computer work do you do?" he asked. "Or did. Or whatever."

"Scientific programming and systems. My degree is in environmental and ecological science," she said, a bit puzzled by this interest.

"In other words, you can use computers to figure out how to stay alive in a hostile world," he said.

"Yeah. But I have no computer."

131

"I have dozens. The best in the world. And a job for you when this is over."

"Really?" she said, obviously intrigued.

"On the ship. Want to see it?"

"Yeah. Is the ship in the harbor? Nobody saw her come in."

"That was the idea," Donovan replied.

The tour of *Liberator* that Donovan gave to Embarcadero and two of her top aides lasted an hour and left them dazzled. At 0300 and not a bit tired she sat in the captain's chair and watched as he demonstrated bridge systems, especially the computers.

"I adore the library," she said at last.

"Like I said, *Liberator* is more than a warship. It's a research vessel, and we have the finest scientific and historical data base that's ever been built into a ship."

"Amounting to three mainframes. That's incredible."

"Our design was predicated upon the emergence of peace among the superpowers," he continued. *"Liberator* was to be the first of a class of ships that would carry Western learning as well as might around the world. Now we seem to be the best chance for a rebirth of civilization."

"If you could only lose the weapons," she said.

"I'm afraid we'll need them for the foreseeable future. So . . . will you join us?"

She was tempted, and strongly. But she was a bit frightened. For weeks all her energy had revolved around keeping the San Francisco survivors alive and well. Now strangers had come from the sea and were offering to take her away to do great things elsewhere. Events were happening so fast.

"I *am* a science specialist . . . I *did* publish two books on the scientific principles behind the coop-

132

eration between man and nature in the development of communities. But that was *theory*. I've never had the chance to work it out in the field."

"When we're done in San Francisco . . ."

"We're needed here so badly."

"San Francisco is only the start. Once we clean up this town we can move on. We *have* to."

"Then we *will* succeed here?"

He rested his arm reassuringly on her shoulder. "We'll start first thing in the morning," he said.

12

The dawn scene on the dock nearly gave the impression that the tourists had come back to Fisherman's Wharf.

Liberator was tied up to the protected side of the pier, the first time in living memory that an American nuclear submarine still on active duty had pulled into a commercial dock.

Crewmen found an outlet for their pent-up frustrations. They had a project as well as the chance to get their land legs back. Chief Smith ordered the generators hot-wired to the dormant wharf electrical system, and lights and refrigeration went on in there for the first time in weeks. Electrical feeds went to working areas set up outside on the pier as well as to a workshop that the survivors built in a former gift shop.

Liberator's machine shop crew set about setting up a machine shop and wood shop at the wharf. Dr. Martin treated minor ailments among those wharf personnel who were too busy to walk to Coit Tower for treatment by the doctors there, and took blood and urine samples for newly begun research into the effect of radiation exposure on the survivors.

Charlie began organizing a fighting detail. From the many recruits he selected half a dozen who had prior police or military experience and, having just survived a holocaust that consumed their loved ones, weren't afraid to die for what was right. He set up a target and quick-fire range on Pier 43, nearby. And others in the crew helped in the refit of *Priscilla* on that same pier. Some of the survivors would leave, to spread the good work elsewhere.

And at strategic locations surrounding Fisherman's Wharf, a Percy-organized system of lookouts and sentries did an immensely better job of securing the perimeter than Embarcadero's volunteers had managed.

By 0900 Donovan found himself leaning against a mooring post smoking a Lucky Strike from a pack of them that he had liberated from the tobacconist. He had changed from his uniform to a more casual set of clothes that allowed him to run and stretch and that also looked less out of place with the Franchi strapped to his thigh and the Colt in a shoulder holster.

Jennings and his men spent several hours wiring the crew and survivors for UHF; each carried hand units that connected them to one another and *Liberator*, with Jennings on the topside bridge acting as liaison. Far from being left out of what was shaping up to be an urban guerilla battle, Weapons Control modified two of the antiship missiles for short-range effectiveness. Donovan decided that, faced with a Barbarosa force of hundreds as well as untold thousands of white-shirts, simple hand weapons might not be good enough.

At 0930 Donovan heard a car engine turn over and roar to life. It was a sound he hadn't heard in a long time, and he listened while the engine was tuned and settled down. Then it was put into gear and crept forward, breaking small bits of plaster that had come down in the last shock wave from Oakland, and moved around the corner.

Embarcadero was behind the wheel and Smith in

the passenger's seat. She pulled it up to Donovan and he replaced Smith. Charlie came running over from Pier 43 and hopped in the back.

"I got you a red Toyota," Smith said. "How do you like it?"

"I wanted the Mercedes."

"That's mine. I told you. This one is a beauty. Got ninety horses and a three-speed automatic. It's not great on the freeway but terrific on the hills. Use it well."

"Where'd you get gas?" Donovan asked.

"From a filling station by the Presidio. We carried a portable generator over there and loaded up some barrels. You know, a lot of the systems work in this town—they just don't have any juice. We solve that and we've gone a long way."

"Keep at it, Flaze."

"Fixing up the Mercedes is next. Then I'm gonna go in search of beer. We'll have ice to put it on by noon."

"See you later," Donovan said, and the car roared off with Charlie poking a Franchi out the window in preparation for a fight.

She drove out onto the Embarcadero and turned left for the drive around the waterfront to the Trans-Bay Tube, where the food and medical supplies were kept, and for a look at the wall.

At the sound of a car, the survivors poked their heads out wearily from the partial decimation of San Francisco. Donovan was reminded of photographs of Berlin after World War II: few houses untouched, most a pile of bricks and bare walls, occasionally a campfire and a crude attempt at carrying on with life.

The Embarcadero was, as she warned, mainly a cow path around piles of rubble, but it was passable.

"Where were you when it happened?" Donovan asked.

"At my apartment working on a problem: designing software for a guy in Berkeley who was studying the settlement patterns of Micronesian islands. It was about ten in the morning when it hit, and I thought it was another damned earthquake. I was five years old in the earthquake of '89 and I recall the same low rumble. The earth was shaking. Then the windows blew in, everything went flying, then were was this heat. It went over in a flash—maybe a second, no more. I remember it singed my hair, even my eyebrows.

"It got very bright for ten or twenty minutes. You couldn't look out the window. And there was a weird smell, like lemon juice and vinegar. When I finally got to look out the window the city was on fire. No one fought the fires. They just burned. I lost consciousness and must have slept for three days. I don't think I ever felt so weak . . . like I had the flu. When I finally was able to go outside the city was like you see it now."

"What about the white-shirts?"

"They came a few days later, just as we were getting organized. Barbarosa was getting organized too, and he fought them. I guess he saved us from them. But then he turned on us, on everyone. Padre—that's my father—says he was made sick by the radiation."

"He was," Donovan said. "Dr. Martin is studying a cure. Maybe your brother, Peter, can help him."

"Maybe. Peter is a brilliant medical researcher and a terrific surgeon. We'll see him later, at Coit."

"Is your apartment still okay?"

"Not bad. There's water but no lights. I use a lot of candles. I'm not there much these days—I've set up an apartment above HQ in the wharf. I'll show you later. We cope as best we can. I make a mean

Irish oatmeal over cans of Sterno. Would you like some?"

"Love it."

"I guess you don't get good food on *Liberator.*"

"On the contrary, we get terrific food. Submariners are obsessed with cooking and eating. There's not much else to do. On *Liberator* we can also work out, watch tapes, listen to music, or read. We do a lot of reading. Are there any bookstores still standing?"

"Yeah. We do a lot of that, too."

"I'd like a complete Shakespeare. We have all his plays and sonnets on CD, but it's not the same as reading them on paper."

"There's a bookstore on Chestnut that we've turned into a lending library. We can swing by there later if there's time. So tell me, Donovan ... what are you doing in San Francisco?"

"Helping, or trying to."

"Is that what you do, help?"

"Sure. I mean, there's no one left to fight, so why not help?"

"No one anywhere?"

"There *is* another submarine, but she ran away the last time we chased her. I wonder if she isn't a figment of our collective imagination. Really, *Liberator* is now the most advanced force on earth. We owe it to the world to do what we can to help."

"I'm glad you came," she said, letting her hand fall on his leg and giving it a quick squeeze.

As the car made its way east and then south around the inner corner of the peninsula, it drew nearer to Oakland and the primary target zone, the industrial/technology corridor leading down through Silicon Valley. Damage to houses increased as they got nearer to the target. A greater proportion of the houses were down, and those that still stood were burned as well.

The marks were there of a brief, searing heat that scorched exteriors and flash-melted metal without totally decimating anything. Donovan came to understand more of the reason for the schism between the two cities—south of Market, being nearer to the primary target, got the worse of it. In the final half mile leading up to the BART tube and the survivors' cache of food and medicine, the streets of San Francisco looked like an ash pile poured over an archaeological dig.

Once inside the tunnel, Donovan found a monument to the ingenuity of everyday people. The multichannel tube that crossed the bay between Oakland and San Francisco had been turned, in a few short weeks, into a naturally refrigerated warehouse for food and medicine. The food was in cartons stacked one upon the other (and also in BART subway cars and on platforms). The medicine was in the cool places beneath the tracks, where cold condensation gathered and preserved freshness. With candles and makeshift torches providing the only illumination, the BART tube was like a modern architect's vision of a cathedral, with long shadows and slow-moving figures carrying a great burden.

Embarcadero had worked out a terrific system for making order out of chaos. She had done in San Francisco what Donovan did on *Liberator*—inspire greatness in others. And she had done it without the benefit of a billion dollars worth of hardware and software. It was easy to inspire greatness when you were riding around in the world's most advanced submarine. It was another thing to do it with nothing but a blown-down city and a subway tunnel.

"We have no way of defending the supplies so we threaten to blow it up," she explained to Donovan and Charlie, sitting in the dust outside the tube watching a line of citizens wait to pick up food and medicine. "We got dynamite from a construction site and wired it up in the tunnel. Barbarosa knows that we'll blow it up before giving control of it to him."

"What's he done?" Donovan asked.

"Nothing. He's insane but not crazy. He knows how determined I am. I let his people come and get food like everyone else. I thought that would create dissension within his ranks, but it didn't. So he's planning to kill me, destroy our HQ and the hospital at Coit Tower, and get my men in the tunnel to turn over the keys."

"How do you know he plans to kill you?"

"He threatens, of course ... sends volunteers up to Coit with messages. They haven't got anything to lose—he'll kill them if they don't come. And my father takes care of them."

"This guy's really got you by the throat," Charlie said.

"That's why I need you—to help me get rid of him."

They drove uphill and onto the passable north side of Market and, a few blocks inland, came to a halt and got out.

"The wall," she said, and led them to it.

The drop was, at that point, forty feet, and below it was a scene every bit as desolate as what they'd found in Seattle. Virtually nothing remained standing in the dead zone except white-shirts, and they roamed the wasteland sometimes like zombies, other times in semiorganized bands. Bodies wrapped in dusty rags lay in odd piles here and there, and many fires burned as far as the eye could see.

"The vultures, cleaning up," Donovan said.

"The wall keeps them on that side. Toward the center of the city it's only ten feet high, and they

140

build ladders and try to come over. Barbarosa's men usually fight them off, but a few get through."

Donovan said, "This is not good. The good people of this city are faced with a choice between a homicidal megalomaniac and hordes of dying scavengers. If it's any consolation, Barc, the white-shirts are dying."

"They are?"

"Dr. Martin says it's just a matter of time. They're suffering from radiation insanity, which will kill them eventually."

"Do they have to take so long to drop?" Embarcadero asked.

"Look at it this way—their continued presence gives Barbarosa something other than you to think about. Charlie—we have to get the doctor up here to see this."

"I want to see that gun shop."

"You can't see it from the wall," she replied. "You'll have to go over. I'll show the way."

"Like hell you will," Donovan said.

"Come on, Donovan. I run this show."

"You run the show on this side of the wall. We're the professional fighters."

"You said you had never fought," she argued.

"We learn quick," Donovan growled.

"So do I, and I'm going."

"We'll discuss it later. Take us to meet your father."

She was still simmering when they got back into the car, and halfway up the next cleared street, asked, "What did you call me before?"

"Barc," he replied. "Embarcadero is too long to shout at you in the middle of a fight."

There was a strange appropriateness to Padre's use of Coit Tower as a post-Apocalyptic haven for the sick and homeless.

Built by a wealthy eccentric to celebrate her fireman lover, the tower atop Telegraph Hill was in the shape of a fire hose nozzle, and its inner walls were decorated with 1930s social realist paintings of the glorious workers in the fields.

"It's always good weather for picking apricots," Donovan mused, then his eyes coursed down the wall to the rows of hospital gurneys and patched-together medical gear. As in the Trans-Bay Tube, candles and torches cast long shadows.

The sound of a small gas motor kicking to life outside was followed by the electric lights flicking on.

Patients, nurses and doctors cheered. Padre said, "Well, all right!" and strode across the room to clap Chief Smith on the back.

He looked nothing like his twin children. A tall, burly man with brown hair that reached below his shoulders by way of a ponytail tied with a sailor's knot, he had a round face with soft features. Alexandra had high cheekbones, a narrow face, and dark brown almond-shaped eyes. Peter was nearly identical to her, only an inch or two taller. He had long hair like his father. The two men in the family seemed to be unreconstructed hippies from 1960s San Francisco, though only the father was arguably old enough to qualify.

"So you're the man who came from the sea," Padre said, shaking Donovan's hand hard enough to crunch a weaker man.

"Glad to know you."

"The people have been talking about you all day. I'm grateful to you—and to these wonderful lights."

"Think nothing of it, Father," Smith said.

"Can I get you some coffee?"

"There's never enough of that," Donovan said.

They sat at an old canasta table with three metal folding chairs and candle drippings all over the top and had mugs of coffee brewed on an old tin pot atop a Sterno stove. As they talked, patients and medical workers moved in and out of the landmark building and half a dozen guards patrolled with baseball bats and hockey sticks.

George Henry Fisher was fifty years old, an Episcopalian priest who had been pastor of St. Agnes Church on Nob Hill before the war. A onetime Army surgeon, he raised his children to the intellectual life and that of caring for others. Peter, two minutes Alexandra's senior, was the chief emergency surgeon at San Francisco Interfaith as well as an epidemiologist with a specialty in the exotic tropical viruses that might be expected to come into a Pacific port city from all over the world.

"I lost my wife in the war," Padre said. "She was a doctor too, working with the poor and homeless in Oakland."

"The primary target around here," Donovan said.

"Yes. I'm afraid she's dead. Of course, it was instant, and I guess that's a consolation."

"But you don't know for sure," Smith said, think-

143

ing of his own family in San Diego, also a primary target.

"I know in my heart. There's no need to go there and risk my life finding out what I already know. Especially when I can be of use to the survivors if I stay alive. That's what life is all about ... being of use."

"We're trying too," Donovan said, patting his old friend on the arm.

"So, can you help me get rid of Barbarosa?"

"We can certainly try."

"I mean, Christian charity does have its cutoff point, don't you know? This man is quite insane and means only the worst for the good people of the city. I wouldn't lose any sleep over killing him myself."

"You do your job and we'll do ours," Donovan said. "We were trained at that sort of thing. This is hardly the battlefield we were trained to fight in, but any old battlefield will do. The fight is primal—good against evil. We'll win."

"Golden Gate Park is where he lives and trains his men. They're all young and all killers. Some of them are no better than the white-shirts. I have an idea of the layout of his place, which is in the Panhandle. You may have heard of that place."

Donovan hadn't.

"I was ten years old when my mother took me to a be-in there. It was a communal gathering that was supposed to clear the air of all things evil."

"I guess it didn't work."

"It seemed to for a while. But that's history and this is the present, and we have to kill Barbarosa. You'll need guns."

"We have more like these," Donovan said, showing the Franchi.

"That will do nicely. But we need ones that we can operate. I'm not foolish enough to think that

144

all evil will die with the death of one man. There will be others, and we must be ready."

"I plan to raid the gun shop near the bus station. Can you tell me about the habits of the white-shirts?"

"They don't like the dark," Padre said. "I don't know what it is about it that frightens them, but they never attack at night. They stay indoors, in the ruins and tumble-down buildings, and seldom stir unless provoked. That we avoid doing."

"For good reason. So you'd go in tonight?"

"And do it fast. Try not to get caught there. I take it you've seen them work."

"More than I care to remember," Donovan said, adding, "There is a no-fail option for dealing with Barbarosa. We could have *Liberator* stand off in the harbor and lay a ship-to-ship missile on top of the bastard. But since that would wipe out a quarter of the remaining city . . ."

"We'll save it in case all else fails," Smith said.

Donovan hadn't spent that much time with candles since being taken to hear Christmas carols at the cathedral by his parents, and that was longer ago than he cared to remember.

Embarcadero's apartment, on Greenwich Street not far from Telegraph Hill, had more candles than most cathedrals. Chief Smith's magic with generators and cable might be fine for essential areas, but her apartment would have to do with simpler lights.

It was a small but modern place, one bedroom with a terrace looking up at Coit Tower. The living room was filled with books and two computers, and a small eat-in kitchen held boxes of provisions, including candles.

"There's running water in this part of town," she said. "So pretty much everything in this apartment works except the lights and the computers. You can't run computers on candles."

145

"You're welcome to use the ship's computers," Donovan said, pushing aside his largely finished bowl of Irish oatmeal.

"You're very good to make the offer and I love you for it, but my work is here."

"This week," he said emphatically.

"And maybe for the rest of my life. There's easily a lifetime of work. What are you offering me? The job of scientist aboard *Liberator?*"

"Yes. What's wrong with that?"

"I didn't know that submarines had women crew members."

"They usually don't, but these are unusual times. And *Liberator*'s crew plan calls for the addition of women eventually."

She poured two glasses of Evian water, and mused, "It won't be too bad being the only woman along with . . . how many are in the crew?"

"Forty-five," he replied, smiling. "Forty-six now."

"I haven't said yes yet. Will there be other women?"

"Eventually. And we'll need a place to live. A permanent base where we can build something."

"I can help you there. I've studied the design of communities in Micronesia and Polynesia. You know, aspects of traditional communities that are common to the region. Houses oriented to the trade winds, the creation of harbor facilities, that sort of thing."

"Which is exactly what we'll need," Donovan said, "if we can't find a permanent home in the States."

"With the white-shirts around that could be a problem."

"They'll die eventually, like the doctor said. We just have to prevent them from doing more damage while they're alive. Radiation insanity seems to erupt spontaneously and be sweeping down the Pa-

146

cific coast from Alaska, where we first saw it. I presume it's happening on other coasts of other continents, too. Dr. Martin might be able to find a cure and save a lot of lives, but we have to stay healthy for that to happen."

"*I* want you to stay healthy," Embarcadero said, and Donovan blushed.

He felt her dark eyes on him, and in a way he hadn't felt in a while. Ever since he knew he would be taking command of *Liberator*—the better part of a year before—there had been no time for women. Before then he had a series of encounters. He would be hard-pressed to describe them as relationships, for none lasted more than a few months in the hot stage and maybe lingered for a year or more as a fraternal sort of thing.

When *Liberator* became the woman in his life, Donovan acknowledged to himself that he would be a solo act for life. He was too much at sea, and when he wasn't he found himself preoccupied with thoughts of getting back to sea. It was no life to bring a woman into. Centuries of sailors knew that, and some of the best avoided things like marriage.

But now the world had changed, and Donovan was taking his world to sea with him. There was no life for him outside *Liberator,* and as far as he knew there was little life of any kind. What remained alive was messed up, scared, and on borrowed time. In what remained of the future he would have to take the good things in his life to sea with him and not think of life on land.

Alexandra Fisher was 25. *Twenty-five!* Almost a child, but then the last woman he'd cared even a little about had been thirty-five and scared half to death that she would make it through the last of her child-bearing years without a mate. She was so scared about it that she made it happen, and at last report was still living alone and angry at the world.

Alexandra—God save us from code names like Embarcadero, he thought—was young and unafraid in a world practically over.

"What do you like to be called?" he asked, a bit out of synch with the portentous tone of the conversation, but it turned out that she was thinking along the same lines as him.

" 'Embarcadero' was a necessity. I didn't know how long I could broadcast on that police radio, and I wanted to identify myself with something indelibly San Franciscan."

"Very wise."

"I got your attention, didn't I? But to answer your question, I always preferred 'Alex.' It ain't ladylike but I love it. What do you like to be called?"

"Tom."

"Not 'Captain'?"

"Not when I'm off duty."

"Are you off duty now?" she asked, her mouth forming a delightfully wicked smile.

Donovan looked at his watch, and said, "Until ten o'clock, when we have to meet Charlie and the others."

She stood and extended her other hand to him. He took it, and pulled her to the edge of his chair.

Alexandra's calm was gone, her demeanor as a leader of men smashed. Instead she had begun to quiver, and the words that came so easily to her all her life were nowhere to be found. Donovan knew the look, but not recently and certainly unexpected in the ruins of San Francisco. So this is the future, he thought.

He pulled her down onto his lap, and her arms snaked about his neck.

Donovan stood by the window, looking out at the city of San Francisco, which lay before him nearly black except for occasional fires and, nearby, candles in blasted-out windows.

Down in the street below, occasional curious survivors came out of their homes to watch the two sets of headlights making their way up the hill from Fisherman's Wharf. The cars moved slowly, turning from one side of the cleared path to the other to avoid larger bits of rubble. Turning an ear to the window and listening hard, he thought he heard a CD player in one of the cars.

"Charlie," he said.

Alex came out of the bedroom carrying his shirt. She handed it to him.

"Your brother? How can you tell?"

"He found music and something to play it on. That's Charlie."

Donovan slipped on the shirt, turned, and watched her as she dressed. Alex had a good body for a scientist, with large breasts with perfect nipples, and athletic legs. She spent her share of time in the gym, but lately had gotten her exercise on the street, organizing the survivors.

She pulled on a black sweater and handed him the same. "It's a large. It should fit you."

She kissed him on the lips, then helped him pull the sweater over his head and gave him a hug.

"You're a saint," she said.

"You too."

"Not me. I'm just a poor sinner who's found a man at last. I could be pregnant, you know."

"That fast?"

"I wasn't protected and I haven't been counting the days," she replied. "There have been other things on my mind. No matter. We'll deal with that in time. Now I have to get you and the others to the wall."

"I always wanted to have a kid."

She laughed, and said, "Did you ever think it would happen like this?"

"Sort of. I was conceived on a patch of grass in a forest. It must run in the family."

The cars pulled to a halt outside and a horn sounded twice. "Time to make war," Donovan said, and led her down the stairs.

14

By the light of a map light in Chief Smith's Mercedes, Donovan perused the partly burned copy of the San Francisco Yellow Pages.

" 'S and R Guns, open seven days, eleven A.M. to seven P.M. Buy, sell, trade. Over twelve thousand guns in stock.' "

"This must be the place," Smith said.

" 'We have the products you want when you want them and the price is right.' That's for sure. 'Aimpoint, Assault Systems, Beretta, Bianchi, Browning, Colt, Dan Wesson, Falcon, Interarms, Martin, Remington, Ruger, Smith and Wesson . . .' This place has more stuff than an armory."

"The citizens often were better armed than the military. So, are you bringing her with us?"

"Who?"

"Embarcadero. How many women do you know?"

"She likes to be called 'Alex.' The other thing was a code name. Yeah, she's coming with us."

"You're taking her on the raid?"

"I'm also taking her on board."

"What?" Smith exclaimed.

"She hasn't absolutely made up her mind, but she's inclined toward it. Look, we need a science specialist. Everyone says it."

"Yeah, but . . ."

"She's more than qualified. And what are you complaining about? You were always pushing me to get involved with someone."

"I'm not complaining," he said quickly. "You're the boss. I only hope you know what you're doing."

Charlie stuck his head out of the back seat and said, "There's family history here, Chief. Mom and Dad lived on a boat, too."

Donovan closed the Yellow Pages and peered at the street map stretched across his lap. "To get to Mission and Seventh we have to go past the bus terminal, which is crawling with white-shirts."

"They're supposed to be dormant at night," Charlie said.

"Yeah, but we're gonna have to blow our way into the gun shop, which will wake up the bastards. Percy laid it out for me. We take the twelve men that Alex gave us and place them along the route: two each at strategic corners along the route and on the wall, and three to cover our backs while we're inside. Three to carry guns and ammo back to the wall, with the help of the three bodyguards. Bring up four more from two of the corners and we have ten guys carrying guns back to the wall, plus two to haul it up."

"Not bad for a night's work," Charlie said.

"In and out in twenty minutes, not counting time spent blowing the gun shop open."

"If it isn't blown already."

"No way. The white-shirts can't get it together to do that. They use brute force, knives and ropes. The only guns they have is ones they scavenge from wrecked houses. No way they can blow down a wall."

"Barbarosa could have gotten the guns."

"He hasn't or he would already own the city. His men do a good job of keeping the white-shirts on their side of the wall, but don't have the balls to go in and rob the gun shop. They also may not have the ordnance—Padre says they use shotguns and occasional pilfered handguns; nothing heavy and no explosives. The gun shop door will require C7 and a detonator."

"I got it here," Smith said, patting a satchel on his lap.

"Okay," Donovan said, folding the map and sticking it in a pocket. "Are you guys ready?"

"Just about, boss," Smith said.

Charlie, by way of response, cocked his gun.

Donovan plucked his transceiver from his pocket and brought it to his lips.

"Captain to *Liberator,* do you copy?"

"This is *Liberator,* Executive Officer speaking."

"Mr. Percy, is there anything on sensors?"

"Negative, Captain. No radio. No sonar contacts. The fire has burned out at the base of the Oakland Bay Bridge and there is no visual sighting of whiteshirts."

"Okay, we're going in. Did you make the arrangements I asked for backup?"

"Backup?" Charlie asked.

"Affirmative . . . we're standing off in the harbor with one Mark 97B missile targeted on the Panhandle, as ordered. One torpedo targeted on Fisherman's Wharf."

Donovan explained. "Just in case this whole thing is some weird kind of trap, I want the backup ability to level this town."

Chief Smith smiled evilly. "Like I always said, love women but don't trust 'em too much."

"You don't think that Alex . . ." Charlie said.

"These are troubled times," Donovan replied. "I trust nobody. Except you guys."

It was then that Alex came out of the patched-up door to her building and climbed into the front seat of the Mercedes, next to the captain.

"Hi!" he said, cheerily.

153

The wall by Market and Sixth was only ten feet high, and to keep the Huns from mounting the ramparts, a series of sharp projections had been erected.

There were pointed sticks, broomsticks and hockey sticks (a lot of hockey sticks had gone into San Francisco defense, along with softball bats and mop handles). They were anchored beneath fallen building material—cement blocks and chunks of marble from the facades of ravaged downtown office towers. Additionally, glass panes that had peeled from the towers like autumn leaves in a full gale had been stomped into even finer pieces and the sharp bits strewn along the rim of the wall to discourage handholds from below.

This section of wall, being the lowest in the city, was also the least well patrolled by Barbarosa's men. The white-shirts had become obsessed with piling up rubble and wood on a slightly higher section of wall to the east that also provided swift access to the bay, where they congregated for nighttime bonfires and body-burnings.

That was where Barbarosa stationed his patrols, which in the hours after midnight consisted mainly of four men alternating on two motorcycles who crisscrossed the vulnerable zone, wielding shotguns. Alex led the two cars—the Toyota and Mercedes—to the low stretch of Market between Sixth, where they stopped and got out, to walk to Seventh, where they would find the gun shop.

Eight men awaited them there, having walked to the spot from the staging area at Coit Tower, avoiding Barbarosa's patrols, which stopped five blocks to the east. All were dressed in black, according to instructions, and carried available weapons—bats and more hockey sticks. Charlie handed out two Franchi automatics as well as plenty of ammunition, and Donovan quietly gave instructions.

154

Donovan took a long look at the terrain below, using night-vision binoculars. There was no movement to be seen inside or outside buildings, most of which were too blown-down to have recognizable entrances. The Greyhound bus terminal, which spanned two blocks, resembled a great blockhouse that had been battered by a firestorm and only part of which remained. The upper reaches had been eaten away by the ravages of the war, leaving only girders and fragments of wall. Deep inside the structure fires burned dimly, casting almost no light onto the street, which was knee-deep in rubble with the exception of a ten-foot-wide path that had been worn by the tramping of boots and bare feet.

The gun shop occupied the ground floor of a modern office building, all tinted glass and steel, built in the nineties. The shop itself was an ultramodern facility the existence of which in the central city was the outcome of liberalized gun-possession rules promulgated by the Quayle administration. Its defenses were based on the principles contained in the building's security system, which was almost entirely electronic. Once the building was trashed in the war and its three backup power systems failed, the laser security failed to function and all that protected the store were old-fashioned steel shutter-gates that slammed down in the final paroxysm of San Francisco's electric grid.

Those gates were enough to keep out anyone who didn't have C7, and that included everyone in San Francisco with the exception of Chief Smith and some others in the crew.

From his vantage point atop the wall, Donovan felt that the streets were secure. After watching for nearly an hour, nothing was revealed. No one stirred below the wall, and above it the only sound

155

was a periodic far-off rumble from Barbarosa's motorcycle patrol. A final check-in with Percy confirmed that technicians aboard the ship had detected nothing out of the ordinary, so at 0115 the raid got under way.

Charlie cleared away the rampart obstacles along a ten-foot section of wall and lowered a rope ladder and a bosun's chair. He led the way down, with Donovan following, their boots scraping the bricks, torn pavement, and ruined power, water, steam, and gas lines that tore when the land parted. Smith went third, then Alex. The last to follow were ten of the volunteers (two remained atop the wall as lookouts, snipers, and to help the others back up).

Once at the bottom of the ladder, Donovan felt keenly the sense of isolation and terror that bottom-dwellers knew. Above the wall was sunshine and light and places for people to live. There were children and occasionally there was laughter. Below the wall was primal terror and the stench of death, which hung in the air like an early morning fog.

"Does this remind anyone of Navy Harbor?" Donovan asked.

"All too well," Smith said.

"What happened there?" Alex asked.

"The white-shirts stacked some bodies and hung others. Maybe they also burned a few but we didn't see any fires and we didn't stick around long enough to look for ashes."

"This is like war games," Smith said. "The enemy is out there, but you have to guess where."

Donovan had felt the sensation before, creeping through the depths of the ocean in search of an invisible foe. The danger always present was that you could die instantly—no warning, no reprieve, no chance to run or argue about it.

Someone could come out of the shadows below the

wall and kill them as swiftly as an enemy torpedo could burst the wall of *Liberator.* Easier, even. At sea they were the predominant power, with weapons and destructive abilities scarcely seen before on Earth. But in the tumble-down streets of postwar San Francisco they were only safe while the bullets lasted. In the early morning hours preparing to cross several hundred yards of terrain owned by a huge and ruthless enemy, the aura of death fell upon them.

Donovan motioned Charlie to lead the way, and Charlie started south on Sixth toward Mission, walking slowly and deliberately with the Franchi always at the ready. Donovan went second, followed by Alex and Chief Smith. The others tagged along with the rear brought up by Saxon, a former San Francisco motorcycle cop who was the survivors' most handy man when it came to arms and preparedness.

The sky was as clear as the night that *Liberator* steamed into the harbor and the moon shone well. The shadows were long but the street clearly marked, and the gray of the ashfall that covered nearly everything seemed nearly white. The path that they walked in was wide and tramped down by feet. The white-shirts had come and gone from the wall many times.

Fifty feet from the wall, the terrain changed from concrete rubble to piles of glass, the falldown from the office towers on both sides of the street. Sheets of glass had peeled off the buildings and fallen to the pavement, some in curved, partly melted, twisted sheets that resembled potato chips.

The glass piles ran to fifty feet high, but here and there were chipped away by the work of the white-shirts. Smaller paths had been cleared to the entrances to buildings. On the west side of the block, the blasted-out archway of the Crocker Bank was nearly free of glass piles, most of that having been swept away for body removal. The bank itself was laid open, with piles of money lying carelessly around. A hand truck with a four-foot stack of bundled bills sat alone by the door, the war having happened before its handler could get to his destination.

"Anybody care to get rich?" Donovan asked.

No one replied. Charlie moved the group forward down Sixth to the corner of Mission, where he called a halt.

"We're alone," Alex said, pressing her hand against her heart.

"They've got to be all in the bus terminal," Donovan said. "There was plenty of room for them to camp out in the bank if they wanted. The white-shirts are centralizing for some reason. Don't suppose it matters why."

"Comfort in numbers," Smith said.

"You need comfort when your business is picking up bodies," Charlie agreed.

"And when there's more business than you could handle," Donovan added.

"You guys are ghouls," Alex said, poking Donovan in the ribs.

"No. *They're* ghouls. We just need to keep our perspective and sense of humor. None of us asked for this war. We happened to survive it and now are doing our best to pick up the pieces."

The block of Mission from Sixth down past Seventh was wide and relatively clear. A lot of foot traffic had gone down it in recent days. It had a wide central corridor that had been swept clean of debris, and the rubble along the curb was organized into neat piles twenty or thirty feet high. The remains of bonfires were everywhere. Piles of ash and bones littered Mission like horse droppings after a parade.

In the center of the intersection, which had been

swept especially clean to account for the nexus of footpaths running east-west and north-south, was a pile of bones three stories high. The heat had been intense and the duration long. All the bones were scorched clean of flesh and barely emitted an odor. Alex stared at it in grotesque fascination, then felt her stomach coming up and ran away from the group. Donovan followed and put an arm about her until the heaving stopped.

"I can have the men take you back."

"No. I'm here for the duration. If you can take it, I can."

With few exceptions, storefronts were blocked by piles of rubble and the debris that had avalanched down from their facades and upper stories. Always, glass was on top of the pile, being the last thing to fall. It sprinkled the tops of the debris piles with millions of bits of glass that caught the moonlight and turned it to sparkles. It was grotesquely beautiful amidst the desperate loneliness.

Donovan posted men at the corner of Sixth and Mission to augment those he left back by the wall and the pair who would stand guard at the corner of Seventh. Once again Charlie led the way, this time west on Mission, past the mammoth pile of bones in the intersection and out, tremulously, into the middle of the street.

They felt very alone out in the open. The probability that the white-shirts couldn't shoot straight was, at that moment, little consolation. There were thousands of them against the handful in the street.

The absolute lack of wind added to the terror. There was nothing to mask their footfalls, which resounded up and down the block. The ground was covered with a thin layer of broken material—so utterly broken that you couldn't tell what it was. It was broken *stuff* that crunched when they stepped on it.

They made their way fearfully to the second intersection. There, too, a pile of bones and other burned material occupied the center of the intersection. This pile was the same size as the first, and looking south down Seventh Donovan could make out other piles as far as he could see. Every intersection south of Market had a pile for burning bodies. There was an eery neatness to it, the work not of angels of destruction but of vultures of habit. Their lives spinning to a conclusion in the weeks and months following the war, the white-shirts were going about the blasted ruins of urban America, cleaning up the mess that mankind had left as its epitaph.

To the north, the Greyhound bus terminal still had fires burning inside, as Donovan had noted from the wall. But the paths on the south of the building were much broader and cleaner than those to the north. The Market side of the building and of that part of town had been written off by the white-shirts as an impassable waste of time, not to be bothered with after the bodies in it were cleaned up.

But in the section where they stood, the paths were broad, wide enough for two cars at least, and bounded by the ubiquitous debris piles that were capped by sparkling glass fragments. The ramps into the bus terminal also were swept clean, the rubble having been shovelled off into mammoth piles beneath them.

"A lot of people must come and go from that building," Charlie said.

"The whole white-shirt concentration in this town, maybe," Donovan said.

"They go in there at night and hole up," Smith said. "There's no sign of 'em outside it."

"Let me check," Donovan said, and whipped out his transceiver.

"Captain to *Liberator*. How do you copy?"

"Five-by, Captain. Do you need help?"

"Maybe, *Liberator*. Is there any sign of activity south of Market other than us?"

"Negative. I'm getting reports from Fisherman's Wharf, Coit Tower and the wall—your party and Barbarosa's patrol are the only creatures stirring."

"You're sure of that?"

"Affirmative, Captain," Percy replied, his voice showing a slight amount of irritation at having his information questioned.

Donovan looked at Chief Smith, Charlie, and Alex, then sucked in his breath and said, "Inform Weapons Control to fire up another Mark 97N, this one targeted on the bus terminal. If you don't hear back from us in twenty minutes, fire it."

Smith and Charlie stared, wide-eyed, at the captain, and Alex looked surprised. Percy radioed, "Captain . . . you'll be killed."

"I plan to get us out, but if we don't make it carry out your orders."

"Aye, Captain."

Donovan looked at the others and said, "It's the only solution. I can't wait for them to die. They're cleaning up the bodies but they're also killing innocent survivors."

"What's this solution?" Alex asked.

"The Mark 97N carries a field-grade nuclear warhead," Donovan said, matter-of-factly. "It will kill all the white-shirts. It will also level this quarter of town."

"You can't nuke the bus terminal!" Alex whispered. "It will kill everyone."

"No. Just the white-shirts. And us, if we don't get out in time."

Chief Smith said, "The captain's right. A Mark 97N will take out the terminal and ten square blocks. But everything else will be okay. The blast damage goes mostly down and up."

"It's a *field-grade* weapon, designed for use in the Andes. The first targets were the strongholds of drug kingpins. It's an effective weapon. At sea it's supposed to take out an aircraft carrier without ruffling the destroyer escort."

"Donovan, those are *people* we're talking about," she continued to protest.

"Oh, bullshit! They're ghouls, you said so yourself. They're dying anyway. I'm just helping speed the process. Get them before they kill anyone else."

"I can't believe you're going to nuke San Francisco."

"I won't be the first," he said sharply.

"With the white-shirts gone, all you will have to worry about is Barbarosa," Smith said.

"And we can take care of him," Charlie added.

She scratched her head, and sighed, "This is very weird."

Donovan's transceiver crackled and Percy's voice said, "Missile armed and targeted as ordered, Captain."

"Proceed," Donovan replied. "Twenty minutes counting down from now."

He checked his watch. It was 0130. "Let's try to be out of here by oh-one-forty-five," he said.

Charlie took several long looks up and down all streets, and said, "All clear. Let's blow this thing and go home."

With the others following, he ran across the street to the gun shop. S & R Guns was indeed a modern shop, with gunmetal gray steel security shutters that slid and locked in a recessed groove in the sidewalk.

While Alex's volunteers stood guard at vantage points on the corner of the building and across the street, where the view of the bus terminal was better, Chief Smith found the vulnerable point in the security shutter and packed in enough C7 to rip the metal fabric to shreds. That explosive, C7, was a further-generation gelignite, the latest advance in the series of plastic explosives that began in World War II. It was the most stable and compact yet, and required only a .05-volt charge from a watch battery to detonate. *Liberator* carried copious amounts of both C7 and detonators in her stores.

He pressed the thumbnail-sized detonator into the soft material and fitted a blast-direction cap over the whole lot. "Let's give this twenty feet," he said, and ushered the others to safety around the corner.

"This should wake the dead," Donovan said, and cradled Alex's head in his arms.

The explosion was brief and high-pitched. The C7 seared a high-temperature fissure in the security shutter, causing the metal to burn differentially and peel open like a grape. Then there was a lower-

163

pitched bang as the shutters burst to the ground, their pieces rattling like a child's toy.

The acrid yellow smoke smelled of sulphur and mustard seeds. "Make it fast, guys," Donovan said, and followed Charlie into the store.

S & R Guns was huge, modern, and reeked with rotting flesh. "Oh God," Alex exclaimed, backing out faster than she had gone in.

There had been four employees and six customers in the store when the bombs fell, and their bodies putrefied where they fell. Before the gush of fresh air from outdoors swept the inside of the store, the stench overcame three of the volunteers but gave Donovan the chance to make a point.

"If I don't nuke the white-shirts the whole city will smell like this," he said.

"Get guns and let's go," Alex stammered.

Donovan said, "Take stuff that's easy to shoot and reload. Saxon, you tell them what to pick up—basic thirty-eights and shotguns. No fucking around with exotic weapons."

"Got it, boss," Saxon said, turning his voracious appetite for firearms to the task of arming the survivors.

Weapons came out of showcases and went into carrying bags. Boxes of ammo were loaded into backpacks and strapped to backs, two per person. Pistols were strung like beads on quarter-inch nylon rope and hung over necks. Shotguns were loaded into burlap bags and made fast with cord for easy carrying. In ten minutes, all those in the party were loaded with enough firearms to equip a guerilla band, if not a small army.

Even Donovan had a backpack full of 9-mm ammunition for his Colt as well as a hunter's vest with all pockets stuffed with loaded magazines. With *Liberator* seeing modest action in the Pacific and

164

other oceans, he had enough rounds to last several years.

"We got company!" Charlie yelled, accompanying the warning with two quick shots from his Franchi.

"Where?" Donovan asked, running to join his brother.

"The big ramp from out of the bus terminal! Look!"

The two bodies that Charlie had deposited on the tarmac were only the first of an exodus as white-shirts walked zombielike into the early morning air, attracted by the C7 blast that had laid bare the gun shop.

They also poured out of the street-level doors, dozens of them, and behind them could be seen hundreds or thousands more pressed against the doors and windows. They were packed inside the terminal—doing what? Donovan had little idea ... recharging or something like sleep. Now they were awake and some were coming after him.

"Home the way we came!" he shouted, and urged the others in the party out the hole they had blown in the wall and across the street. The guard posted there had opened fire, aiming selectively at the nearest white-shirts.

They walked and half-ran, some carrying axe handles and others guns, others simply with clenched fists and furied grimaces upon sore-marked faces. They came straight at Donovan's party, which ran across Seventh and back down Mission, with Charlie in the lead and Donovan bringing up the rear along with Alex and Saxon.

"This is how it was in Navy Harbor?" she asked, frantically loading a .38.

"Pretty much. Do you know how to use that?"

"I learn fast."

The first wave of white-shirts tried to catch up

with them as they made their way down Mission, retracing their footsteps. Donovan shot the first one in the chest and dropped a second with a leg shot. Alex aimed the .38 with both hands at first, and missed wide with two shots. Cursing, the adrenaline flowing in her, she held the gun in her right hand and plugged the first white-shirt that came around the corner.

"Way to go," Saxon said, squeezing off two shots of his own.

The men and women (for the first time, Donovan noticed strange, gaunt women among his pursuers) were still dressed in white, more or less. They had started out with white T-shirts and bleached slacks two weeks ago and now were consumed by dirt as much as by radiation insanity. They were white-shirts only in the sense that their clothes once were that color. Now the shirts and pants were the color of pus, blood and grime. All that remained of the original being was the rage.

Even burdened with hundreds of pounds of ordnance, Donovan and his party were faster than the white-shirts. Moving laboriously, they made their way back to the wall, picking up support as they ran from the men they'd left behind. The other men pitched in with carrying and, as the goods were being hoisted up to the civilized side of the wall, with throwing up a picket line for defense.

Percy would freak out, Donovan thought. They made a classic military formation from out of the British army of the seventeenth and eighteenth centuries, with massed guns protecting a perimeter around the retreating troops and supplies. The white-shirts never fired the weapons some of them carried. Probably the guns wouldn't work. They waved them and would use them as clubs if they got close enough, but none of them did.

Donovan and company stood (or kneeled) and

fired, reloaded and fired again. White-shirts dropped one upon the other until the bodies began to accumulate in a semicircle around the retreating survivors.

There was no apparent end to them. While Smith helped Alex up the rope ladder and then clambered up himself, moving amazingly fast considering his bulk, Donovan and Charlie held off the remainder. Of the original two or three dozen who came after them, only four were standing. Only one of them was armed, with a broomstick.

"I want one for the doctor," Donovan said.

"The one in Seattle died too quick," Charlie said.

Donovan holstered his Colt and moved away from Charlie, a bit to one side. The man with the broomstick came after him, holding the stick as if it were a baseball bat. Donovan ducked a freewheeling blow that came accompanied by a hiss of venomous rage.

A second blow also missed. This time Donovan pivoted and drove a strong right hand into the man's face. It was like sucker-punching a melon. As the knuckles hit, the man's face crumpled inward, teeth collapsing with bone and oozing flesh. Donovan jerked his hand back, frantically shaking it to get rid of the oily substance that clung to his fingers.

The white-shirt crumpled to the dusty ground. A bellow of disgust and anger came from Charlie's mouth, and in a half-second of rapid fire the other three figures were cut down.

Off down the block several more white-shirts had come out of the bus terminal and were moving slowly, picking up the bodies of their fallen comrades and carrying them off to be burned.

Donovan fumbled for his transceiver, and when he had the ship on the line, yelled, "Blow them up! Blow them the fuck up!"

"Are you safely away, Captain?" Percy asked.

"Give us two minutes," he replied, and followed Charlie up the rope ladder.

The others had loaded the guns and ammo into the two cars and the engines were running. Donovan and his brother climbed into the Mercedes, which Smith frantically turned around and drove as fast as he could away from the wall.

Careening off the piles of rubble on both sides of the street, the two cars raced north toward the protecting warmth of the civilized part of the city. They were still driving when Donovan spoke again into the transceiver, giving an order.

Twenty-four seconds later, that part of San Francisco centered around the bus terminal shook with yet another mighty spasm. A brief, concentrated fireball seared the sky, turning darkness into high noon. In a millisecond, the scourge of the white-shirts in San Francisco was ended, and as the decades passed this would be recalled as the first chapter of the rebuilding of the great city.

Compared with what they were accustomed to, the electric lights strung up in the barroom were positively brilliant.

A CD player, resuscitated from an early death and rigged up to speakers above the bar, played songs by the Grateful Dead. At bar stools and tables in the large room, survivors and crew members from *Liberator* caroused and carried on in a style befitting the best shore leaves of U.S. Navy history.

Liberator was once again docked at Fisherman's Wharf. Not only docked, but dressed for a port call, with decorative lights and pennants. The wharf itself, that part outside of the buildings, was well lit and festive, with couples strolling and children playing in the early evening air. It was the ship's second day in town, and the evening after the defeat of the white-shirts. Donovan had called a celebration, and it had been raging since sundown.

The bar was a rogue's gallery of officers and survivors. Chief Smith and Helmsman Hooper were engaged in a loud argument about targeting methods for Mark 97N missiles. Charlie was arguing firing range scores with Saxon, the former cop, who had just been put in charge of weapons by Alex. She was talking computers with Jennings, and throughout the room men and women let down their hair for the first time since the war.

Donovan sat at the end of the bar by the cash register, an old brass model stamped with an ornate pattern, playing with the keys and ringing up phantom sales. Everything was going as he wanted. The white-shirts were defeated, and the bomb that killed them had sent a powerful message to Barbarosa that a new boy was in town.

To augment that message as well as to blow off steam, he dreamed up the party. Bringing *Liberator* into dock, dressing her up, and throwing a party on shore with the survivors made it clear to any prying eyes that might be about that Donovan was unafraid. To make sure that his message wasn't answered too forcefully, Percy had posted lookouts at strategic points overlooking Fisherman's Wharf and linked them by transceiver to the topside bridge of *Liberator,* where men also stood guard with automatic weapons.

Most of the guns taken from south of Market were locked up at the survivors' HQ, but some had been rationed to those volunteers who either had experience with firearms or were willing to learn from Charlie and Saxon. Training classes had gotten under way within an hour of the guns' arrival, and would continue until everyone who needed proficiency got it.

Sitting smoking a Lucky Strike and nursing a bottle of Harp (true to his word, one of the first things that Chief Smith made with his electricity was ice), Donovan watched Alex as Communications Officer Jennings gave her his predictable sales pitch on *Liberator* computers. Absentmindedly, Donovan sketched her on a bar napkin. She was happening so quickly in his life. Too quickly, he thought for a moment, then realized that from a certain point of view his life had been going on scarcely more than two weeks.

Acting on impulse, he strolled out of the bar and across the wharf to alongside *Liberator*. The ship was again tied up port-to-dock. A work crew was on the foredeck, swabbing it down, the suds running into San Francisco Bay. A hundred yards out into the water, a young couple rowed a small boat. Seagulls hovered overhead and sat upon mooring posts, waiting for food to come their way. To them, tourists had returned to Fisherman's Wharf and tidbits of food couldn't be far behind.

Donovan felt a special joy. Normalcy was back, at least to a degree. The harbor looked much as harbors should. It was only a matter of time until more ships and free ones plied the waters. He finished his beer and left the bottle atop a mooring post, displacing a seagull.

On adjacent Pier 43, the work of refitting *Priscilla* was nearing an end and had been suspended for the evening. Donovan stared wistfully at the old wooden ship, realizing that she was about the first wooden ship he had seen since the war. Her sails had been recut and put back on, and were furled against the booms. She rolled lightly with the current, and a kerosene lamp burned enticingly near the companionway.

"Hi, sailor," Alex said cheerily, surprising Donovan by slipping a hand into his back pocket.

"How was your computer lesson?"

"I gave him the lesson, Donovan. Be real."

He kissed her on the forehead. "He knows a few things."

"Sure. How to follow menus in programs that the Office of Naval Research wrote for him. I knew the guys who wrote those programs."

"Did you come out here to brag?" he asked.

"No. I came out here to get laid. What are my chances?"

"Pretty good. Want to take a walk?"

She nodded. He slipped an arm around her waist and walked her over to Pier 43 and out onto the deck of *Priscilla*. The schooner had low freeboard and a flat deck that curled up toward the bow. Amidships, the companionway led down to a spacious cabin that once was a hold for oysters. The cabin had been cleaned up and bunks added, with foam-padded cushions covered with vinyl. A candle sat atop a low centerboard trunk. Donovan lit it, and the cabin was bathed in a warm glow.

"Is this your personal yacht?" he asked, unbuttoning her blouse.

"Everything here is mine," she said. "Including you."

She tore open his buckle, thrust a hand inside his pants, and held him tightly in her hand. "I take good care of what's mine," she said, and pulled him down onto a bunk.

The building used to be a food factory or at least a major distributor. Saltwater taffy was everywhere, boxes and boxes of it. There also were three kinds of fudge; four types of caviar; six varieties of Alaskan king crab; and as many kinds of shrimp, scallop, hard clam and, curiously, Siberian cream tart. All were packed in crates stacked neatly on rows and rows of industrial shelving. Address labels showed customers in all fifty states and much of Canada.

Charlie Donovan and Tom Saxon had taken their argument about firing range scores out onto the street for some practice shooting at tin cans, then moved it up to the third floor of what had come to be called the candy building. The original idea was to shoot out street lights—there was no hope of getting them working anyway—and it was something that both men had wanted to do since they were kids.

So they went up to the third floor of the building, which was on the Embarcadero two blocks to the west of Fisherman's Wharf, to settle their argument about marksmanship using the as-yet-unbroken remains of the city's street-lighting system, when the store of food was discovered.

Food to a submariner is Topic A on the news. Word that the cook has devised a new and better way to make muffins ranks right up there with shore leave and the successful completion of a mission. But a storeful of gourmet food? That was something certain to get the whole off-duty crew running, even away from the celebration that the captain had called on the wharf. And Charlie had just gone to the window to radio down the news when he spotted the caravan coming down the Embarcadero from the west.

A white, 1961 Mercury convertible in amazingly good condition travelled slowly down the waterfront highway, surrounded by a handful of motorcycles in not-so-good shape. All the vehicles in the convoy had white rags tied to their radio antennas, and regally placed in the back of the convertible was another white-garbed figure, but this one was in clean clothes.

He wore robes made of bedsheets or something like that and had a black beard and long hair that flowed down onto his shoulders. He sat on the back of the car with his sandalled feet on the back seat. He was accompanied in the car by two young women who also wore white robes, as well as a driver and an armed guard. The motorcycle drivers wore black and leather, and were also armed.

"Who's that?" Charlie asked.

"Barbarosa," Saxon replied, lifting his rifle and

sighting in on the man, who was an easy target for an assassin's bullet.

"Don't shoot!"

"But he's so easy to kill," the frustrated ex-cop protested.

"That's because he's driving slow and showing the white flag. We can't kill him now."

"This is a strange time to think of chivalry."

"I'm thinking of the rules of war. Never discount options no matter how implausible they may seem. He may have something useful to say. I'm going to call this in to my brother."

As a young man, Donovan occasionally accused his younger brother of being a Jesuit. Certainly he was a spoilsport. Nothing had changed to alter that opinion.

When the transceiver emitted the captain's call code, Donovan was lying in the bunk toying idly with the nipple of Alex's left breast, teasing it with a fingertip, while she rested her head under his arm.

He scowled at the radio for a moment. "Remind me to fire the maid," he said.

"You'd better answer. They'll only come and drag you away."

"It used to be easy in the old days, before the war. You could slip away for a weekend, maybe not in Tahiti, maybe at a motel on the San Diego Freeway, but at least you got away."

"I don't want to hear about your old girlfriends," she replied.

"They're all dead."

"Nonetheless, I don't want to hear about them."

"It was fun then, after the AIDS thing was cured and the sexual revolution came back. A lot of people had hot times."

"I was born too late," she said, squirming out

174

from under his arm and reaching for her blouse. "We'll have to start our own revolution."

Donovan brought the transceiver to his lips.

"Liberator, this is the captain."

"Executive Officer here, Captain. Please report to the ship."

"What's up?"

"We have guests, Captain. It's Barbarosa, with an armed guard. They're flying the white flag."

"On my way," Donovan replied, jumping off the bunk.

They dressed in record time and hurried back to Fisherman's Wharf, ignoring the stares of survivors and crewmen who were suddenly made aware of what they were up to.

Barbarosa's caravan had stopped at the foot of the wharf. The engines were shut down on both car and cycles, and the man himself was sitting with his arms folded, waiting for an audience. Padre had come down from Coit Tower to talk to him, and Donovan and Alex joined him at the foot of the pier.

A growing crowd of curious survivors gathered cautiously around, respecting a fifty-foot circle that *Liberator* crewmen were enforcing. Included in the crowd were ten crewmen, all of them armed with Franchis that could be used at a moment's notice to blow away the little dictator.

As the circle of onlookers opened to let them pass, Donovan, Alex and her father walked up to the side of the car, giving scant attention to the thugs on motorcycles who accompanied it.

Donovan wasn't impressed with the looks of the fellow. He was a small man with thin features and a weak chin that the scraggly beard failed to conceal. Even sitting on the back of the rear seat he looked small, and only his black, beady eyes stood out as being extraordinary. They were magnetic in a way, capable of giving the long and penetrating

175

stares that served preachers so well in captivating their audiences.

"What do you want, Jim?" Padre asked, his arms folded in a defiant pose.

"My name is Barbarosa," he said, in a voice surprisingly deep and full. " 'Jim' is a forgotten apparition, a shred of the past."

"What do you want?"

Barbarosa sneered, and said, "I heard about this marvelous visitor from the sea and wished to see for myself. I presume this man is the captain?"

He gave Donovan a contemptuous look, to which the captain didn't respond.

Padre said, "Captain Donovan is here to help all the survivors of San Francisco."

"Yours or mine?"

"All of them."

"I suppose I should accept. The captain is a powerful man. I admire the way you handled the white-shirts. It would have taken me years to rid the city of them."

Donovan replied, "I repeat Padre's question— what do you want?"

"To see the new boy in town, what else? Do you think I'm here to kill you, Padre?"

"You tried once."

"We were just over the war and I was unenlightened," the robed man suggested. "Now I am a man of peace."

"Let's hear it," Alex said.

"I bring you an offer that is an extension of my first offer—share resources with me and there will be peace."

"I tried that," Padre said. "You tried to kill me and take over."

"As I said, I was unenlightened. Now I am willing to let you and your people live in peace. Moreover, the captain and his crew are welcome to stay with you, which I presume is his intention."

"No," Donovan said. "It is not."

"And why, may I ask?"

"This isn't the only town with problems. It's a big world out there and lots for us to do. After we've cleaned up here we'll move on."

"Cleaned up what? The white-shirts?"

"They were first. Now it's your turn. So, Jim . . . or Barbarosa, or whatever you'll be calling yourself in the afterlife, are you going to shape up or not?"

Rattled by Donovan's nonchalant but pointed threat, Barbarosa said, "Move on if it suits you. Go tilt at other windmills. Leave the people of San Francisco to settle their arguments alone."

Donovan looked over and nodded at his brother, who raised his Franchi just enough for the motion to catch Barbarosa's eye.

"Lay down your arms. Live in peace. Or die. That should be easy enough for you to understand."

"Are you going to drop a bomb on us too if we don't?"

"It was a missile and, yes, I'm prepared to use one on you, too."

"You're a representative of the U.S. government. What about fair play?"

"The war changed everything," Donovan said.

"That is correct. It left me as the savior of this city, which was brought down by the evil it has lived with for years. If this"—he looked disdainfully at Padre—"man of the cloth gets in my way, he will be crushed."

"There are two ways to do this, the easy way and the way you saw yesterday south of Market," Donovan said. "The choice is yours. Make up your mind. I give you twenty-four hours to lay down your arms and begin to live in peace."

Several of Barbarosa's men looked at him, ex-

177

pecting the signal to do violence, but the only violence in the offing came from the evil glare emitted by the man's eyes.

"You will have my reply," he hissed, and drove off.

Liberator withdrew to a secure anchorage, dropping the hook halfway between the wharf and Alcatraz Island, where the six-to-nine-knot current and cold seas ensured protection. No swimmers could make it, and it was unlikely that Barbarosa—or anyone else in San Francisco—had boats capable of the journey.

Just to be sure on that last point, Donovan sent parties out in two motor rafts to reconnoiter. One went west under the Golden Gate past the Presidio to the sea side of Golden Gate Park and back. The other went south along the inside of the peninsula, checking the waterfront as far as five miles past the remains of the Oakland Bay Bridge.

There was activity on the ocean front of the park—encampments occupied by Barbarosa's followers, including some crude fortifications meant to forestall an invasion from the sea. These were new; put up since Liberator arrived, in a ridiculous effort to make sure that no invasion forces hit the beach successfully.

Of this effort Donovan said, "It has nothing to do with defense. It has everything to do with keeping the work force occupied during times of stagnation. That was the real reason why the pharaohs built

179

the pyramids. It kept the peasants laboring in the sun, where they were too busy to think treason."

"Whatever you say, Donovan," replied Alex.

The boat that went down the inside of the San Francisco peninsula found nothing south of Market, only that some of the wreckage and all of the dust had been rearranged by the missile that ended the white-shirts' reign of terror.

A stiff breeze that came up from the west by midnight ruffled the whitecaps on the bay. The motor rafts that shuttled crewmen and survivors between *Liberator* and Fisherman's Wharf provided wet and cold rides, but still the traffic was brisk.

The party didn't end with Barbarosa's threat, although disrupting the celebration was at least part of his motive. It went on in even higher gear, but with a goodly party of extra guards joining those already on duty. Donovan wasn't worried; it was unlikely that Barbarosa would launch an attack until he was back in his compound.

Meanwhile, work proceeded apace. Chief Smith and his men worked to repair as many of the city's systems as possible. One of the projects was to turn a windmill, found in the museum as part of an exhibit on the alternative energy movement of the 1970s, into a working electricity producer on the Hyde Street Pier. Charlie and Saxon were increasing the firearms proficiency of the survivors, and Dr. Martin had found a way to make himself especially useful.

He never got the chance to peek over the wall and see the white-shirts at work, but did on that second night make it as far inland as Telegraph Hill. He came armed with medical supplies—as many as he felt the ship could spare, and was prepared to throw himself into the struggle, as a medic, for as long as the ship remained in port.

Coit Tower had been transformed miraculously

in such a short time. Two generators ran in shifts, supplying the hospital inside with more than enough power to meet needs. The long shadows cast by the torches and candles had become quaint memories, and the orderlies had new, clean clothes to wear. With light and power, sanitary procedures weren't the mess they had been before, and even the patients looked cheerier. More and more of them were being treated, as a result of which the lines outside were shorter.

With Padre's attention shifted to HQ and the need to focus on defense of the community rather than its healing, that work was left to Peter Fisher, Alex's brother. His long hair tied in a ponytail and tucked inside a white robe, he scurried about the hospital looking after patients and scheduling surgery.

Dr. Martin helped him for half the night—six straight hours until four in the morning, when both men turned the work over to assistants and went out into the early morning light to drink coffee and look out at the lights. That was a newly rediscovered treat, looking at city lights. The small glow made by Smith's lights at the wharf and the lights on *Liberator* moored out in the harbor were extraordinarily comforting to men and women who had seen only darkness since the day there came a great flash of light and everything died.

"You try to help but you always wonder," Peter said, finally, breaking a long silence.

"Wonder what?"

"Wonder if I'm doing good."

"You are."

"And if I'm doing *well*. My main strength is not emergency surgery, although I learned it and am good at it. I'm a researcher, and feel a little uncomfortable out of the lab."

"I've always been a clinician," Dr. Martin admitted. "Research isn't my strong point. I learned enough of it to work the computer banks, but no more. Now I find myself in the position of doing it full-time. Working here at the hospital has been a welcome break for me. I get tired of staring at those monitors."

"I wish I had mine back," Peter said, managing to evoke sympathy for the notion of missing the company of computers.

"You're welcome to try mine. Unfortunately, Mohammed will have to come to the mountain. *Liberator* can do many things, but coming onshore and climbing Telegraph Hill is not one of them."

"What research are you into?"

"Radiation insanity. I'm trying to find a cure. I know that may sound laughable—a cure for something that is, in effect, a side effect of global thermonuclear war."

"It's not laughable at all," Peter said, a knowing look on his face. "Not in this city after all we've been through."

"We first saw it in the Aleutians. Then again it appeared in Seattle. It seems to be working its way down the coast. Then San Francisco. The computer theorizes it should be in Santa Barbara by now, or even L.A."

"Where no one will notice."

"My point is that I have to find a cure. When it appeared that no one would survive nuclear war, curing the effects of radiation insanity seemed pointless. Now that it's clear that some percentage of the population survived, it's our duty to do what we can to cure them. All over the world, not just in the States."

"How it the research going?" Peter asked.

"Not well. I got organ and tissue samples from the Seattle victim, but they deteriorated by the time I got the diagnostic software set up. The white-shirts deteriorate very rapidly after even minor injury. I understand that the captain punched a man to death just twenty-four hours ago. Well, after the Seattle victim died his tissues fell right apart. Of course, I had the software set up beforehand—but when I put to sea I never expected to be doing ROM diagnostics."

Peter perked up so fast he spilled some of his coffee on his knee and didn't even notice.

"You c-can do ROM diagnostics?" he stammered.

"Of course. Why are you surprised?"

"I thought *Liberator* was a Navy submarine."

"She is. But we have an advanced medical facility, especially the library. When she was built, part of the justification for the budget was that she would be partly scientific—just in case *glasnost* lasted forever."

"It didn't," Peter said bitterly.

"Don't be so sure. The Russians may not have been behind the war. The captain suspects the Germans. But that's neither here nor there. We have ROM diagnostics as part of her mission to be able to go anywhere and do anything. If need be, we could put into a tropical island and cure malaria."

"My first research was into malaria—the resurgence in it late last century, after Third World nations burned down the forests to plant crops, including drugs, they upset the global ecology and started a new malaria pandemic."

"I'm set up to take blood, tissue and organ samples, and do diagnostics. I can even test water, air, and native plants for pharmaceutical potential. I can develop drugs in the wild by analyzing roots and bark of native plants. All I need is a breakdown chromatograph of a substance for the computer to compare with the millions of possibilities stored in ROM memory. If you prick your finger I can run a sample and tell you what you had for breakfast. Well, almost."

"I thought only major land facilities had ROM diagnostics. I've used the one at Berkeley . . ."

It was Dr. Martin's turn to get excited. "Then you can show me how to use it for epidemiology? The computer designers never anticipated that I would be faced with a pandemic."

"Between the two of us we can figure it out."

"I only need some tissue samples. Unfortunately—it sounds odd to say that—the white-shirts are all dead."

"Yes, but their tissue lives on. I preserved samples from a dozen white-shirts who died after scaling the wall. Don't ask me why I did it—force of habit, I suppose. But whenever I see a question I have to know the answer, or at least preserve a bit of the question for future research. I guess in the back of my mind I thought maybe Berkeley was spared. It wasn't, I know."

"Then we have to go to the ship!" Dr. Martin said. "When can we start?"

"Now. Come into the tower with me and I'll get the samples."

The library of *Liberator* had been turned into a war room. The flat-top monitor, used mainly for navigational exercises and simulations, displayed chess board–like a street map of that section of San Francisco that still stood.

Whereas Alex used a paper street map and shot glasses to mark positions, Jennings had rigged up a horizontal display of key blocks. Important intersections were marked in yellow, and survivor positions in green. Barbarosa's known locations were designated red, and Percy had drawn upon his military knowledge to mark areas where he thought the battle might be fought. Those glowed red on the screen.

The red zones were the blocks of Powell, Taylor, Hyde and Van Ness coming down the hill from the south, and the Golden Gate National Recreation Area from the west. The latter route was considered the probable invasion route, for the relatively flat and uncluttered-by-debris regions of the National Recreation Area and the Presidio lay along it, on a more-or-less direct route between Barbarosa's camp in the Panhandle and Fisherman's Wharf.

The food and medical supplies in the BART tube were probably safe. So was Coit Tower, although newly trained guards had been posted just to be on the safe side. Barbarosa was thought unlikely to risk the destruction of the supplies in a frontal assault on the BART tube, and even if he did take them he would have to fight survivors anyway. Percy theorized that he would come after Padre and his supporters at Fisherman's Wharf first, and all agreed with that assessment.

In the library, Drs. Martin and Fisher were happy as kids in a candy shop. The CD Rom memory of the computer was being turned inside out, as ionized tissue samples from the white-shirts were analyzed and compared with all known medical knowledge of different diseases across recorded history. Everything related to radiation poisoning was examined: from Hiroshima victims and survivors to natives of Bikini Atoll to U.S. Army volunteers from White Sands in the 1940s to Colombian peasants affected by the nuclear shelling in the South American War of the 1990s.

"Look at this one," Dr. Fisher exclaimed, pointing at the demonstration curve of a tissue sample. "This is a whole-body dose of five thousand rads: cerebral edema, shock and extreme neurological disturbances. This other one is only three thousand rads, more or less. Death within days."

"That's all?" Dr. Martin said, sarcastically.

"Severe vascular damage, loss of fluids and eleccrolytes into intercellular spaces and the G.I. tract. Death within ten days."

"Most of these white-shirts lived for two weeks or more after exposure."

Fisher nodded: "This other one is about one thousand rads: bone marrow destruction and demolition of the autoimmune system. Total susceptibility to infection. Death within five weeks, if it occurs at all. Some of these least-severe cases can linger indefinitely; for years."

"I can see necrosis all over the body in these men. Note the sores on the faces. It's the neurological damage that puzzles me."

"There does seem to be a pattern," Dr. Fisher agreed. "From what you observed in Navy Harbor and what we've seen in San Francisco, the victims share psychotic symptoms."

"And not only share them, they become symbiotic ... feed on each other. Maybe necessary to withstand survivor's guilt. At any rate, this is the first time in history that we've had mass survivors to radiation damage."

"And not only survivors, but in a position of power over their environment. In masses they're *strong*. The biological symptoms are in league with the psychological and sociological ones. There still must be a biological cause underlying the insanity. Your job is to find it."

Dr. Martin said, "My job is to be ship's doctor. Research is your strong point."

"This cure could take all your energy for a prolonged time," Dr. Fisher said.

"I have to treat the survivors," Dr. Martin insisted.

"You will be. Radiation insanity is a global problem."

"Then *we'll* cure it," Dr. Martin said. "Come with me on *Liberator.*"

"But I'm needed here," Fisher protested.

"Your assistants can take over. There are four good medics at Coit Tower who can fix broken legs and cure fevers. I need you to help me cure radiation insanity. There's no doubt we can do it together."

Peter Fisher looked at his older colleague and at the brilliant array of research tools around him. The attraction of *Liberator* was nearly overwhelming. A few weeks after the world came crashing down, here was the opportunity to get into a first-class lab and tour the world, doing research and helping cure ills. And Martin was right—the medics *could* take over at Coit.

"What about my family?" he asked.

"Family is an outdated concept," Martin said, surprising himself with his words. Like many others in the crew, he had come to accept almost totally the new reality.

"My father needs me here."

"When we finish cleaning up San Francisco," Martin said, "there will be little left for your father to do other than minister to souls."

"And my sister?"

"Alex? She's coming with us. To run the science labs. We have a new world to build."

"She mentioned the possibility," Peter said. "She hasn't made up her mind."

"Donovan is very persuasive. She'll come."

18

Charlie's red Toyota had been turned into a small armored personnel carrier.

The roof had been cut off and plates welded over the windows as blast guards. More plates covered the wheel wells down to three inches from the pavement. Percy figured that Barbarosa's men, armed mainly with shotguns, couldn't do damage to the tires or blast through even one-eighth-inch sheeting except at close ranges. And considering the newfound firearms proficiency of the survivors, the enemy would never get close enough.

Several cars were outfitted in this manner. Two guarded Coit Tower and the BART tube. Four roamed the city, keeping to a route laid out by Percy: down the Embarcadero to Lombard, where the patrol linked up with the Telegraph Hill patrol; down to the BART tube, where the second linkup took place; up Washington to Chinatown; along Columbus to Beach; and back across Jefferson to the Embarcadero. These were the best strategic streets that could be cleared of rubble well enough to run patrols.

Liberator's machine shop and the one set up at HQ did the welding, and Charlie and Saxon trained the guards. By daybreak on the third day eight three-man cars were driving the routes laid out by

Percy. In addition, lookouts had been posted in buildings along the expected attack routes, and command posts were set up on Powell, Taylor, Hyde, and Van Ness. Percy was aware that he was fighting a defensive war and was not at all crazy about defending the low ground. But the survivors had the advantage of firepower and initiative. Barbarosa had to attack soon and there were limited ways in which he could do it.

As things stood, it would be an Alamo-type defense, with barricaded survivors at three locations holding off a much larger force that had the advantage of time. While it was thought that Barbarosa would attack right away in order to stifle the insult laid upon him by Donovan's threat, he could wait indefinitely. *Liberator* wouldn't stay in port forever. Perhaps he figured that out. Or maybe he preferred to believe that the new boy in town was staying and had plans to take over.

"There are too many questions," Donovan said, standing atop Fisherman's Wharf and scanning the horizon through binoculars.

A roof-access port used, before the war, mainly by cleaning crews and electrical repairmen, had been reopened so that the roof could serve as an observation post high atop HQ. While only three stories high and on the waterfront, the vantage point was better than that in most buildings, for those that remained standing were pretty much devastated above the second level.

Percy said, "Where the enemy will attack is now a matter of odds. He can't come by sea or air—at least we don't think so. And his vehicles can't be much better than ours. He's got to come by one of the land routes, and that restricts him to four—Powell, Taylor, Hyde, and Van Ness. All of them are covered by patrols."

"Yeah, but not at frequent-enough intervals. He could slip through anyplace."

"Captain, you have got to stop thinking of San Francisco as being a city. Think of it as a huge rubble pile crisscrossed by trails. The possibilities are many but only four are likely—and we have command posts on those streets and patrols on the trails."

"Where are the patrols now? It's dawn of the third day. I have a feeling we'll be fighting soon."

"Red One—your brother—is coming down the Embarcadero from Pier Thirty-nine. Red Two—Chief Smith and Mr. Hooper—is at Van Ness and the Recreation Area. Red Three—Saxon and his group—is at Taylor and Bay. Red Four—Padre and Alex—is on its way back from Telegraph Hill. I'm going out in Red Five in ten minutes. Want to come along?"

"Where are you going?"

"To inspect the fortification at the BART tube. I really don't want to blow it up just to keep it from falling into enemy hands."

"You go do that," Donovan said. "Have Mr. Jennings call Red One and tell him to go to Van Ness and the Rec Area. I'll join him there."

"Reason, Captain?"

"Intuition. My brother is good at it. I think the enemy is coming out of the Presidio and down Van Ness."

"Why, may I ask?"

"It's the direct route. Barbarosa strikes me as being unbearably linear."

"And predictable. Let's hope so."

Donovan checked his transceiver, running radio checks with *Liberator* as well as with the command posts, then went back down through HQ and out to the street, where the 750-cc Honda that Chief Smith had tuned up for him stood ready.

Donovan had done a little motorcycle riding as a young man, but never pursued it once he figured out how easily he could break bones. But his early days with trail bikes served him well in postwar San Francisco. The little Honda was ready-made for dodging rubble piles and negotiating narrow trails strewn with bricks and crushed mortar.

He gunned the engine and cruised slowly off the wharf, acknowledging the waves of survivors who knew he was going off to war on their behalf. Once on the mainland he gunned the engine along Jefferson to Hyde, and from there along Beach to Van Ness.

The Golden Gate Recreation Area was the nearest of a series of parks and open spaces built in the latter years of the twentieth century to link Golden Gate Park with the green spaces of the Presidio and the marina district of the city. Their effect was to make a green belt stretching along the west and north sides of San Francisco, and in the immediate postwar days they provided an open pathway, or battleground, that was relatively free of debris.

Not that much stood there to be knocked down, other than trees, most of which were uprooted and lying on their sides as if a hurricane had been through. The ground was gray with soot and most of the leaves were gone, making the "Green Space," as city park planners called it, more like the dark side of the moon.

It was the perfect place for a battle, at least if you had all the automatic weapons. Donovan was sure that wasn't the case, but it made a comforting thought as he dismounted and stood by the side of that particular wasteland, dreaming body counts.

He could see about five hundred yards into the green. That was a tiny fraction of the length of the green, which went all the way from Van Ness to the Presidio along the northern rim of the penin-

191

sula. The feeling he got was creepy. A vast expanse of open land, marked only by dead trees and uprooted shrubs, flanked a dead zone of crushed buildings. The road on which he got there seemed little more than a rabbit trail when compared to the scope of the devastation.

Ten minutes after Donovan got there Charlie pulled up, alone in Red One. Donovan smiled at the sight of the Toyota, which looked like a cheese box on tiny wheels.

"What's up, boss?" Charlie said.

"What's going on this morning?"

"All is as planned with the troops. I didn't inspect 'em all, but the streets are clear and no Indians in sight. The run from the BART tube to the wharf is down to twenty minutes. The Embarcadero is that clear now."

"Good. What do you make of this green?"

"Looks gray. Remember Mount Saint Helens after the eruption?"

"Which one? Thirty years ago or ten?"

"Either."

"It looks like that except it's flat. I don't like the looks of it much. You could hide a hundred men behind those rocks and dead trees, and the scrub bushes growing everywhere make great cover."

"But you *could* move troops through it."

"Possibly. Is that what you think Barbarosa is doing?"

"Yeah. He lives in the other park, Golden Gate. It's logical for him to think of parkland as a way of moving troops."

"He does know we're organized and have the streets," Charlie agreed. "He could be planning to come around through the Green Space and take us from the side."

"My thought exactly. What do you say we go in and take a look?"

192

"In there?"

"On the bike. I'll drive."

"Let's go," Charlie said eagerly.

Donovan got on the bike with Charlie sitting behind, one hand around his waist and the other holding the Franchi at the ready. They looked like latter-day Mexican bandits getting ready to hold up a gas station.

They motored a hundred yards along a winding path among knocked-down trees and tossed-about scrub, and soon found an ironic virtue of the landscape. Dust covered everything, especially the spaces that were open enough to walk in. Anything that walked left footprints.

Donovan stopped and they got off the cycle to inspect. "This is a bonanza," Charlie said, looking down at the ground. "There's no way you can move through here without it showing. Look at these tracks."

There were many in the dust, which was three inches thick and covered his boots just like moon dust did Neil Armstrong's in the lunar pictures from 1969. Charlie knelt and inspected close-up a variety of prints in a heavily travelled trail between fallen tree trunks.

"Lepus californicus," he said.

"A jackrabbit," Donovan said.

"Very good, big brother. Already there's an amazing example of ecological adjustment."

"Explain."

"Nature abhors a vacuum, right? Rabbits ain't native to San Francisco, Jack. This one must have migrated since the war, probably onto the peninsula from the coastal mountains. I wonder what else has moved in since man gave up the land."

"You mean we might be facing a takeover of the animals?"

"Why not? The nuclear planners didn't target

193

wildlife preserves, so far as I know. The animals are free to move wherever they like."

"What's that small hoofprint?"

"Peccary. *Javelinas.* Wild pigs. Definitely not normally found in San Francisco."

"Alex will want to know about this," Donovan said.

"She may also want to know about *this,*" Charlie said, taking a hasty look around before returning his attention to the ground. There were a series of large footprints. Charlie traced a finger around one.

"That ain't no dog," Donovan said, picking up on his brother's apprehensiveness.

"Canis lupus lycaon. Timber wolves."

"Wolves?"

"Yeah, and a lot of them. There must be a family of twenty or thirty living in this section of the park. All these uprooted trees make perfect den areas, and also cover for hunting."

"Hunting what?" Donovan asked.

"The jackrabbits and wild pigs, for starters. Stray humans. There must be a lot of stragglers after the war."

"Jesus Christ!"

"He can't help us now, big brother. These wolves are handling the body clean-up that the white-shirts didn't get to."

"That's one thing the war planners didn't count on: scavengers after the dust has stopped falling. I wonder if Barbarosa knows about this development."

"I don't see how he could avoid it. Unless he's so obsessed with killing Padre that he didn't stop to look around him in his own park. If there's one family of wolves, there's hundreds. We'll have to warn the survivors against straying into the Green Space."

Donovan's fingers involuntarily tightened around

the grip of his Colt, and the automatic weapon that also was strapped to him suddenly seemed more comforting than ever.

"There are no human prints," he noted.

"We've only covered a small section of park," Charlie answered, looking around the bleak landscape. "Let's check out that high ground . . . maybe get a better look around."

They left the Honda and proceeded on foot another two hundred yards, following the wolf trail that wound up a hillock to a stand of freshly stripped maples. The hill was windswept and relatively free of dust. One thing that hadn't changed in San Francisco was the localized weather conditions, where it could be sunny in one neighborhood and foggy next door. The hill was windy and the dust had mostly blown away.

The vantage point was good. From that spot they could see the whole sweep of Green Space in that part of town, from the edge of the buildings along Van Ness to the start of the Presidio. The land was flat but there were some hills, most of them covered with uprooted trees. Donovan used his binoculars to scout around.

The proliferation of wildlife was amazing. Everywhere he looked in the Green Space, animals abounded. Jackrabbits were everywhere, browsing in the rubble for nuts and grasses. Small herds of peccaries prowled beneath fallen trees and uprooted brush. At the lip of another hill located to the north, eight or nine larger figures prowled.

"Timber wolves," Donovan said, handing his brother the binoculars. "Seven or eight of them."

"A family group," Charlie added. "Two adult males, six adult females, several juveniles. They're stalking jackrabbits."

"The revenge of the animals," Donovan mused. "Is there any chance those wolves will notice us?"

"If we stand here long enough it's inevitable."

"Wonderful. Let's go."

It was then that a shot rang out and tore a chunk of bark out of the tree next to Donovan's head.

"Jesus Fucking Christ!" he hollered as he hit the dust.

Charlie was right next to him. "Where did that come from?"

"Ten o'clock! Bandits coming into the park from the south."

Donovan raised his head far enough to see a stream of people moving into the Green Space from the rubble on the other side of Divisadero. Then another shot tore up the tree trunk.

Charlie jumped up long enough to fire two shots that let him and his brother leap backwards behind a fallen maple.

"Behind the leaning tree—fire!"

Donovan caught a glimpse of a dark-clothed man trying to hide behind a tree that was too narrow for the purpose. Donovan aimed his Colt deliberately and squeezed off a shot that ripped some bark from near the man's head.

He jerked backwards, too far. His body backed up from behind the tree, and Charlie nailed him in the shoulder with a solo shot. The man went down screaming.

"First blood," Charlie said gleefully.

There were five men in the group, all of them big and hairy, with full beards and tattered clothes mostly or entirely soiled with dirt and motor oil.

"Those guys don't look very religious to me," Donovan said. "They look like they came out of a motor pool."

"Barbarosa may be religious but his followers aren't up to snuff," Charlie agreed.

A second man knelt over the one that Charlie shot, not tugging him back to safety so much as trying to relieve him of his rifle. The others carried shotguns; no good at long range.

Donovan took aim and shot him, and he tumbled over and out of sight.

"Nice shot."

"Thanks. Did you notice the fighting over the rifle?"

"I did indeed."

Charlie fired a burst from the Franchi that kept the three others hiding.

Donovan spoke into his transceiver. "Red One to *Liberator*, do you copy?"

"Aye, Captain."

"Red One under attack by five bandits in the Green Space near Divisadero. Two bandits are down."

"Do you need help?" Jennings's voice asked.

"Not from three bandits," Charlie replied, reacting to the offer over the radio.

"Negative, *Liberator*. We're doing fine. Report to Mr. Percy that the Green Space is porous, but not severely at this point."

"Aye, Captain. All other points report quiet at this time."

"Acknowledged. Red One out."

Charlie said, "Two bandits are moving to the left, one to the right. Which ones you want?"

"Left."

"Are you up to this, big brother?"

"Don't worry about me," Donovan snapped, substituting the Franchi for the Colt.

He ran in a crouch along the side of the fallen maple, scurrying across an open space to a stand of mulberry that still had some leaves on it. He slammed himself down on his belly, sighting over a clump of grass toward the area of tree logs and scrubs toward which the two men had been circling, trying to get behind the *Liberator* men.

These two were shorter than the first two, but still formidable, brawny and angry-looking. Donovan saw the fire in their eyes and wondered what drove them. Salvation? Fear of the Lord? Or the promise of a stake in running San Francisco once the good people who rallied behind Padre were driven out? The latter was more likely, Donovan thought as he sighted in on them.

They were a hundred feet away, running toward two oak trees that had fallen upon the other to create a natural lean-to.

Donovan stood, holding the Franchi at his waist. "Hey! You!" he yelled.

They spun towards him. He pulled the trigger and a short burst from the automatic cut the men down.

Off to the right there was another shout and a

single shot, followed by a war whoop that Donovan recognized as his brother's.

The first encounter with Barbarosa's men was over in less than five minutes. Donovan looked around to ensure safety, then walked the distance to the two bodies he had just shot and looked down at them.

They were youngish men, thirty or perhaps thirty-five, with tanned skin and workingman's hands. The hands were calloused from long work outdoors. The clothes were similarly worn, from doing honest labor.

Donovan emptied their pockets onto the grass. He found wallets, a money clip, chewing tobacco, cigars, a Swiss army knife, a nail clipper, car and house keys with chains from the Ford Motor Company and the Seattle Seahawks, and $4.65 in silver. Both wallets carried Washington State driver's licenses with Seattle addresses and ID cards from the International Longshoreman's Union.

"These guys are working stiffs," Donovan said in surprise as Charlie ran up.

"No longer working but definitely stiffs," Charlie added.

"Longshoremen from Seattle."

"I see a pattern developing."

"Yeah, ain't it the truth? Two blue-collar guys from Seattle who seem as normal as you or me, but . . ."

"They migrated all the way to San Francisco two weeks after the war and wound up willing sacrifices in a mad crusade," Charlie said. "Am I missing the point or is something contagious?"

"Dr. Martin is working on a cure for radiation insanity," Donovan said.

"I thought that was about the white-shirts."

"So did I. Maybe they're just the worst-case scenario. These guys could be affected, too."

"The problem with these guys is they don't look crazy. How do we tell the crazies from the good guys?"

"Beats me. I only shoot 'em. From now on we may have to shoot everything that moves. Dammit, Pirate . . . we're trained to think that global thermonuclear war is the end of everything. It's damned disconcerting to find out that it isn't. Problems continue; grow worse."

From a few hundred yards off came a bloodcurdling scream. They turned in that direction to see the man who first shot at them, the one they left wounded, trying vainly to struggle to his feet as three timber wolves tore at his flesh with their fangs.

"My God!" Donovan swore.

Charlie lined up a long shot in what seemed like a millisecond and put the fellow out of his misery.

The wolves skittered away for a few seconds, glaring at Donovan and Charlie with fierce yellow eyes, then tore into the corpse.

"Liberator to Red One."

Jennings's voice was becoming synonymous with the struggle of the survivors. It so often appeared bearing bad news.

"Red One here."

"Red Two is reporting bandits at Hyde and Bay. I have the same report from the Hyde command post. Can you back them up?"

"On our way, *Liberator,*" Donovan radioed.

Donovan remounted the Honda and, with Charlie casting a wary eye over his shoulder at the wolves, roared out of the Green Space, the tires cutting narrow grooves in the deep dust.

Charlie jumped off and got back into his Toyota, then turned it around and followed Donovan to Bay.

They paused at the corner and peered around it, listening to the sound of gunfire down the block.

Two old Fords and a Chevy pickup truck had tried to drive down the five blocks of Hyde leading down the hill to the wharf, but were stopped by fire from the command post and Red Two—Chief Smith and young Mr. Hooper.

Bandits were behind the stopped cars, firing shotguns. Donovan counted twenty-two of them.

"Red One to *Liberator.*"

"*Liberator* here."

"Tell Red Five that there are twenty-two guys in three vehicles that may have come from the southwest. The five bandits we encountered in the Green Space came from that direction."

"Will do, Captain. Mr. Percy says it's too quiet along the Embarcadero. He'd like to stay there if you don't need him."

"Let him stay there. I think this is a probe from the southwest. We'll handle it."

"I'm glad you're confident," Charlie said. "There are getting to be a lot of bandits in this town."

"Alex thinks that Barbarosa has two hundred followers, half of them warriors. Are you turning quitter on me?"

"No way. Get behind the wheel and give me your Franchi."

They went back to the Toyota and Donovan took the wheel, with Charlie half sitting, half standing on the passenger's seat holding both automatics. Donovan put the pedal to the metal and steered the car around the corner, and as soon as the bandits turned in their direction Charlie opened up, firing through a slit in the front blast shield.

Six bandits fired shotguns; the pellets peppered the Toyota, and Donovan instinctively hunkered down as low as he could. Charlie emptied the clip of his Franchi and then began firing Donovan's.

The Toyota roared up to the intersection of Hyde and Bay and then stopped. They got out, flinging the doors open as shields and tucking themselves down behind.

Four bandits were down; other men scrambled to retrieve their weapons. Nobody ran at first. Then Donovan, firing his Colt, picked off two men who, in succession, tried to pick up a fallen shotgun. Seeing this, five others turned and ran up Hyde to safety. A few others followed.

When they were gone, only the vehicles remained, their idling engines filling the tumble-down brick-and-mortar piles that marked the four corners with an otherworldly sound.

Donovan walked to the center of the intersection and looked up Hyde at the running-away figures of eight bandits.

"Well, some of these guys don't want to sacrifice themselves," Donovan said, looking then at the fourteen bodies on the ground.

"Maybe not all of Barbarosa's men are nuts," Charlie added.

"Some could be going along based on the assumption that he's the likely winner. Maybe they'll change sides."

"This one's not dead yet," Charlie said, touching a body with a toe. The bandit was especially young, maybe fifteen or sixteen, and alive despite a stomach wound.

Donovan looked at the youngster, then looked harder. As Smith and Hooper ran up, Donovan knelt and pulled the navy blue watch cap off the kid's head. Her long black hair tumbled onto the dusty pavement. On her denim jacket was stitched the name Lisa.

"This one's a girl," Donovan said, astonished.

"She's the one you shot with the Colt."

"While trying to pick up a shotgun. Dammit, I thought it was a guy."

He touched her cheek to comfort her and it seemed like she wanted to talk. He moved his head closer to hers, and heard her say, "Die, die die!"

He stood and spoke into his transceiver. "Red One to *Liberator*. The corner of Hyde and Bay is secure. The body count is now nineteen bandits. No casualties on our side. Get Dr. Martin up to this corner—I have a bandit he will want to look at."

"Affirmative, Red One. Please be advised that an assault is taking place at Embarcadero and Beach. Red Five is holding by itself. Many bandits."

"On our way," Donovan said.

"What now?" Charlie asked.

"Percy is in deep shit and needs our help."

"I didn't think he needed anyone," Charlie said.

"Turn this corner back over to the survivors and follow me," Donovan said, running for the Honda.

Embarcadero and Beach was one of those intersections that suffered more than most from the war and the concurrent seismicity.

A curiosity of the local rock strata caused that part of the northern city to shake more than its surroundings, and nothing at all stood standing. Buildings on the land side of Embarcadero had fallen down and were no more than gigantic piles of stone debris. On the water side, wharves collapsed and waterfront buildings tumbled into the bay.

The trail through that section was a ten-foot-wide path that ran around the curves of the debris piles, rather like a mountain road following the curves of the terrain.

Percy was alone, having stretched the defenses by loading up gunmen in the other cars and keeping only a single, unshielded Volvo for himself. His theory was that he would be running from position to position and always within range of protection, but he didn't count on running into a horde of Barbarosa bandits who were trying to turn the eastern corner and come down toward the survivors' HQ from the other direction.

He realized his predicament only at the last moment, when he decided to stay on in case the bandits tried to come that way. There had been two attacks from the southwest, making one from the southeast a distinct possibility.

Sweeping up the Embarcadero from the north this time, Donovan and Charlie stopped fifty feet short of the embattled executive officer, who was firing sporadically from behind his car, just often enough to keep the enemy back.

"How many are there?" Donovan asked, joining him behind the car.

"Ten or twenty. I can't be sure. They're firing in shifts, like they were using muzzle-loaders."

"Barbarosa must have gotten his idea of warfare from watching old movies," Donovan said.

"Those shotguns are single-loaders and double-barrels. There isn't a five-shot in the whole bunch. I don't know where they found the stuff."

"They probably took them off dead white-shirts," Charlie said, ducking down as a shotgun blast knocked out the windshield of the Volvo.

"Dammit," Donovan swore, standing and pegging two shots at the enemy, who were behind a two-story pile of bricks that previously had been a four-story garden apartment building.

"War wagon!" Charlie said, running back to the Toyota and getting behind the wheel. When he brought it up, Donovan and Percy climbed quickly in and Charlie drove it around the Volvo.

Donovan and Percy fired out the right side, through the firing slits and over the top of the welded-on shield. Barbarosa's men, seeing the small armored car coming, began concentrating their fire on it. Wave after wave of pellets hit the side of the Toyota, buckling in the sheeting until grapefruit-sized blisters pocked it.

Charlie drove slowly directly out into the line of fire, around the corner of the debris pile that served as cover for the bandits. Then he slammed on the brakes and rolled out, holding the Franchi in front of him and blazing away.

It was a slaughter. Bodies fell on bodies and no-body screamed, until suddenly hands went up in the air and the air fell silent of bullets.

Three bandits gave up, looking nervously both in front and in back of them. Smith and Hooper had worked their way behind the carnage and surprised the bandits. They stood dumbly with arms in the air.

Donovan and Percy got out of the car and called the ship to report on eleven more casualties. The body count was up to thirty, with no dead or wounded among the survivors or *Liberator* crew.

20

Barbarosa's troops may have been dedicated but
they were far from invincible. Thirty dead in the
first hour of the conflict showed that none of them
were great soldiers. They weren't even good shots,
and their weaponry was meager.

Dedication was all they had. Their leader had
sold them on the oldest bill of goods in the world—
suffer and die for their leader, and be rewarded in
the afterlife. The problem was that Barbarosa's
preaching was better in the fire-and-brimstone department than it was in the afterlife-reward department.

The troops had a good idea how to suffer, but only
a meager vision of heavenly skies. As soon as they
ran into an obstacle, they found themselves faced
with the inevitability of pain and only dubious
promise of salvation. In short, they gave up easily.
When his bullets didn't smite down all his enemies,
his soldiers wearied.

One of them, a skinny kid named Jake with a
puffin tatooed on his arm, was laid flat by a bullet
crease to the temple and taken to Telegraph Hill
for repair. There, sitting on a hospital cot next to
Lisa, the teenager Donovan had winged on Hyde
Street, the young man recounted his woes to an ap-

preciative audience of survivors and *Liberator* personnel.

"I signed up with him in Vacaville," he said.

"Where's that?" Donovan asked.

"Up towards Sacramento. My dad was manager of a horse ranch there, but everything was blown away in the windstorm."

"Wind only? No fire?"

"Fire to the east and west. Only wind where I lived."

"How did you hear about Barbarosa?" Dr. Martin asked, applying antibacterial film to various untreated wounds on the boy's arms and chest.

"Some friends of mine from up the valley told me about this great man who was taking over San Francisco and planning a renaissance of God on earth."

"How did you get here?" Donovan asked.

"We walked. There were lots of us on the road, and everyone was fleeing south to get away from the white-shirts."

"They came from the north?"

"They seemed to come from everywhere, but yeah, mainly from the north. Alaska, I heard. Man, they're sick."

"We noticed," Donovan said dryly.

"We managed to get into San Francisco just ahead of them. They tried to come over the bridges, but they were out and a lot of them fell off. Eventually they swept around the bay and up the peninsula. We've been fighting them ever since. Until yesterday."

"Their demise was my doing," Donovan said. "Now Barbarosa can free up troops to attack us."

"That's what he said," Jake confirmed. "Barbarosa told us that once the white-shirts were out of the way, we could kill the survivors. He said that all we had to do was point our guns in your direction and you would fall over."

"They aren't great guns," Charlie said.

"How many of you are there left?" Donovan asked.

"Two hundred. No, less. About fifty of us went into battle."

"Thirty are dead already. Where are the rest?"

"The last I heard they were gathering somewhere in the city, waiting for orders. God, none of what he promised came true."

"Some of what he promised did. Thirty of your friends have met their maker and another twenty are doomed if they keep up this bullshit. Either we'll find them and kill them, or they'll attack and be slaughtered. There is an alternative, you know."

"What?"

"Help us get to Barbarosa. We'll lock him up and keep him there until he agrees to behave."

"You can do that?" Jake said, interested.

"Killing actually is a fairly small part of what we do. Until the other day, we hadn't done any at all. I would like to return to those days. Help us nail your boss."

"Okay," Jake said, a smile of relief crossing his lips.

The smile faded instantly, as the girl on the cot next to him shrieked, "No! You will know the wrath of Barbarosa."

"Who's this?" Donovan asked, startled.

"The girl you shot. Lisa."

"Is what she has catching, Doctor?" Donovan asked.

"Unknown. I'm checking. It doesn't seem likely, though."

"You will die! You will all die!" she spat, glaring at Donovan as if he were evil incarnate.

"At the moment, she doesn't seem to have any-

thing that can't be attributed to the bullet wound,"
Dr. Martin said, fixing a sedative and giving it to
her intravenously.

"They all talk like that," Jake said, relieved once
Lisa calmed down and slipped into sleep.

"All the women?" Dr. Martin asked.

"And some of the guys. All the people close to
Barbarosa, anyway. The group leaders of his legion."

"Legion?"

"That's what he calls the fighting men and
women. The group I belonged to. I thought I was
doing good, working for the new leader. Oh God,
can you help me?"

Donovan said, "Tell us how to get at him. Describe the layout of his compound. There has to be
a way in."

The Pacific Ocean was a crystal-blue mirror at
the hour of dawn on the fourth day.

From one horizon to the other, from the campfires
on land to the cirrus clouds forming a haze over the
far western horizon deep at sea, the world was calm
and the sea flat as a pancake. Even the seabirds
were quiet, as if ducking down in fear.

Expectation hung in the air, permeating the
bridge of *Liberator* as the teal-colored hull rose ver-
tically, breaking surface and shedding water in silence, unseen.

Jake cooperated with Donovan and his men to
the extent of giving a complete debriefing about life
in the compound. This was taped for the history
banks of the computer, one of Donovan's side projects being the assembly of an oral history of World
War III.

The debriefing also allowed Donovan and Percy
to assemble a plan of action. Which was, in its simplicity, to sneak out of San Francisco Bay at night

while submerged and resurface before dawn on the ocean side of the peninsula to put parties ashore in Golden Gate Park. They would walk into the compound from the rear, taking advantage of Barbarosa's myopic vision of reality—that the threat came only from the direction of the enemy camp, in this case, northeast.

Liberator surfaced west of Barbarosa and put two boats in the water, one of them sporting the outboard motor confiscated from the man who attacked them near Seattle. Donovan led one party, which included Alex, Charlie, and Dr. Martin (whose interest in radiation psychosis had increased to the point of wanting to see the compound where a mild form of it seemed to be breeding). Percy led the other party, which included Chief Smith and Hooper. Saxon, Alex's right-hand man, was now capable of defending HQ by himself and was back at the wharf, just in case Barbarosa pulled a surprise attack while *Liberator* was out of the harbor.

Both parties were armed to the teeth (with the exception of Dr. Martin and Alex, who were armed with video cameras to record the symptoms of radiation insanity). Both took advantage of Barbarosa's affinity not only for ignoring his flank, but also for sleeping late. No one associated with him, save for a few guards who were natural insomniacs, got up before mid-morning. One unplanned legacy of the war was that, with little social planning in mind other than survival, the necessity of waking up early was entirely a matter of personal choice.

There was no activity on the ocean front of the park. The encampments occupied by Barbarosa's followers, as well as crude fortifications—logs piled up above the high-water mark and strewn half-purposefully over bulkheading, to forestall an invasion from the sea—had been abandoned.

Donovan said, "He kept the peasants laboring in

the sun, where they wore themselves out and currently are sacked out in the tall grass."

"It sure looks like nobody's home," Alex said, trying to keep her balance while taping the approaching landfall.

The expanse of the park was dark and sleepy. The campfires that, from the water, looked as if they were right up on the beach, were in fact far inland and seemed to be dwindling.

Above a ten-foot breakwater where in the previous days Barbarosa's men had laid horizontal ramparts of birch trunks, sharpened at the sea end as if to stave off Viking longboats, a large herd of peccaries roamed. Dark birds roamed the skies above the park, riding thermals and cruising languidly in the dawn air.

"Thomas?" Charlie said, a touch of apprehensiveness in his voice.

"What?" Donovan asked, taking his attention away from the wild pigs.

"Buzzards."

Percy had found a stretch of bulkhead used, now and again, as a boat dock. Ladders climbed down the stone face to a narrow platform at the high-water mark. They maneuvered their boats to the platform and tied up.

The key piece of information in Jake's testimony was that, in the days since *Liberator* arrived, Barbarosa moved his compound from the Panhandle to a stand of birch surrounding a small bandshell. The bandshell had been used for chamber music concerts under the stars, and now was home to Barbarosa and his crowd.

With Charlie in the lead and Donovan behind, the combined parties climbed the steps to the top of the bulkhead. The sun was rising over the rubble piles of San Francisco as they poked their heads up into the light.

Grass, mostly dead or dying and with a fine sheen of gray dust, stretched from the bulkhead to the bandshell. Blankets covered bodies, apparently still sleeping, but it was dark and hard to see.

Alex tried to shoot tape, but it was dark and the iris had trouble adjusting. Peccaries roamed here and there among the clumps of bodies. A trio of campfires set the night before smoldered. Buzzards circled overhead.

"I got a bad feeling about this," Charlie said.

"You can say that again, Pirate," Donovan replied, his fingers tightening on the grip of his Colt.

"What's the matter?" Alex asked. "They're sleeping."

"Stay here where you can get back in the boat," Donovan snapped.

"Why?"

"Trust me."

Donovan and Charlie walked slowly, dead slowly, toward the bandshell. As the sun came up and the shadows disappeared, what they only feared as a possibility became real.

They were all dead, some beneath their blankets. With many, what looked like blankets in the dark were really pools of blood. Everywhere were signs of violent struggle. Skin was ripped up; jugulars torn out. In a scene of incredible savagery, Barbarosa and all of his followers had been slaughtered by the newest visitors to San Francisco—the timber wolves. Killed in their sleep in the middle of the night.

Under the bandshell, where a few weeks before gentle audiences heard the *Brandenburg Concertos,* blood was caked over ripped-up carcasses. Only the men of *Liberator* and the buzzards overhead were alive. Donovan looked at the other men with wild eyes.

"And the beasts shall inherit the Earth," he said.

Off in the stand of birch was a howling and a scuffling of underbrush.

"They're back," Charlie warned.

"Back to the boats!" Donovan ordered. "Go! Go!"

Seeing the men of the party charge away from the bandshell and across the grass toward her, Alex piled back into the boat and revved up the engine. When everyone was back on board and the boats were away, making all deliberate speed for *Liberator*, Donovan looked behind him and saw a line of wolves, gray and menacing with yellow eyes, looking hungrily from the bulkhead.

"I don't think we can do any more good in this town," he said.

"You're sure I can't talk you out of this?" Donovan said, inhaling deeply on a Lucky Strike while walking down the pier with his friend.

"I've made up my mind. I'm staying," Dr. Martin said.

"With the wolves and everything?"

"Saxon says he can keep them confined to the Green Spaces. Once they run out of food there, they'll leave. Go back to the mountains."

"It will be years before this city—or anything like it—is functioning again. It may never be like we knew."

"Nonetheless, there's work for me here. Good work. I'm a clinician. You know that. On *Liberator* there's not much for me to do. Here I have real injuries to real people who can't live without medical care. On *Liberator* everything is possible; here it's a struggle to stay alive. But that's what life is all about."

"You'll be missed, Dr. Martin."

"Dr. Fisher will serve you well. And with him in the research library, your chances of finding a cure for radiation psychosis are better than ever. So it works out; he's in his element, I'm in mine."

Donovan said, "Keep the batteries charged for your transceiver. When he finds the cure you'll be the first one to know about it. You'll get the formula for the antidote over the radio."

"And I'll be able to make it in the lab I set up on Telegraph Hill. Really, Tom ... this is the best thing that ever happened to me. I feel like a doctor again."

"Padre can use you. The world can use his children."

"Take good care of Alex."

"I will," Donovan said, leaving one doctor for another. As Dr. Martin got into a car for transport to Coit Tower and his new medical facility, Dr. Fisher escorted two patients—Jake and Lisa—to *Liberator*. Jake looked happy as a sow in the mud at his new adventure. Lisa was sullen, still sedated. Crewmen escorted them down into the ship.

"My father is very happy with the way things turned out," Peter said.

"Me too. I'll miss Dr. Martin, though."

"He'll be doing what he does best. Me too. I spent a couple of hours alone with the computer, and it's incredible. Between ROM diagnostics and the incredible analytic ability, I would expect a cure for radiation psychosis before too long. And Dr. Martin is prepared to make the medicine here."

"All is as it should be," Donovan mused. "Even the wolves have their place."

"When will we be leaving?"

"At seventeen hundred hours—five o'clock. Where is your sister?"

"Saying good-bye to the party aboard *Priscilla*. Now *they're* off on an adventure."

"So are we all," Donovan said, taking his leave of Peter and drifting over to the pier where the old sailing ship was getting under way for its greatest voyage.

Fifty people, men, women, and children, were piling onto the schooner for a voyage of colonization like those made by other sailing ships at earlier times in man's history. Once again, in the dark days after World War III, it was necessary to sail across oceans in search of new and safer lands that perhaps were untouched by man's firestorm.

No one knew if such places existed. No one had the news. Every place but the one you stood in was unknown and alien. There could be paradise across the sea, or just another wasteland ruined by war and eaten up by white-shirts and wolves. Were there people elsewhere living in peace and happiness, or had the animals really inherited the earth? All these things awaited discovery.

Liberator left San Francisco rid of the terrors that beset it in the days after the war. Now it was up to the survivors to pick up the pieces and rebuild, maybe this time making things better for future generations.

And fifty of them set out to make new lives elsewhere, across the sea. They had charts leading them to the South Pacific and favorable winds to get there. Enough provisions to last a year. Navigational gear. Extra sails for when it blew and diesel fuel for when it didn't. Working the computers aboard *Liberator,* Alex produced profiles of island groups likely to have gotten through the war unscathed. These profiles went to the colonists aboard *Priscilla.* They also went into the navigational computer on *Liberator.* Once again, Donovan had a plan.

She was in the bow of the ship, sitting on the aft end of a long bowsprit that helped carry the three foresails, checking things off on a clipboard. The provisions were aboard and now, as couples and their children arrived, they were assigned sleeping places and jobs and their names checked off.

Donovan stepped over the rail and onto the deck,

helping himself to a seat beside her. He was amazed that, after all they had been through, she could sit calmly checking off names on a list while waiting for people to sail off where she would never see them again.

"This has got to be like marrying off the children," he said.

"Something like that."

"It's amazing to me how these people can sail halfway around the world in a hundred-year-old ship and expect to find something."

"It's a hundred and twenty years old, and they expect to find something wonderful—a place to live and raise future generations. There," she said, closing her notes. "That's all of them. She sails in an hour."

Alex kissed Donovan on the cheek and wrapped her fingers around his arm.

"Are you packed?" he asked.

"Floppy disks and everything. Thanks for taking me into your world, Thomas Donovan."

"I'm delighted. So is Peter, I hear."

"Oh yeah, he's got his lab back. I can understand that perfectly. I always wanted to work with him, you know. Our careers are compatible—medicine and computers, public health and environmental planning."

"I'm counting on it," Donovan said.

"How so? For me to have someone to talk to?"

"Not only that. We are sailing this afternoon, but we can't sail forever. We need the ability to stop and rest, and that means a place to stop and rest in."

"There are lots of ports in the world," she said.

"True, and all of them overrun with white-shirts or wolves. Or totally demolished. No, we need a place to be alone, to recoup and regenerate between missions of exploration and rescue."

"And where will this place be?"

"That's where you come in. You and Peter. You know all there is to know about planning communities in the tropics. He knows medicine and how to treat exotic diseases. The memory banks in *Liberator* contain man's accumulated knowledge, including medical knowledge."

"We're starting over," she said, wild-eyed.

"These people are starting over," Donovan said, indicating the families settling in aboard the schooner. "Mankind isn't dead, no matter how bad things seem. Maybe mankind isn't even *close* to being dead. We'll do what we can to help survivors, but we also have to ensure the future."

She laughed, and said, "You're playing Adam and Eve."

"We are," he said. "And why not?"

"Why not indeed," Alex replied, kissing him again.

The departure of *Liberator* from San Francisco took place at 1700 hours as planned, two hours after *Priscilla* left the dock to begin her long voyage of colonization across the ocean to the South Pacific.

Liberator left a city that was in immeasurably better shape than before. The white-shirts were history, scarcely a bad memory. Every day the thought of them receded further and further into the consciousness of the good people of the city.

Barbarosa also faded from memory, and soon would be recalled as just the first of many would-be despots who tried to take advantage of postwar America. His short reign of tyranny ended as bloodily as it began, and appropriately it ended in another tyranny, that of the animals.

The wolves left. Eventually they, and most of the other wild animals, were driven from San Francisco. They never went back to the mountains, though, but stayed south of the fault line that had broken along Market Street.

In a great burst of appropriateness, mankind was never again allowed to dominate the Bay Area, as throughout the world nature conspired to prevent his ever again dominating a region. In San Francisco there was a stone barrier between man and the animals, with man trapped on the north end, surrounded on three sides by water. Both man and animal thrived, each in his own section and each respected by the other.

In the human quarter, Padre, with the help of Dr. Paul Martin, helped the survivors raise themselves out of the rubble and rebuild the city. It did not happen quickly or easily. Years went by and then decades, but eventually the debris was cleaned up and the city rebuilt. Ships again plied the waters of San Francisco Bay, at first fishing for whatever could be caught, then later carrying goods for trade with other ports where lived other survivors.

Aboard the *Liberator,* Donovan ordered a tour of the bay, which Mr. Hooper made, keeping in the channels while taking the ship on a roundabout course meant to let all who lived see her and remember. After an hour of this slow steaming, and with the schooner *Priscilla* now three hours in the lead, Donovan put the ship to sea.

She crossed under the Golden Gate Bridge for the final time and turned onto course 270, to the southwest and away from land. Donovan and Alex joined the other officers on the topside bridge, watching the coastline of the United States disappear from sight behind them, perhaps forever. The evening was cool and a breeze blew in from the deep sea. The sky was filled with diamonds, clear of the gray haze that stained it for so many days after the war. Birds flew by the bridge, land birds and gulls at

219

first, then terns and blue-water birds. A frigate bird drifted by on an idle wind.

At 1900 hours the sun was setting on the outline of *Priscilla,* her masts and shrouds outlined against the orange-red disk of the sun. Oddly enough it was Donovan, who did not have the sharpest eyes in the crew, who saw it first, and he gaped for several seconds, his breath caught in his throat.

"A ship dead in the water, half a mile to the starboard of *Priscilla!*"

Jennings reported, "Radar has nothing!"

"It's *Nemesis!*" Donovan exclaimed. "And she's menacing the colonists. Executive Officer, call alert stations!"

"Alert stations! All hands to alert stations!"

As the alarm sounded, officers rushed down into the body of *Liberator,* carrying a stunned Alex along with them. Once back down in the bridge, she glued herself to the wall behind Donovan's swivel seat.

"Listen on fourteen-twenty hertz," Donovan ordered.

"Sonar reports emissions on fourteen-twenty," Jennings reported.

"Dive to one thousand! Ahead full! Lasers on! Make ready tubes one and two!"

"Lasers show weapons status. Tubes one and two are activated. Acoustic sensing, fourteen-twenty hertz."

"Who are they?" Alex asked. "What do they want?"

"Unknown who they are," Donovan replied. "But they want us."

Hooper reported, "Levelling off at one thousand. We are making fifty knots."

The reports came to Donovan fast and furious.

"Distance to target, six thousand yards."

"No screw signature evident, just the fourteen-twenty hertz."

"We have sonar contact, Captain. She's still dead in the water."

"How far from *Priscilla?*" Donovan asked.

"I show point-seven miles."

"Is *Priscilla* in danger from our fish?"

"Negative unless *Nemesis* gets any closer."

"We have laser lock. Switching off active sonar."

"Target is still dead in the water. No! She's starting to move, heading south-southwest at negligible knots."

"Let's get her before she goes too far," Donovan said.

"Weapons Control shows receipt of laser lock. Feeding in to torpedo guidance."

Once again the bridge lights dimmed as the crew, now battle-seasoned, did their jobs efficiently and without prompting. Soon the Cyclops monitors turned half the bridge into the equivalent of the cockpit of a fighter plane that was equipped with a heads-up display. Leaning forward from his seat, Donovan immersed himself in the display and watched as *Nemesis* grew in size and speed.

"She's moving toward *Priscilla,* Captain," was the report.

Another voice in the general clamor said, "Target is diving beneath the schooner."

22

"Damn her," Donovan swore, pounding the armrest.

"Target is holding beneath the schooner."

"Torpedoes are ready."

"Hold your fire."

"Captain, this may be our best chance," Percy complained.

"She's using the colonists as cover. We can't fire on her now."

"What the hell does she *want?*"

"Distance four thousand yards and closing."

"Slow to one-half speed. Sonar, is there anything else from her?"

"Negative. No screw signature. No machine noises."

"This is not possible," Donovan swore. "No ship can function without making noise of some kind, and don't tell me about a fourteen-twenty hertz whine."

Jennings said, "That's it, and it's not even associated with a particular part of the ship, which is what you would expect for such a well-defined tone."

Hooper reported, "Three thousand and closing."

"Slow to one-quarter," Donovan ordered.

Suddenly Alex, who had pushed away from the

wall and begun to peer at Jennings's communications monitors, asked, "What software are you using on this?"

"What? I don't know," Jennings replied, caught off guard. "Whatever the Navy put in. Standard sonar recognition software on that monitor you're looking at."

"It gives us the screw signatures on all major vessels," Donovan added. "Is there a problem?"

"Yeah. It's not made to recognize that fourteen-twenty hertz whistle. The Navy programmers weren't looking for a white noise generator."

"A *what?*"

"This is not new. Three years ago the Marine Biosphere Living Experiment in Australia created a white noise generator that emitted fourteen hundred and twenty hertz—a harmonic off the white noise frequencies emitted by lyrefish as a defense against shark attack."

"Lyrefish?" Donovan asked.

"Yeah, which produces an incredibly efficient acoustic barrier against shark attack—against acoustic recognition by all predators, as a matter of fact."

"Two thousand yards and closing," Hooper announced.

"Reduce speed to dead slow. Mr. Jennings, give me a laser scan of that submarine. Laser on probe status."

Alex said, "The Marine Biosphere experiment was off the Great Barrier Reef, which as you know is lousy with sharks. Their fourteen-twenty hertz generator successfully prevented sharks from recognizing the Biosphere and its inhabitants. It allowed them to blend into the background."

"Are you suggesting that the submarine out there is generating noise like a fish to avoid detection?"

"It worked for the Biosphere." She shrugged. "Apparently it's working now."

Jennings interrupted, saying, "Laser probe is inconclusive, Captain."

"Can the same thing interfere with laser and sonar?"

"Unknown, but then the whole field of bioacoustic damping in the marine environment is very new."

Hooper said, "The target is holding depth seven hundred yards below *Priscilla.*"

Donovan bristled, and said, "New? We're the newest thing going. How come we don't know about bioacoustic damping, lyrefish, or whatever the fuck it is? How come the guys in the other sub do?"

"You accept whatever science the Navy gives you. You wait for someone to hand you technology. Maybe they go out and get it themselves."

"We've only been on our own for two weeks," Donovan said.

"That's long enough to start looking," Alex retorted. "When I get the chance I'll update the software on your computers. In the meantime, and just so those guys in the other sub don't harm the colonists, why don't you look for a white noise generator located amidships. That's where the Biosphere experimenters put theirs for the widest possible dispersal."

Donovan looked at Jennings, then said, "Laser to weapons status. Fire in bursts, targeting amidships. If there is a generator, let's blow it to shit."

Jennings replied, "Weapons Control reports a good lock on the starboard beam of the enemy. Commencing fire."

As Donovan watched the representation of it on the Cyclops display, the laser cut loose with bursts of blue-green light that hit the side of *Nemesis* just aft of the tower. On the display, hits registered as

224

short bursts of blue-green light against the slate gray of the hull.

"Come on, damn you," Donovan coaxed, and Percy clenched his fists.

Jennings's eyes were glued to his monitors, sweat forming in droplets on his brow. Then he smiled. "Machine noises!" he announced. "Circulating pumps and turbines!"

"Got him!" Donovan yelled, raising a fist in the air.

"Cavitation noises, Captain. A screw turning. Holding on for the computer match."

"She's under way," Hooper said. "Heading southwest."

"Ahead slow," Donovan said.

"Weapons Control is recalibrating for the new acoustics," Percy announced. "Torpedoes are ready."

"As soon as she's clear of *Priscilla*, Mr. Percy," Donovan said proudly.

"Enemy is turning onto two-seven-six, speed increasing to twenty knots."

"Stay with her, Mr. Hooper. Ahead half."

"The schooner is safe now," Percy said.

"Fire one!"

Liberator shuddered perceptibly as the torpedo was hurled into the sea and kicked to life yards from the bow. As she raced toward her target, all ears were on the sonar.

"Torpedo is running true, Captain. Guidance is holding. The enemy is now at thirty knots."

"You won't get away so easily this time," Donovan swore.

"The laser lock is holding," Percy said. "The torpedo is homing on amidships and the acoustic shield is down. She sounds like a regular sub now."

And she'll die like one, Donovan said to himself.

Jennings reported, "She's jamming the fish. At least she knows we're here, Captain."

"I expected jamming. Mr. Percy, set torpedo two to ignore acoustics—respond to the laser lock only. Proximity fuse."

"What does that do?" Alex asked, gripping the back of Donovan's chair.

"The second torpedo will ignore the enemy's attempts to jam the acoustic sensor. It will follow the laser track and detonate within three hundred yards of the hull. If we get that near her we may not sink her but we'll do damage. At least we showed her she can't hide from us anymore."

"*I* showed her."

"Medals will be given out later," Donovan said sharply.

"Torpedo two is reset and ready to fire."

"Fire two!"

Liberator raced through the sea, keeping pace with *Nemesis* as both accelerated into the deep ocean.

Alex moved her hands from the back of the seat to Donovan's shoulders, and gripped them. He sat with his eyes fixed on the Cyclops display, which showed the other submarine from aft on as it retreated at increasing speed. Who were they? What did they want? Would they be destroyed without ever answering those questions?

"She's holding course, Captain. She may not be aware of the second fish."

"Dependence on technology can breed overconfidence," Donovan said, looking over his shoulder at Alex.

"She's at forty knots," Hooper said.

"Stay with her."

"Aye, Captain. She may be faster than us, but she's no giant."

"She may not be faster, either. This hasn't been a fair fight until now."

"The first fish has swung to starboard and is veering away," Percy said.

"And the second?"

"On target and accelerating. The enemy is aware of it now and she's turning to port. The fish is turning with her. Ten seconds to impact."

"Hold on," Donovan said. "This could be rough."

"Nine . . . eight . . . seven . . . six . . ."

"I'm turning to stay with her," Hooper said.

"Five . . . four . . . three . . ."

Alex dug her fingers so deeply into Donovan's shoulders that the bruises didn't come out for days. As *Liberator* held her collective breath, the second torpedo detonated one hundred yards from the starboard skin of *Nemesis,* touching off a shock wave that rocked both ships.

On *Liberator,* those on their feet braced themselves, while containers fell off shelves and the engines surged to maintain thrust through the turbulence.

When the shaking stopped and Donovan was again able to look at the display, little had changed. *Nemesis* was apparently undamaged, with not so much as a solitary hull plate scarred. But she had increased speed and dived, and was pulling away from her pursuer.

"Seven thousand yards, Captain," Hooper said. "She's accelerating too fast for us and is now at fifteen hundred feet depth."

"She's running again," Percy said, a large tinge of satisfaction in his voice.

"We made our point, gentlemen," Donovan said. "Let's not waste any more torpedoes on her. Not today, anyway. We know now that she's no giant, and she has a fatal weakness—she sticks around and lets us take shots at her. Eventually one will get through."

"How could she survive a detonation one hundred yards from her hull?" Charlie asked.

"We're rated to survive a near hit," Donovan said.

"It would be nice to know who she is," Percy said.

"Still think she's Russian?"

"Do you still think she's German?"

Jennings was peering at a monitor, shaking his head and almost smiling. "She's us, Captain. The screw signature match I ran? Her signature is identical to ours."

"That's impossible," Percy exclaimed. "No two boats are alike. We're unique."

"Nonetheless, her signature matches ours. The computer doesn't lie."

Donovan turned to Alex. "Does it?" he asked.

"No. Not simple sound-comparison software."

"I can't explain a direct match," Jennings said.

"Ten thousand yards and accelerating," Hooper said. "This time her acceleration-diving curve is identical to the one we ran in tests off Cape Hatteras. She is a lot like us. Maybe she is the *Nemesis* everyone talks about."

"Enough of that," Donovan swore. "Mr. Hooper, slow to one-quarter and reverse course. Let's see how the colonists are faring."

23

Priscilla bobbed gently in the cusp of the swells, her sails partly luffing to reduce speed yet maintain headway. *Liberator* steamed alongside, moving just fast enough for Mr. Hooper to steer.

Donovan had just returned from an inspection tour and pep talk, and stood on the topside bridge enjoying a mug of coffee and a cigarette while the motor raft was taken apart and stored. With him were Charlie and Alex; she had gone with him to the schooner to provide the pep talk.

Actually, the colonists were barely fazed by the encounter, which one of them described as a "nonevent." *Nemesis* had surfaced nearby and watched the schooner, knowing that her appearance would attract *Liberator*. There was never any spoken threat. Whoever was manning *Nemesis* didn't even appear on the topside bridge, but may have watched from the slit window. Just the machine itself appeared; no men.

"I have no idea who they are or what they want," Donovan said, lighting one Lucky Strike while a second was still falling toward the water.

"You know that's going to kill you," Alex said.

"I survived World War III," he said. "What do you want from me?"

"You're going to be the father of my children. You have to live forever."

"Immortality is too great a burden for me to contemplate right now. Are you sure that the colonists are going to be okay on their own?"

"Sure. They know that *Nemesis* wants us, not them. You said it yourself. And we'll be waiting for them in the South Pacific, having scouted prospective islands for colonization."

"Tell me about islands," Donovan said, watching as the sails on *Priscilla* began to fill again, driving the sharply defined bow into the waves as speed picked up. They made quite a pair sailing along rail-to-rail, the world's oldest working ship and its newest.

Alex unfolded a batch of computer printouts that were hot from *Liberator*'s research library and read from them. "Here's a nice one," she said. "It's in the Society Islands, in the Windward group. Thirty-three miles long and sixteen miles wide. Most of it is slightly above sea level, but the dormant volcano rises seven thousand, three hundred and fifty-two feet at the peak. There are numerous streams running off the mountain and the soil is fertile, producing bananas, oranges, coconuts, sugarcane, and twenty-two other species of edible and nutritious fruits and vegetables.

"The temperature range is sixty to ninety degrees Fahrenheit and the natives, assuming there's any left alive, are friendly."

"Does it have a deep-water port?"

"No. Do I have to provide everything?"

"We *need* a deep-water port. We're a submarine, remember, and it may behoove us to come and go undetected on occasion."

"I thought you said you could blast one."

"We can blast a channel, not a whole damn port.

230

And we don't need natives. I can't deal with the concept of radiation-crazed natives."

"We simply won't know how much of the population has survived until we get there. The computer projection is that the Society Islands escaped the worst of the firestorm, but we won't really know until we arrive. The morning papers didn't come out the day after the world ended."

"Meaning?"

"Meaning that we have no objective way of knowing what things are like in the rest of the world. All we know is what we've seen—what you've seen—and that limits our knowledge to Navy Harbor, Seattle, and San Francisco. We can't really know what things are like in Washington, London, and Moscow—or the South Pacific. We have to project."

"If Washington, London, or Moscow were still on the face of the planet, I think we would have heard of it."

"And the computer projection is that, where the geography and man-made structures survived, the human populations didn't. If the Society Islands still have trees and streams and bananas, there are no surviving natives. Why don't we just *go there,* Donovan? Empirical research remains the best way to find things out."

"Well, the colonists are already on their way," Donovan said, watching as *Priscilla* bore off under full sail and resumed her course to the southwest and the Society Islands.

"Which means that we have to get to the South Pacific at least six months before they do."

"We can get there in a week," Donovan said. "Now, what's the name of that island you told me about?"

"Otaheite," she replied. "Tahiti to you. But we don't have to go there. It was overbuilt in the last century, with all the hotels and landing strips. There are thousands of other islands in the group."

"I always wanted to sail to Tahiti," Donovan said wistfully. "I figure that the Isthmus of Taravoa would make a fine sub base, with a little blasting to open it up."

"You know about this island?"

"You're not the only one who reads. So, the Society Islands it is, maybe Tahiti. The group is ideally located, near the equator and within fast sailing distance of Asia, Africa, and North and South America. It should also have escaped the worst of the war."

Priscilla was well under way, and said good-bye with a long blast from her air horn.

"I'm going below to do some more research. Perhaps the Marshals would also be a good place to look. They're on the way to the Society Islands, and checking them out wouldn't take long. On the other hand, Christmas Island is nice."

Once she was gone below deck, Charlie fished a cigarette from his brother's pack, and said, "You'll have to present this decision to the crew."

"I already have, in general terms," Donovan said. "And?"

"The fact that we have to find a base is well understood. We can't sail on forever without a home port. Every ship needs one."

"Chief Smith wants a home port in the States."

"So do Hooper and Percy. It's the only thing they've all ever agreed on. Jennings is on my side along with most of the crew. Weapons Control is with me. They know that if we have a secure base we can last forever, given our weaponry and speed."

"Security is the main issue," Charlie said.

"It's high on the list. We can't live if we have to be on guard duty twenty-four hours a day for the rest of our lives, which is how it would be if we had to expect white-shirts coming over the walls at any time. There simply are too many surprises living in the States. We also need a local food supply that gives us a broad nutritional range. There's no such thing as markets anymore, at least not as we knew them."

"And there's the problem of radiation."

"Which seems to have affected the States in different and unpredictable ways. According to the computer model of the war, every place we go to in the States will be a new ball game with a new set of conditions. The South Pacific is the only region of Earth in which the predicted radiation is within tolerance levels. The flash effect may have decimated populations, but living and growing conditions should be good."

"Tahiti it is," Charlie said.

"Or thereabouts."

Donovan took a last look around, at the just-set sun and the bright visage of Venus hovering in the western sky, then at the now-distant sails of *Priscilla.* There was something eternal about sails in the sunset, he thought. Wooden ships and the men that sail them would always be with mankind one way or the other. Hardly the image presented by *Liberator,* with her titanium-composite hull and nuclear propulsion. Hers was a different kind of image, but one just as powerful.

He ordered a course change to the southwest, following the schooner, and a dive.

Dr. Peter Fisher had an excited look on his face, and the excitement quickly became contagious within the ship. It drew a crowd of the curious and hopeful, and when Donovan got to the research library Alex was there with him.

"Look at this," he said, pointing at a set of figures displayed on a color monitor.

"So?" Donovan asked.

"Your computer banks are great. The ROM diagnostics have come through for me. I know this is only a start, but I think I have a handle on radiation psychosis."

"That's great. Using the samples you took in San Francisco?"

"Yeah. I found a connection with the data assembled during the South American War. I'm more hopeful than ever for a cure. Remember AIDS?"

"Not personally. It did have something to do with Mom and Dad getting married and settling down, though."

"Well, the HIV virus was neurotropic—it displayed a remarkable affinity for attacking nerve cells. In the terminal stage—assuming the patient wasn't killed by an opportunistic infection—it attacked the sectors of the brain responsible for cognition. Psychosis often resulted.

"Well, the development of the AIDS virus pretty much ended that plague, but during the South American War a very similar virus erupted suddenly in the Andes—about the only region in the world where AIDS inoculations weren't made."

"As I recall, the Red Cross inoculation teams weren't admitted to the war zone," Alex said.

"My theory is that the radiation spread in that war caused the AIDS virus to mutate in the Andes, with its new principal action being an attack on those sectors of the brain that control aggression."

"Do you have a cure?" Donovan asked.

"Not yet. I don't even know the means of transmission yet. I don't think it's airborne, though. So casual contact is ruled out. It may be a contact virus."

"That's nice to know," Donovan said, rubbing his knuckles where they had pushed in the face of a radiation-psychotic white-shirt.

"So we have a start," Dr. Fisher said, tapping the monitor as a jockey might pat a favorite racehorse.

"Isolation of the specific agent will be the next step," Alex said. "I can help my brother with the computer work, but it will take time—a few months at least. So if you could provide us with peace and quiet and a nice place to work . . ."

"Join me in my quarters in half an hour," Donovan said to her.

Siberian cream tart and Alaskan king crab were only two of the gourmet foods that Charlie had liberated from the building off the Embarcadero that Saxon and he had used for firing practice.

Donovan had saved them for a special occasion, and the departure of *Liberator* on a mission to find a new port of call in the South Pacific seemed as good a time as any. When Alex came into his cabin and closed the door behind her, Donovan gave her a glass of zinfandel and a tart.

"What's the occasion? Peter's discovery?"

"No. I'll celebrate that when he finds the cure. We're preparing to set course for the Society Islands. I thought you'd join me in a toast."

"You saved my life and helped the city," she said, sipping the wine. "I'll join you in anything."

He held his glass aloft. "Cheers," he said.

"That's the best toast you can think of? Cheers?"

"Two weeks after World War III, if you got 'cheers' you got it all."

"I'll drink to that," she said, and did. Then she gave him a long kiss that meandered to his earlobe and back.

"We didn't do so bad on our first outing," he said, patting the bulkhead by way of congratulating the ship.

"You did great. And you'll do even better in the months and years to come. *We* will."

235

"The crew voted fifteen minutes ago. It's the Society Islands. I convinced them that making a home there is the best thing we can do."

"Did you have any trouble convincing them?"

"Not really. When all is said and done, I *am* the captain."

"How long will it take us to get there? You said before it would take a week."

"More like four days at forty knots. That's if we don't stop and sightsee."

"What's to look at?" she asked.

"The same thing we've been looking at for weeks—the world and what's left of it. The more I see the more I'm convinced we can make a difference."

"We can," she said.

"I have to go to the bridge to give the word. Want to come?"

"I'll wait here for you to come back," she said, more than a little dewy-eyed. "Don't be long."

"I won't," he said, leaving the cabin and walking down the corridor to the bridge.

Ceremonial departures were always a big deal. That much hadn't changed, even on the advanced U.S.S. *Liberator*. The first of the Omega-class nuclear submarines was no different from the U.S.S. *Constitution* when it came to ceremonial departures. All hands turned out, even if they had nothing more to do than look over the shoulders of the on-duty personnel.

Gathered on the bridge were Executive Officer Percy, Systems Chief Smith, Communications Officer Jennings, and the other officers whose job it was to head up departments and assist the captain in the making of major decisions. With Helmsman Hooper glued to the wheel they made quite a team, one that would be remembered and featured prominently by historians writing the history of the early twenty-first century in the (truly) New World.

At 2100 hours a fortnight after the old world ended, a simple exchange between officers began *Liberator* on a lifetime of adventures. Mr. Percy, summoning up all his dignity, said, "Course is set for the Society Islands, Captain. First port of call is the King George Group."

To which Captain Donovan replied, "Very good, Mr. Percy. Ahead full."

"What have we got?" Donovan queried as he sat in his swivel chair.

"Seven contacts, Captain," Percy informed him. "Eight miles off. Bearing two-eight-two."

"Mr. Hooper, come to course two-eight-two and bring us to periscope depth. Let me know when we're within visual range."

"Two-eight-two, and coming to periscope depth, sir," the helmsman replied.

"What can you tell me, Mr. Jennings?" Donovan asked.

"They're dead in the water, but they're not dead, Captain."

"Explain."

Communications Officer Jennings scrutinized a meter on his right. "I'm registering concentrated heat generation on board several of the ships."

Donovan leaned forward. "Engines?"

"No, Captain. I'd say heaters or lanterns, or else someone has set fires on board."

"Put them on the screen," Donovan commanded. He watched a series of blips materialize on the horizon.

"Each ship is two hundred feet in length," Jennings stated.

"The same size as that Japanese trawler we saw."

"A Japanese fishing fleet, you think?" Percy asked.

"Could be. Japan had one of the largest on the globe. Almost half a million ships afloat, as I recall. We'll know in a minute."

Minutes later Helmsman Hooper called out, "Periscope depth and close enough for visual, Captain."

"Raise periscope and the antenna mast," Donovan ordered. He checked his watch. Only 1000 hours.

Once the radar-receiving mast had been elevated, Communications Officer Jennings employed the radar receiver to determine if there were any signals from the ships. "No signal readings, Captain."

Nodding, Donovan peered through the periscope at the small fleet. He pressed a button so everything he viewed would be videotaped. Sure enough, the ships were similar to the fishing boat *Liberator* had run into before. That ship had turned out to be little more than a scorched hull adrift at sea. These were in much better shape. Their masts were gone, and there were scorch marks on the decks and wheelhouses, but overall the fishing boats were seaworthy. The big question concerned whether there might be Japanese fishermen on board. He saw no sign of life. But there was only one way to find out for certain. "Mr. Percy, we're going to surface and investigate. Sound alert stations, if you please."

"Aye, Captain," Percy stated, smiling, and pressed the button that activated the alarm heard throughout the sub. Monitors strategically located in the living quarters, the work spaces, and the corridors displayed a message for all the crew to see, which was programmed by Communications Officer Jennings, and read: "Multiple contacts off the starboard bow. Japanese fishing fleet."

Alex and Charlie came onto the bridge and took up positions near the swivel chair.

"Mr. Percy, I'll be taking a boarding party onto the nearest trawler. Chief Smith, Alex, and the first gunnery officer will be going with me."

"Begging your pardon, Captain. I'd like to go along."

"Sorry, John. Not this time," Donovan replied. He looked at Jennings. "Are those trawlers hot? Will we need radiation-protection suits?"

"Negative, sir."

"Mr. Hooper, bring us alongside the first fishing boat."

"Aye, Captain."

Donovan swung toward his brother. "You can break out the weapons, Pirate."

"Four?" Charlie asked, his tone tinged with excitement.

"Three. Alex will carry a video camera to record whatever we find."

"See you topside," Charlie said, and exited the bridge.

Smiling at Charlie's transparent eagerness, Donovan watched his brother depart. He'd bestowed the title of First Gunnery Officer upon Charlie because Pirate happened to be one of the best shots in the Navy. Twice Charlie had been the Navy pistol champ, and he loved guns.

"Where'd your brother ever get a nickname like Pirate?" Alex inquired.

"He adopted it after seeing *Raiders of the Lost Ark*," Donovan disclosed. "A seaplane pilot in that flick had the words 'Air Pirates' on the back of his shirt."

Alex grinned. "Pirate and Sinbad. Quite a team."

Donovan turned his attention to the scope, scrutinizing the fishing fleet as Hooper brought the sub to within boarding range. He failed to detect a trace of life. "Down, scope," he directed. "Surface."

The teal-colored hull of the *Liberator* broke water gracefully, and within two minutes the boarding party, Percy, and four armed crewmen were on the foredeck. The boarding party and the crewmen all carried the same type of weapon, the new Navy version of the Luigi Franchi 9-mm automatic. The compact submachine gun sported a thirty-two-round box magazine and could fire 250 rounds per minute. For over a decade the Franchi had been the weapon of choice for leftist guerilla groups in Africa, Latin America, and Southeast Asia because of its reliability and rugged construction.

A four-man raft was placed in the water, and Donovan, Charlie, Alex, and Chief Smith quickly climbed into it.

Percy stood on the starboard diving plane, gazing warily at the trawler. "Be careful, Skipper. We'll cover you as best we can."

"You do that," Charlie spoke up. "I've got a bad feeling about this."

Donovan glanced at his brother, disturbed. Past experience had taught him the value of Charlie's intuition. If Charlie sensed there might be trouble, then there damn well would be trouble. He wondered if he was doing the right thing by bringing Alex along, but it was too late to change his mind. "Let's go," he said.

They paddled the dozen yards to the trawler, which lay perfectly still in the quiet sea. A fishing net hung over the port side within four feet of the water, rendering the use of grappling lines unnecessary. Charlie went up first and fast. He stood guard on the deck while the others joined him.

"This is spooky," Alex whispered.

Donovan had to agree. The door to the wheelhouse stood wide open. Except for a pile of nets and a few scattered tools, the deck was barren. A fishy odor permeated the air.

"Somebody is home. I just know it," Charlie declared. He moved toward the wheelhouse.

"Flaze, you stay with Alex," Donovan ordered, and followed his brother. They peered into the wheelhouse and discovered everything in apparent order. One of the glass panes had been shattered and another cracked, but otherwise little damage had been done.

"We've got to go below," Charlie said, clearly not enthused by the idea.

Together they walked to a companionway and descended carefully. At the base of the stairs a flickering lantern hung on a gray hook. The brothers exchanged glances and advanced along the narrow corridor. After the luxurious accommodations on *Liberator,* the confined space in the trawler seemed particularly constricting, almost claustrophobic.

A dozen yards ahead a door hung ajar, and light emanated from the room beyond.

Donovan slowed, gripping the Franchi tightly. He nearly gagged when a disgusting, putrid stench assailed his nostrils. Halting, he pressed his left sleeve over his nose and saw Charlie do the same. He'd smelled the rank stink of death before, but never as bad as this. Dreading the sight he would find, he advanced to the doorway.

They were stacked neatly like plates on a shelf, one on top of the other, from the floor to the ceiling. There were eight Japanese seamen, and they had died horrible deaths, their throats slit or their chests and abdomens cut to ribbons. Blood and bodily fluids had seeped onto the floor and formed a foul pool, congealed now into a reddish, oily film. Shriveled intestines dangled from the right side of the man on top.

Donovan felt his stomach start to heave. He staggered away, a few yards down the passage, and fought the urge to retch. A hand fell on his right shoulder, and he inadvertently jumped.

"Are you okay?" Charlie asked.

Donovan gulped and nodded. "Doesn't that get to you?"

"Sure. But after seeing what those wolves did to that crowd in San Francisco, I can handle it."

"The next time I board a ship like this, I think I'll bring nose plugs."

They continued deeper into the trawler, passing several lanterns, only two of which were lit. Eery shadows danced on the walls. Sibilant whispers seemed to issue from the murky corners. The fishy odor became stronger as they neared the hold.

Donovan inspected a cabin they found, a clean room containing a small bunk and a wooden table on which rested a bowl of raw fish and cooked rice. He stuck his finger in the bowl and found the rice warm to the touch. The short hairs at the nape of his neck tingled. "There's definitely someone home," he whispered.

Charlie nodded, then stiffened. "Listen!"

Donovan cocked his head, and it took a moment for him to distinguish the low, raspy laughter emanating from the bowels of the vessel. The laughter rose in volume, then tapered off.

"God!" Charlie exclaimed.

"I feel as if I'm in a Boris Karloff movie," Donovan commented nervously.

"Just so Frankenstein doesn't pop out of the woodwork," Charlie said.

They moved along the gloomy corridor until they reached another flight of narrow metal stairs. Below them yawned a black pit, an inky expanse of emptiness, from which wafted an intensified aroma of fish.

Donovan scanned the chasm and deduced they must be at the hold. He thought of the laughter and wondered if there might be someone down there, watching them. His skin felt as if it wanted to crawl from his body. What if there were white-shirts on board? he asked himself, and the question provoked a torrent of memories.

Liberator's crew had encountered the dreaded white-shirts several times since the war. The first incident occurred in the Aleutians, at Navy Harbor on Unalaska Island. Donovan and a landing party were attacked by four of the demented bastards. Then, in San Francisco, Donovan and company had to contend with an army of white-shirts who were determined to wipe out the few normal survivors. The desperate situation had called for drastic measures, and Donovan had called up a Mark 97N to obliterate the white-shirt headquarters. Used during the nuclear shelling of the Andean coca fields ten years before the war, the Mark 97N carried a field-grade nuclear warhead.

No one knew exactly what caused normal survivors to transform into crazed white-shirts. The prevailing medical theory attributed the transformation to the radiation insanity. Many of the survivors simply became hopelessly psychotic. But the psychosis alone failed to explain certain puzzling aspects about the white-shirts. Why, for instance, did they all wear white shirts or some semblance thereof? Why did they go around meticulously collecting bodies and burning the corpses? And why did the white-shirts attack anyone who wasn't a white-shirt?

Donovan stared at the black abyss and pondered. Surely there couldn't be white-shirts on board the trawlers? Perhaps several of the crew had gone off the deep end, their sanity shattered by the horror of the nuclear holocaust. That didn't necessarily mean they would become white-shirts, did it? He sighed in frustration. There were too many questions and not enough answers.

Charlie knelt and peered into the darkness. "Should we go down?"

"Not by ourselves. We'd be inviting grief," Donovan said. "Let's return to Alex and Flaze."

They quickly retraced their route, and they both smiled when they finally saw the sunlight streaming down the companionway to the deck.

"I never knew sunshine could look so good," Charlie said.

Donovan opened his mouth to reply when a maniacal laugh rent the air to their rear. He whirled, leveling the Franchi, and it was well he did, for there, less than twenty feet away, stood a scrawny Japanese fisherman attired in filthy black pants and nothing else. His face and chest were caked with grime and crimson stains, his black hair oily and plastered to his head. In each hand he held a slender ten-inch knife, the kind used to slit the belly of a fish with consummate ease.

The Japanese, his brown eyes wide and unfocused, smirked and waved the knives in circles.

"Hello," Donovan greeted him, attempting to communicate but feeling foolish doing so. "I'm Captain Thomas Donovan of the U.S.S. *Liberator.*"

Snickering, the fisherman tilted his head and uttered a string of words in his native tongue.

"We mean you no harm," Donovan said.

Without warning, the Japanese hurled his emaciated frame at the Americans, both knives upraised for a fatal thrust.

Charlie shot him. The burst chattered short and sweet, and the rounds caught the man in the torso and hurled him from his feet to crumple on the floor in a heap.

Donovan edged toward the fisherman, the eight-

248

inch Franchi barrel pointed at the Japanese. He saw blood oozing from holes in the man's back, saw the chest had ceased moving, and knew the man was dead.

"Do you think he killed all the others?" Charlie asked.

Before Donovan could respond, from the deck outside came a screech and the blasting of Chief Smith's Franchi.

FROM PERSONAL JOURNALS TO BLACKLY HUMOROUS ACCOUNTS

VIETNAM

DISPATCHES, Michael Herr
                            01976-0/$4.50 US/$5.95 Can
"I believe it may be the best personal journal about war,
any war, that any writer has ever accomplished."
                            —Robert Stone, *Chicago Tribune*

M, John Sack
                            69866-8/$3.95 US/$4.95 Can
"A gripping and honest account, compassionate and
rich, colorful and blackly comic."
                            —*The New York Times*

ONE BUGLE, NO DRUMS, Charles Durden
                            69260-0/$4.95 US/$5.95 Can
"The funniest, ghastliest military scenes put to paper
since Joseph Heller wrote *Catch-22*"
                            —*Newsweek*

AMERICAN BOYS, Steven Phillip Smith
                            67934-5/$4.50 US/$5.95 Can
"The best novel I've come across on the war in Vietnam"
                            —Norman Mailer

WORLD WAR II
Edwin P. Hoyt

STORM OVER THE GILBERTS: 63651-4/$3.50 US/$4.50 Can
War in the Central Pacific: 1943
The dramatic reconstruction of the bloody battle over the Japanese-held Gilbert Islands.

CLOSING THE CIRCLE: 67983-8/$3.50 US/$4.95 Can
War in the Pacific: 1945
A behind-the-scenes look at the military and political moves drawn from official American and Japanese sources.

McCAMPBELL'S HEROES   68841-7/$3.95 US/$5.75 Can
A stirring account of the daring fighter pilots, led by Captain David McCampbell, of Air Group Fifteen.

LEYTE GULF   75408-8/$3.50 US/$4.50 Can
The Death of the Princeton
The true story of a bomb-torn American aircraft carrier fighting a courageous battle for survival!

WAR IN THE PACIFIC: TRIUMPH OF JAPAN
      75792-3/$4.50 US/$5.50 Can

WAR IN THE PACIFIC: STIRRINGS   75793-1/$3.95 US/$4.95 Can

THE JUNGLES OF NEW GUINEA   75750-8/$4.95 US/$5.95 Can